The
honorable
Barbarian

The honorable Barbarian

• • •

L. Sprague de Camp

A Del Rey Book

BALLANTINE BOOKS ◆ NEW YORK

A Del Rey Book
Published by Ballantine Books
Copyright © 1989 by L. Sprague de Camp

All rights reserved under International and Pan-American
Copyright Conventions. Published in the United States of America
by Ballantine Books, a division of Random House, Inc., New York,
and simultaneously in Canada by Random House of Canada
Limited, Toronto.

LIBRARY OF CONGRESS CATALOGING-IN-PUBLICATION DATA
De Camp, L. Sprague (Lyon Sprague), 1907–
    The honorable barbarian / L. Sprague de Camp. — 1st ed.
        p.   cm.
    "A Del Rey book."
    ISBN 0-345-36091-5
    I. Title.
PS3507.E2344H6   1989
813'.52—dc19   88-92810
                                                    CIP

Text design by Mary A. Wirth

Manufactured in the United States of America
First Edition: July 1989
10 9 8 7 6 5 4 3 2 1

Contents

The
honorable
Barbarian

· I ·
Eomer's Cowbarn

"Hold me closer!" whispered Adeliza to Kerin, Evor's son. "Put your hand here—What's that?"

"Who's there?" roared Adeliza's father Eomer. "Is someone with you, Adeliza? I'll come in to see."

Adeliza whispered: "Run, Kerin!"

Kerin scrambled up. A glance at the floor of the barn below the hayloft revealed, by moonlight streaming through the open door, Eomer's bearded face staring up the ladder and a knotty, brawny hand upon a rung.

Kerin's sight had become adapted to the darkness of the barn. Perhaps, he thought, the farmer's had not. In any case, he could not stay put; nor could he descend the ladder with the burly Eomer starting up. Stepping to the end of the loft, he sprang and came down on the planks below in a crouch.

The impact shook him; but then he was on his feet and running. Behind him came Eomer's bellow:

"I know you, Kerin son of Evor! Come back here!"

The boards of the cowbarn boomed beneath the farmer's boots. Clear of the portal, Kerin risked a backward glance. Into the moonlight lumbered Eomer, waving a sickle and roaring:

"Come back, ye losel! I'll serve you so ye'll deflower no more virgins!"

Younger and leaner, Kerin quickly outdistanced his pursuer, who stopped for want of breath. Kerin heard his final shout:

"I'll shoot you down on the highway! I'll bring an action at law! I'll tell your mother on you!"

Reaching the road, Kerin settled down to a steady jog, breathing hard. He cast a resentful upward glance at the silvered moon, whose light had betrayed him. He thought: What now? I shall soon return to Kortoli with my brothers; but that wouldn't stop Eomer from lodging an action. And I fear the toils of litigation worse than I do Eomer's sword or crossbow, or even than his accusing me to my mother. Or he'll hire a witch to bespell me. . . .

Kerin sat with his kin in the house of his sister and brother-in-law in Ardamai. His sister and her husband were present; so were Kerin's widowed mother and his two brothers. Kerin's sisters-in-law were elsewhere; Jorian's wife Margalit managed the clock business during the brothers' holiday in their native village.

Sillius, the tall, graying elder brother, said with an irritating air of superior logic: "At least, Kerin, you might have avoided a full-moon night with a cloudless sky. Then you could have told Eomer it was one of Adeliza's other swains. They're ever slinking about, I hear."

"So I was an ass," said Kerin, angry at himself. "But what to do? Submit to a crossbow wedding?"

Jorian, the big, burly middle brother, grinned through his black and bristling beard. "Na, na, laddie. We don't crave a fanatic like Eomer in the family."

"What's he fanatical about?" asked Kerin.

"It's the new cult that fellow Ikbar brought from Fedirun. His deities, I understand, are a desert god and goddess, daft about modesty. I hear a lawfully wedded pair must ask the priest's permission to enjoy their connubial privileges. And he would abolish the public baths, having a horror of nudity. The devout are forbidden to bare the least smidgin of skin to a fellow sinner. Speaking of which, my lad, art sure you went not in unto the lusty Adeliza?"

"I am sure, Jorian. I ought to know. Actually, all I had in mind was a little kissing and fondling. But she—ah . . ."

"Had more advanced ideas," put in Kerin's sister Basina. "Adeliza's a lass with a hot notch in her crotch. Were she to conceive, none but the blessed gods would know, of a dozen swains, which yokel was truly sire."

"And Kerin's an obvious target," said Sillius, "since 'tis known in the village that our business prospers. But for Eomer's intervention, our lad's virtue had gone with last year's snows."

"Eomer yelled something about deflowering virgins," muttered Kerin. "My conscience wouldn't have let me—"

"Ha!" said Basina. "She's no more virgin than I. If anyone had been deflowered, 'twould have been our Kerin—unless he have already taken care of that unbeknownst to us. Eomer doth but lay the foundation for a claim against us, either a legal alliance or a payment in cash. He knows as well as the next that Adeliza's been playing the local charity box, so he watches for a chance to marry her off."

"The world hath gone rotten," said Kerin's mother Ethelin. "In my day, nice girls didn't. That is how one told them from the rest."

"It's that easy contraceptive spell," said Sillius. "Morality has gone to the seven hells since Doctor Mersius' secret got out. But ere we settle the kingdom's social problems, let's deal with Kerin. We lust for neither Eomer nor his loose-lived daughter in the family." He gave Kerin a stern, thin-lipped stare. "For months we've talked of sending one of us to the Far East, to return with the secret of the Kuromonian clock escapement. Kerin has spoken of making the quest."

A little appalled, Kerin gulped. "Forsooth, I did but jest. Still and all, if all think I should. . . ."

"Oh!" cried Ethelin. "Ye maun not send my babe into unknown perils—to lands where they roast and devour a stranger!"

"As long as he stays out of reach of the Paaluans," said Jorian, "he's safe from that peril."

"But he is too young!"

"No younger than I, when I signed up for a hitch in the Grand Bastard's army."

"And he hath no such training for perilous adventure, as ye have—"

"Mother!" said Kerin, his backbone stiffened by his mother's attempt to baby him. "I may not be so big and brawny as Jorian, nor so seasoned in business as Sillius; but I am fit of body and sober of mind."

"And," added Jorian, "I'll teach him the tricks of the trade, such as gaining entry to a locked and bolted house. He managed that Estrildis business in Xylar featly enough, and we must all take our chances betimes. We'll send him forth with the best protective spells that money can buy; my friend the wizard Uller will give them to us at a discount." Jorian turned to Sillius. "We hoped to stay two more days; but methinks we'd best be aroad tomorrow, eh?"

Back in Kortoli City, Kerin heaved his duffel bag into the luggage rack on the back of the diligencia for Vindium, drawn by four glossy bays. He was as prepared for his adventure as a month's intensive training under Jorian could make him. He could handle the sword at his side, scale a wall, pick a lock, lie with a straight face, and speak rudimentary Mulvani and a few words of Salimorese. Several pounds of Kortolian golden eagles rode in a compartmented belt against his skin.

At the first overnight stop, Kerin, knowing he had to be up at cockcrow, turned in right after supper; but his roommate lingered in the common room, drinking beer. Kerin was glad, since the roommate, a beefy man named Garic whom chance had assigned to the room with Kerin, had not bathed lately, if ever.

Kerin stood before the spotted mirror above the washstand, scrubbing his teeth with a frayed twig. In the mirror he saw a young man of slightly above average Novarian stature, rather slim, with light-brown hair that hinted at Shvenish blood. He envied Jorian's blue-black mop and bristling beard. Looking at his own unlined and rather unformed countenance, Kerin resolved to try again for a beard. His previous effort had foundered when it came in patchy, fuzzy, blond, and barely visible. Perhaps this time. . . .

A tinny little voice, like a tinkle of tiny bells, made him start: "Master Kerin!" Kerin was not sure whether he heard it with his ears or inside his head.

He whirled. At first he could see nothing by the single candle's amber light.

"Master Kerin!" said the voice. "Here I am!"

At last Kerin located the source. It was a floating spot of bluish luminescence, which rose and dipped like a hovering insect. Looking more closely, Kerin thought he saw something resembling a big butterfly fluttering about. But the pearly body supporting the glassy wings was not an insect's. Although not sure, he had an impression of a tiny naked woman, not much taller than the breadth of his palm. The apparition seemed translucent; when it fluttered between Kerin and the candle flame, the light was dimmed but not completely occluded.

"Now what—" began Kerin, recovering from his initial fright. "Who, pray, are you?"

"I am your guardian spirit," it said in a voice like the screak of a nighttime insect.

"Forsooth? And who appointed you?"

"My mistress; Erwina the Enchantress."

"You mean the witch of Ardamai?"

"Pray, Master Kerin! Call not my mistress a witch, any more than you'd term King Fridwal's queen a drab."

"As to that," said Kerin, "I've heard tales of Queen Clotsinda—" He broke off, remembering Jorian's caution against loose talk. The walls were thin; and in any case, how far could he trust this little spook? He continued: "Did Eomer's daughter put Erwina up to this?"

"Aye, spending gold she filched from her father's hoard."

"And what do you here?" persisted Kerin.

"I am to watch and ward you from harm, so you shall safely return to claim your bride."

"Meanst Adeliza . . ."

"Aye, Master Kerin. She is bound and determined to have you for spouse; for she holds you the prettiest of all her swains."

"Pretty!" snorted Kerin. "I never so much as hinted at wedding."

"She hath a different tale."

"In any case, I do not wish a guardian spirit. An iatromagus in Kortoli laid a protective spell upon me. So begone!"

"Oh, but Master Kerin, I dare not defy Erwina's express command—"

"To the afterworld with your mistress! Aroint! Vanish!"

The sprite's glow dimmed, and Kerin heard a tiny sniffle. The tinkly little voice persisted: "You are a beast, Master Kerin! Here am I, essaying to carry out my duties; and far from appreciating, you spurn my earnest efforts! You are a harsh, unfeeling brute who hath wounded my deepest feelings!"

"Oh, stop sniveling!" said Kerin, touched in spite of himself. "Just keep out of sight and sound."

"How can I perform my duties—"

"Hush!" said Kerin, hearing the heavy tramp of his roommate in the hall. "Be invisible, spook; the other fellow's coming in. Hast a name, by the way?"

"Aye; 'tis Belinka. Now shall I—"

"Just disappear, Belinka!"

"But I must ask—"

"Not now; we'll talk when we're alone. Good-night!"

The door opened and the roommate lurched in. "Whom were you speaking with just now?" growled the man in an ale-thickened voice.

"Merely practicing a speech I must give," said Kerin. "Goodnight, Master Garic."

The man grunted, sat on the stool, and wrestled off his boots. Kerin lay with closed eyes, hoping for no further converse. Then Garic rose with a muffled expletive.

"Some damned insect," he said. "Where's something to swat it with?"

"Merely a big moth," muttered Kerin.

"I can't stand bugs," snorted the man. "By Imbal's brazen balls, I'll get something!"

9

The man left on bare feet. Kerin said: "Belinka, if you disappear not, he'll smash you against the wall."

"Fiddle-dee-dee, Master Kerin!" came the bell-like voice. "He cannot touch me, because we Second Plane spirits do not here completely materialize. I fear him not! Anyway, why should you care? You like me not; you have no sympathy. . . ."

The tiny voice broke off as Kerin's roommate bulked in the doorway, carrying the paddle-shaped bat employed in the game of paddle-ball. He peered about in the scanty candlelight, then swished the bat through the air.

"Missed the damned thing," he growled.

"Calm down, Master Garic," said Kerin. "It's harmless."

Ignoring Kerin, the man took another swing. "Cursed thing's bewitched," he mumbled, his puffy visage crimson in the candlelight.

Kerin sat up to protest when a futile backhand fanned his hair. "Hey!" he cried. "You nearly brained me! Now put that thing away and come to bed quietly or get yourself out!"

"Futter you!" said Garic, bracing himself for another swat. "The fornicating thing's *laughing* at me! I'll not stand for that!"

He swung again. Enraged, Kerin climbed out of bed in his loincloth, stepped to the corner where his clothes lay piled, and seized his sword. "Now get out!" he snarled.

Garic took a step towards him, hefting the bat. Then the gleam of candlelight on the blade checked him. After a heartbeat's hesitation, Garic blundered out the door and slammed it behind him, leaving his distinctive odor awaft in the room. Presently Kerin heard his voice and that of the taverner raised in anger.

Kerin got back to bed, apprehensively awaiting Garic's return. A reaction made him shaky. Although he had traveled about Novaria, he had never threatened anyone with a sword. He thought of the horrid things that might have ensued if Garic had closed with the bat, including placing his neck on the block on a murder conviction. He had certainly bungled that encounter. Jorian would have known how to shrug off Garic's antics with a jest or an improvised verse.

It was all Adeliza's fault, thought Kerin, for setting the sprite upon him—but then it was his fault, too, for making up to Adeliza. Although he had not confessed it, he had taken her to the loft with a secret hope, despite pangs of conscience, of losing his irksome virginity. This many young men had done by his age—at least, if one believed their boasts of prodigious fornications.

"I told you he could not hurt me, he-he!" tinkled Belinka, turning on her full cerulian luminescence and dancing wildly about.

"Ha! You might have gotten me slain!"

"'Twould have served you right, you unfeeling monster!"

Kerin sighed. Jorian's training had not included the getting rid of importunate sprites. "Please, Belinka, quiet down so I can get some sleep. What would Erwina say if, thanks to your help, I came back home in a box?"

"Oh, very well, O mighty Lord Kerin. Good-night!"

Garic did not return; the taverner must have found him other quarters. But Kerin still found slumber hard to attain. He cursed himself for having broken one of Jorian's rules. His brother had said:

"Above all, youngster, move briskly but quietly, drawing the least attention. No public displays, no boasts, no complaints, no disputes, and above all no brawls. And remember that flattery gets you almost anywhere."

Throughout the rest of the journey, he and Garic ostentatiously ignored each other. On the second night, the taverner ear-

marked for Kerin a room with an elderly bank clerk from Me-
touro, who kept his own cousel and ignored Belinka's flittings.
Late on the third day, the diligencia rolled up to the northern
gate of Vindium City, capital of the Republic of Vindium.

The passengers got out and lined up. The captain of the guard,
splendid in crested helmet of gilded brass, went down the line,
asking each passenger his name, origin, occupation, and other
data, while a guard made notes on a tablet. Another guard busied himself with tying swords, including Kerin's, fast to their
scabbards with scarlet strings.

The captain stood back and said: "Welcome to Vindium, ladies and gentlemen! May your sojourn in our famous city be
pleasant! We have historical monuments, libraries, and a zoö-
logical park. We have theatrical entertainments, ranging from
those suitable for children to those appealing to the most—
ah—sophisticated tastes. A revival of Physo's *Tinsel Crown* is
playing at the Empire; the poet Edredus will give a reading of
his epic *The Sea of Blood*, in eighty-four cantos, at the Hall of
Culture; while at Atrax's Palace of Pleasure they have Madame
Ziska, who picks volunteers from the audience, and . . . but
what she does with them you must see for yourselves.

"We have an athletic field, where amateur teams of ball players practice decamerally; visiting foreigners are welcome to
take part. We have a drill field, whereon sections of the army
and the civic guard drill daily; two days hence the army band
will give a concert, weather permitting. If you hie yourselves
north along the coast for half a league, you will find a splendid
beach.

"For tonight, it were well to keep to your quarters. Today
our paddle-ball team defeated that of Othomae, and certain
citizens may celebrate with excessive enthusiasm. Moreover,
elections to the Chamber of Burgesses will occur six days

hence, and the candidates are campaigning. Disturbances sometimes ensue when rival partisans meet."

The passengers reëntered the coach, which rolled on into the city. Compared to respectable, staid Kortoli, Vindium seemed livelier and more colorful. Some were already celebrating the sporting triumph, weaving along the pavement shouting and waving mugs.

On buildings fronting the street, posters had been put up here and there. They bore such legends as "Frithugis, the people's choice!" or "Vote for Beonnus, friend of the downtrodden!" or "Victron—experience—integrity!" or "Ithmar, foe of the establishment!" Similar slogans had been painted on many walls.

The coach passed a man with a paintbrush and pail, interrupted while painting a slogan by two members of the civic guard. With these he was engaged in a furious argument. As Kerin craned his neck to watch, the slogan painter hurled his pail at a guardsman, drenching him with butter-yellow paint. The three ran off, the guardsmen after the painter, waving their truncheons and yelling.

As the parting rays of the setting sun touched spires and domes with ruddy gold, the vehicle halted at the principal square, flanked by the Senate House, the Magistracy, and other public buildings. In these structures, the austere plainness of classical Novarian style was adulterated by a touch of florid, fanciful Mulvani ornateness. From the square, Republic Avenue sloped gently down to the waterfront, where Kerin glimpsed a thicket of masts and yards. Across the square, a man harangued a crowd from a wooden box.

Kerin was reared on tales of Vindine corruption and public scandals. A traveling Vindine had given him the other side of the story:

"The difference, Master Kerin, lies not in you Kortolians' superior virtue but in the fact that, under our system, misdeeds are more easily brought to light. I daresay there be quite as much wrongdoing amongst the popinjays of your royal family, and amongst the hangers-on of the Royal Council, as with us. But your rulers, not having freedom of speech and publication to contend with, are in a stronger position to smother news of transgressions."

Kerin sat over a mug of ale, on the end of a bench in the common room of the inn to which Jorian had referred him. As his first task in Vindium, his brother had told him, he should find the harbor master to ascertain what ships were sailing when and whither. But, by the time Kerin had alighted in the square, the sun was out of sight behind the buildings. Sure he would find the harbor master's office closed, Kerin had gone instead to the inn.

Sounds of revelry wafted in from the street. Kerin kept repeating Jorian's advice: to keep his eyes and ears open and his mouth shut. He suppressed a small resentment that his brother possessed a more imposing façade than he. When someone cheated Jorian, all the latter had to do was loom upon the man, beard a-bristle, and quietly ask for a correction. Being smaller in all directions, Kerin did not feel he could manage that.

He tried to pick up snatches of talk among the Vindines in the room. But the few words he caught were of little import: comments on the weather and the speakers' trades, family problems, and aches and pains. Besides, his ear was not fully attuned to the Vindine dialect of Novarian.

The door banged open, and in came revelers three. They were stout, rough-looking men, led by one as big and brawny as Jorian. They carried little flags of the Republic of Vindium, showing a golden torch on an azure field; the leader had the staff of his flag stuck in the band of his hat.

"Ho, Chundo!" roared the leader. "Flagons of your best beer, to celebrate the glorious victory! And none of that horse piss you serve your ordinary customers!"

Kerin stared, for he belatedly recognized Garic, his odorous roommate on the first night of the journey. Garic stared back in similar recognition. Instead of speaking to Kerin, he shouted again for the taverner.

"Coming, coming," grumbled the proprietor. "I'm no wizard to make the stuff appear out of thin air."

"We'll take that one," said the leader, pointing to the bench on which Kerin sat. His companions slid in behind the table, so that the first to seat himself rubbed shoulders with Kerin.

The bench was not quite long enough for all four. Garic looked at those already seated; Kerin smelled the man's odor. Then the big man lowered one buttock on the end of the bench, saying loudly:

"Oh, push that skinny pup off the end! 'Tis he who so vexed me on the ride from Kortoli."

He applied his shoulder to his nearest companion and shoved, displacing the companion, who in turn forced the third of the trio up against Kerin. Seeing that he was about to be shoved off the end, Kerin rose, picking up his mug. The big man on the other end beamed triumphantly.

Kerin was furious; but his sword was in his room above, and in a rough-and-tumble with these characters he would have all the chance of a snowball in the crater of Mount Sholala. He had read fictions wherein the spindly young hero trounced the hulking bully; but he had seen enough of the world to know that such things did not really happen, unless the hero had the help of magic. Kerin's only magic was the protective cantrip laid upon him by Jorian's wizardly friend, the iatromagus Uller; and that, a mere passive defense against spells, would not hinder Garic's fists and boots.

Keeping a grip on his temper, Kerin sat down at a vacant table. For a while he was suffered to drink his beer in peace, hearing the speech of the three who had ousted him. They endlessly boasted about the might and prowess of Vindium's paddle-ball team. There had been a minor riot at the game, with a couple of players whacking each other with bats, and spectators joining in until the civic guardsmen beat them away with pikestaves. Finally Garic bent a scowl upon Kerin, growling:

"Ho there, you, skinny!" When Kerin looked up, Garic continued: "Do you admit that the Vindine team is the finest, bravest, and ablest in all the Twelve Cities?"

Kerin realized that he ought to agree; but his boiling rage and imp of perversity led him defiantly to return the stare, saying: "I wouldn't know. I follow not that sport."

"Oh, too hoity-toity, eh? If you did, you'd know we Vindines could trample you Kortolian sissies into dirt! We'd grind 'em to powder, as I will now do to you!"

The fellow lurched to his feet and started towards Kerin. One of his companions said: "Garic, let's not start—"

Ignoring the advice, the big man continued his way, clenching and unclenching his fists. Kerin, badly frightened but determined to sell his life dearly, also rose. Then Garic stopped, saying:

"Ouch! Some damned bug bit me!"

He halted, batting the air with his massive arms. Kerin sighted Belinka's misty form, flitting round Garic's head. Kerin raised his voice:

"Goodman Garic! Know that your bug is my faithful familiar spirit. Wouldst force me to exert my full occult powers?"

"Huh? You a wizard?"

Kerin gave a mocking bow. "A mere pupil of Uller of Kortoli. How'd you like a little spell of impotence? Of course, I am not yet a licensed master magician, so the spell may go awry and turn us all to pollywogs or blast us off the planet." He extended both forefingers, closed his eyes, and declaimed: "*Nitrae radou sunandam, noctar. . . .*"

"Ho!" snorted Garic. "That's unfair! I'll take you on with fists or quarterstaves, but not with unholy spells!" When Kerin continued to incant, Garic, grumbling under his breath, returned to his table, saying: "Come on, boys; we like not Chundo's lousy beer anyway."

The three rose and hulked their way out, leaving their undrunk mugs. Weak with reaction, Kerin sat down, blessing Jorian for having coached him in lying. He murmured:

"Thankee, Belinka!"

"Hee hee!" tinkled the sprite, alighting on Kerin's shoulder. "Now you see what I can do for you. Art not sorry you treated me with such mortifying disdain?"

Before Kerin could answer, he found the taverner before him, saying: "Master Kerin, what didst to make those customers leave without paying? I'll not have you spoiling my trade!"

"If I had not, there'd have been a brawl, which would have cost you far more. I'll drink the beer they ordered."

"And pay for it, I trust?"

"Yea," sighed Kerin.

Kerin awakened with a throbbing head. He groaned and sat on the edge of the bed with his head in his hands.

"I warned you!" tinkled Belinka, flitting about. "I tried to tell you four bumpers would give you grief, but you pretended not to hear, you stupid lout!"

Kerin grunted. "I couldn't hear you, after those other people came in and started singing about the Vindine ball team. So let up on the preaching, will you?" He reached for his clothes.

"Oho, Master Kerin, you shall not so lightly escape! You owe me a favor for my defeat of the oafish Garic."

"Eh? What?" said Kerin, pulling on his trews.

"Aye. I demand that you buy me a dress, like unto those that dames on this plane wear."

Kerin stared. "What on earth dost need with a dress? Suffer you from cold?"

"Nay; the temperature of your plane affects me not. On mine own plane our natural forms suffice us; but here, I see that folk go not about naked, even when weather permit. So I would fain be in style with those of my sex in this world."

"But why? I like you as you are. Had you ten times your present stature, I might make lewd advances." He leered and wiggled his eyebrows.

"Ha! You, pretending to like me whom you have scorned and spurned? Anyway, on my plane we love a-wing; and how wouldst manage that? But I will not be out of fashion with those of your barbarous plane!"

"And where in the seven cold hells shall I find a dress for a winged woman a span in height?"

"Have you no folk who sell poppets to pleasure their infants? Find one and buy a poppet's gown, of suitable size."

"And if I won't?" said Kerin defiantly.

"You shall see!" The hovering spot of luminescence vanished.

"Ouch!" yelled Kerin, feeling a sudden stab on his neck, like the bite of a horsefly. He futilely slapped at the place. Another stab assaulted his forearm; another, right through his trousers into his calf.

"Stop, Belinka!" he cried. "Is this your idea of watching over me?"

"I expect recip—reciprocity!" she squeaked. "Now will you be a good fellow?"

Kerin sighed. "I'll ask the taverner if he know of any such shop; but I promise nought."

No, the harbor master said; those exotic Kuromonian ships, with their blunt ends and slatted sails, had not been seen in Vindium harbor for above a year. "They've been satisfied to haul their goods to and from Salimor," he said. "They say that piracy hath become rife betwixt here and Salimor; so I ween the yellow men reckon the game's not worth the horseshoe. Ye maun sail for Salimor and transship there."

"Who leaves next for Salimor?" asked Kerin.

The harbor master, a swarthy man whose complexion suggested Mulvanian ancestry, thumbed through a pile of papers. "Here 'tis: the *Dragonet* of Akkander, Captain Huvraka."

"A Mulvanian?"

"Aye. Ye'll find her about six berths north from here. Says he'll cast off—by Astis' ivory teats, lad, ye are in luck! She hoists up sail this even, if the wind be fair. At least, so saith her skipper; but ye can't always trust these Mulvanians."

Kerin thanked the harbor master and went in search of the *Dragonet*. He picked out the ship, a sharp-ended vessel with black-and-crimson eyes painted on her bows, by her slanting lateen yards.

On the *Dragonet's* pier stood a crane, a tall skeletal structure of beams and ropes and pulley blocks. A treadwheel in the base was powered by six breechclouted convicts inside the wheel. A rigger belayed a rope around a bulky piece of cargo and slipped beneath the rope a hook suspended from the tip of the crane.

An overseer shouted; the six convicts began climbing the curving wall of the treadwheel, which had cleats to make the task easier. With noisy creaking, the burden slowly rose. The overseer shouted again. The convicts ceased their climbing; a pair of workers turned a winch. This slowly rotated the crane, swinging the load out over the deck of the *Dragonet*. More shouts, and the convicts backed down, letting the tread-wheel turn the other way and the load descend to the deck. Other workers strained at a brake to keep the load from getting away. A pair of Captain Huvraka's brown-skinned sailors guided the load through the hatch and into the hold.

Kerin picked out Huvraka by his turban. The shipmaster was a squat, thickset, powerful man with a deep-brown skin and a bristling black beard striated with gray. Besides the turban, he wore a pair of baggy trousers gathered at ankles and slippers with turned-up toes, leaving his upper body bare; the air was balmy during a late autumnal warm spell.

Kerin started up the gangboard. Noticing him, the captain bustled over to the inboard end of the plank. "What would you?" he said in accented Novarian. "Can't you see I am loading?"

"I thought to buy my passage," said Kerin.

"Oh, in that case. . . ." Huvraka shouted to another member of his crew in Mulvani. The man addressed, in loincloth with a strip of fabric around his head, began issuing orders to the deckhands.

"Now then," said Huvraka, turning back. "Whither go you?"

"To Salimor and thence to Kuromon. The harbor master said you sail to Salimor."

"Aye, with stops at Janareth, Halgir, and Akkander. Are you coming alone? No wife or leman?"

"Yea."

"Then your fare will be twenty-six Mulvanian crowns."

"My money is in Kortolian marks," said Kerin. He did sums in his head and said: "That should come to about forty marks."

Huvraka looked doubtful. "That's local market rate, no

doubt; but I am giving only official rate; it is the law. According to that, your fare is coming to sixty marks."

Kerin had been warned to haggle over the fare. He hated bargaining, which made him squirm with embarrassment; but he knew he would have to harden himself. He said:

"I cannot afford such a sum, Captain. Hast any other passengers? I want to know with whom I must needs share quarters."

"Nay, you are only one," said Huvraka. "You are having your cabin to yourself."

"Well, since I'm your only passenger, 'tis either I or none. Under the circumstances, methinks you could give me passage for fifteen crowns, which would bring it down to the local rate of exchange."

Captain Huvraka snorted. "Nay, never! If you are not paying going rate, be off with you!"

"Very well," said Kerin, turning away. "I must needs await the next ship."

As he started back down the plank, Captain Huvraka called: "Ho, not so fast, young man! I am abating my charges somewhat, albeit not to ridiculous figure you named. How about twenty-three crowns?"

A half-hour's chaffer got Kerin his passage for forty-six marks. Then he set out to find the maker of dolls to whom the taverner had referred him.

When he finally found the man's house, he approached its door with lagging steps, horribly embarrassed to ask for doll's clothes. When he hesitated, his hand outstretched to pull the bell rope, a sharp, stabbing pain in the buttocks made him jump.

"Go on, craven!" tinkled Belinka's voice.

He rang the bell. The dollmaker, a stout man with a fringe

of gray hair around a bald scalp, admitted him. Kerin squared his shoulders, stuck out his chest, and told the proprietor:

"Sir, I need a dress for a poppet about so high." He held his fingers apart at what he thought was Belinka's stature. Squirming, he added: "For my little niece."

The man shouted over his shoulder: "Ricola! Have we a spare frock for one of the Queen Thanudas?"

"Aye, methinks so," mumbled a woman's voice. The dollmaker's wife appeared with a mouthful of pins, holding a piece of cloth on which she had been sewing. She rummaged in a pile of miscellany and held up a doll-sized, turquoise-colored dress. Taking the pins out of her mouth with her free hand, she said: "Will this do, young sir?"

Kerin disliked being referred to as "young" but he was so eager to begone from the place that he paid the asking price without haggling. Back at the inn, he whistled: "Belinka!"

"Aye? Let me see!" Kerin felt the dress snatched out of his hand. It bobbed about in midair before the faintly-seen form of Belinka, who chirped:

"Oh, curse of the purple skull! How shall I get the thing on over my wings?"

"If you're an immaterial being, what's the problem?" asked Kerin.

"Not so immaterial as all that. But you would not understand."

"I wondered about the wings, also. How about cutting a pair of slits?"

"'Twill spoil the effect!" she cried. "It won't hang aright!"

"How can I help that? Must these slits go all the way to the bottom, or can you fold your wings, like fans, to get them through narrower openings?"

"Methinks gaps about *so* long would suffice," she said, holding her hands apart. "Here, catch!" The blue-green garment fluttered towards Kerin. "How wilt accomplish this task? By sawing with your dagger?"

"Nay," said Kerin. "My family sent me forth well equipped." From his bag he dug out a small canvas sack containing needles, thread, and small scissors. "They insisted I be able to mend my gear."

He set to work on the gown, saying: "Turn around, Belinka, and make yourself more visible—oh, damn!"

"What's amiss?"

"I cut the slit too far on one side. I fear I'm no tailor. Canst sew a fine seam?"

"Nay," she said. "Not wearing clothes on our plane, we've never developed that skill."

Kerin sighed and addressed himself to threading the needle. After several attempts, he said: "Belinka, your hands are daintier than mine. Could you stick the end of the thread through that little hole in the needle?"

"I will try. . . . Oh, you have the end frayed out, so of a surety it won't go." She licked the end of the thread and twisted it into a point. "There you be!"

Kerin began sewing the edges of the longer cut together. "Ouch!"

"What befell?"

"Pricked myself. Methinks this be my first needle."

For a few seconds he worked away quietly. Then Belinka, rummaging in Kerin's sewing kit, held up a shiny object. "What's this, Master Kerin? It looks like a helm for one of us Second Planers, albeit too small for me."

"That's what we call a thimble. I am supposed to use it somehow in this task, but I know not how." He continued sewing.

Belinka exclaimed: "You've got it all wrong, clumsy oaf! One side of the cut matches not the other, so the fabric will gather in bunches."

Kerin spread his hands. "'Tis my best effort. If it's not good enough, the reason is you distracted me by asking about thimbles."

"That's right, blame me for your clumsiness!" She paused, then said in a less petulant tone: "Why not ask the dollmaker's wife? Methinks she made the dress in the first place."

Kerin grunted. "A fine fool I should look, trailing back across half the city to ask her to repair my botchery! I'll try the wife of our present host."

Kerin went and found the innkeeper's wife. With another rush of embarrassment, he explained his errand. "This poppet for my little niece, now, has wings like unto an insect."

The innkeeper's wife examined the garment; Kerin was sure she was hiding a laugh. "'Tis a quarter-hour's work, an I guess not amiss. 'Twill cost you thrippence, Master Kerin."

"Agreed," he said.

Back in his room, he held out the dress for Belinka's inspection. She took it and flitted about, so that the bit of fabric fluttered this way and that. When she turned on her full visibility, she wore the dress with her wings protruding through the slits. "What thinkst?"

"Enchanting, my dear; though I admit I liked you the way you were. But you cannot wear the garment outside our room."

"And why not, sirrah? I can be invisible."

"Aye, but the sight of the dress fluttering about in midair, without occupant, were quite as arresting as your delectable form."

"Then take your damned dress!" she flung it at Kerin. "You Prime Planers make us work our arses off as familiar spirits, but you never let us have any fun!"

Kerin sighed. "Sorry, Belinka. And now the time for sailing nears, so we'd best be on our way."

·II·
The Ship Dragonet

As the sun sank redly towards the serried roofs and sparkling towers of Vindium, Kerin neared the *Dragonet*'s pier. A baldric over one shoulder supported his sword, while a strap on the other took the weight of the duffel bag on his back. As Kerin climbed the gangplank, Captain Huvraka said:

"Aha, Master Kerin, you are coming in good time. I am showing you your cabin. . . . But what is this?"

Belinka, glowing bluely and visible even in daylight, was flying circles round Huvraka's head, tinkling: "Oh, Captain, what a beautiful headdress! I must find somebody who can make me its ilk!"

"This your familiar spirit is?" asked Huvraka.

"Well, ah, yes it is," said Kerin. "She's quite harmless." Unless provoked, he silently added.

"You are thinking to bring it along on voyage?"

"Aye; she'll be no trouble."

"That may be; but then I am asking five marks more, for her passage."

"What!" cried Kerin. "That's an outrage! We had a firm agreement—"

"Ah, yes; but the agreement is not including other life forms. I am charging you same if you are a cat or dog aboard bringing."

"But she won't eat any of your food—"

"That is no matter. I am sticking to consistent policy. Pay or find another ship."

"Curse it, I will!" said Kerin. Defiantly he strode back down the plank. In his ear Belinka chirped:

"I am glad you won't sail on that ship, Master Kerin."

"Why?"

"There is a feel of evil about it."

"What sort of evil?" Kerin walked back towards the base of the pier.

"I cannot tell; 'tis a feeling I have, as of some evil super-natural presence. We sprites are sensitive."

Kerin drew a deep breath. "Then there's nothing for it but to hunt up the harbor master again. Let's hope he have not closed his office. . . . Oh, oh!"

He stopped. Coming upon the pier were three large, stout men with cudgels, and a smaller fourth man. Although the sun had dipped below the roofs of Vindium City, the sky was still bright above. By its light Kerin recognized Garic and his companions. The remaining man, a slight, gray-bearded oldster, wore a black robe to his ankles and a pointed skullcap.

"Well, fry my guts!" roared Garic. "Here's our little would-be wizard now! Give him the treatment, Frozo!"

The older man stepped forward, pointed a wand at Kerin, and shouted. With a whiplike crack, a jagged streak of blue luminescence shot from the wand towards Kerin. Even as Kerin winced, the streak ended in midair, a foot from his face, throw-ing a shower of sparks.

Again the words of power; again the crack and the flash; again the sparks. The small man said: "He is protected by a counterspell, like that which I put on you. I cannot pierce it."

"Well then," rumbled Garic, "we must needs use simpler means. Come on, boys!"

The trio started for Kerin, cudgels aloft. Kerin seized his sword but found it still affixed to its scabbard by peace strings. By the time he untied or cut them, the men would be upon him with clubs. He ran back along the pier, the duffel bag bouncing against his back.

At the *Dragonet*'s berth, Kerin found a pair of loinclothed sailors preparing to haul in the gangboard and others standing by to cast off the mooring lines. He panted up the plank.

"Well," said Captain Huvraka, "you are changing your mind?"

"Aye," panted Kerin. "I thought that. . . ." He paused for breath.

Huvraka and the mate unhurriedly stepped to the inboard end of the plank, each with a slender, curving sword in a bronzen fist. Huvraka shouted: "Keep off, you! I am not letting you on board!"

He added a command in Mulvani. The sailors cast off the hawsers and dashed back up the plank, which the deckhands hauled aboard and stowed. The *Dragonet* drifted away from the pier. Ashore, Garic and his comrades shouted:

"Coward! Eunuch! Come back and fight! Horse turd!"

Getting back his breath, Kerin asked: "How didst come to be armed so timely?"

Huvraka replied: "We are seeing fireworks on pier, with you and that hedge wizard. So, thinking we might have use for them, I am telling Mota to fetch our tulwars. Now, about your fare—"

"I'll pay as soon as I get this thing off," grunted Kerin, wrestling with his bag. "Fifty-one marks, right?"

"Ah, no, good sir. Since you are evidently dangerous cargo, pursued by enemies, I must be asking five marks more for the risk. That makes fifty-six."

"What? That's a swindle! We had an agreement—"

Huvraka shrugged. "If you are not liking, I am putting you back on pier."

Kerin sighed; circumstances conspired against him. As he fumbled with his purse, Huvraka said: "You should not be sad, young sir. Look, since you are only passenger, will you do me the honor of messing in my cabin tonight?"

Kerin frowned in puzzlement, then said: "Oh, you mean to eat dinner with you?"

"Yea, sir. That is what I am meaning."

"Thankee; I shall be glad to."

When Kerin had stowed his gear in one of the *Dragonet*'s two passenger cabins and emerged from his compartment in the deckhouse, he found the ship well away from shore. Eight sailors heaved on four sweeps to row the *Dragonet* out into the harbor. Others shinnied monkeylike along the yards, which lay in crutches rising from the deck, to untie the brails that retained the sails. Captain Huvraka shouted in Mulvani; sailors heaved on cranks, and the yards arose by little jerks. Other crewmen manned the sheets to give the yards the desired slant.

With popping sounds, the crimson-and-white-striped sails ballooned before the gentle westerly breeze, and the ship heeled slightly and picked up speed. The men at the sweeps shipped their oversized oars and stowed them. Other ships, anchored

in the bay, drifted past: undecked Shvenish single-masters like
magnified canoes; local coasters and fishermen, rigged like the
Dragonet on a smaller scale; beamy deep-sea square-riggers;
and long, low, lethal galleys of war.

As they reached open water, the *Dragonet* began to pitch and
roll with a corkscrew motion. Kerin had been warned of seasickness and apprehensively awaited its manifestations.

Activity on the fantail drew his attention. A knee-high apparatus of copper struts had been set up, and behind it a brown-
skinned woman sat cross-legged. She was plump, past her
youth, and clad in foreign fashion. She wore a length of fabric,
wound round and round her middle to make a short skirt, leaving her upper torso bare. Her smooth, flattish face suggested
the Far East.

The apparatus included a bowl of water a span across, suspended from the apex of the tripod. Beneath it, a smaller dish
hung by slender chains. In this dish, a little fire gave out ruby,
golden, and emerald smokes, which the sea breeze snatched
away. Edging closer, Kerin saw that the bowl was two-thirds
full of water. The bowl and the dish beneath it pendulated as
the vessel rocked.

As Kerin watched, the woman placed on the bowl a short
straw with one end painted crimson. Captain Huvraka also
watched. Trying his rudimentary Mulvani, Kerin pointed, saying:

"What is that?"

"Shh!" hissed the captain. "Magic."

The woman chanted in a tongue unknown to Kerin. As she
sang, the floating straw rotated slowly until the scarlet end
pointed to port. After it had wobbled about this direction and
finally settled down, Huvraka shouted to the sailor at the tiller.
Kerin caught the Mulvani word for "right-hand," and the *Dragonet* swung to starboard.

Huvraka grinned through his sable bush. "Now you see magic, Master Kerin. Janji is calling on her bir—you are saying her familiar spirit—to make straw point north. We go southeast by east. She my navigator is. Member of Salimorese Navigators' Guild." He glanced at the fading yellow-green afterglow in the western sky. "Time for dinner is. You are coming now."

Seated on a cushion on the floor of the captain's cabin, Kerin strove to cross his legs as did Captain Huvraka and Navigator Janji. Used to chairs, he found this posture difficult but hid his discomfort as best he could.

A brown, barefoot man in a skirt came in with pitcher and bowl, and towels beneath his arm. He poured water over his diners' hands, caught it in the bowl, and handed round the towels. Then he glided out, to return with three metal cups and a bottle, whence he poured a drink for each. Gathering up the towels, he slithered out again. Huvraka raised his cup.

"To success of quest, Master Kerin, whatever it be."

"Thanks," said Kerin. The liquor was smooth but stronger than any wine. "Captain, from what my brother told me, I thought Mulvanians drank nought alcoholic. At the palace in Trimandilam, they gave him only fruit juice."

Huvraka wagged a finger. "Ah, you are hearing tales of the strict Mulvani sects. We sailors are not so—so—what is your word? Straitlaced. Since we are belonging to one of lowest castes, what have we to lose by a little fun, like drinking *tari*? Drink up!"

Three drinks later, Navigator Janji asked: "Master Kerin, you are telling us what this quest of yours is."

His tongue loosened by liquor, Kerin talked: "I'm on my way to Kuromon to learn the secret of their clock escapement."

"What is?" said both Mulvanians at once. Huvraka added: "Some device for opening locks, so you are escaping from prison?"

"Nay, nay. As escapement regulates the speed of a clock, so it shall show noon as the same time as the sun every day. My brothers and I make and sell clocks as Evor's Sons. My brother Jorian has made inventions in clocks, but he has not attained a perfect escapement. . . ."

Kerin rattled on until dinner arrived. Then, as eating halted his spate of speech, he heard a tinkly little voice in his ear: "Master Kerin, you have let your tongue run away with you! Be more careful!"

Suddenly conscious of his imprudence, Kerin sat silently eating until Janji asked: "Are you doing aught with methods of navigation?"

"Why, no. I've never been on a ship before, and your spell is the first time I've seen such a thing. I've heard the Shvenites have a kind of crystal. . . . Why dost ask?"

"Oh, I am curious, being in that trade. How are you liking our food?"

"Excellent!" he said. Although he was not enthusiastic about this vegetarian repast, he remembered Jorian's drilling him in seizing every opportunity to flatter his hosts.

As the days drifted past, Kerin settled into his shipboard routine. He rose, ate, exercised, watched the sailors at their tasks, learned something of how the *Dragonet* worked, practiced his Mulvani, learned a little Salimorese from Janji, and went to bed again. On the second day out, Belinka told him:

"He-he, Master Kerin, that brown woman is more to Captain Huvraka than just his navigator!"

"You mean . . ."

"Indeed I do. She enters his cabin of nights. Her bir regards it as a joke, since the captain hath two wives at home in Akkander. He says—"

"Who says?"

"The bir, the familiar. He says they be frightfully jealous, though not of each other. But if they find out about Janji, they will make the captain's life not worth living. But my instincts tell me to beware of Janji! All Salimorese navigators are witches, saith the bir."

Kerin shrugged. "Huvraka's domestic arrangements concern me not."

Belinka tinkled on: "The bir considers it strange that in most of Novaria, none may marry more than one mate. That, he saith, means that where the numbers of men and women differ, some are left mateless."

"He may have the right of it," said Kerin.

Kerin enjoyed a day ashore at Janareth, amid the motley, polyglot crowds. As he returned to the *Dragonet*, he saw that a stranger of about his own size and shape was speaking with Captain Huvraka on the afterdeck. As Kerin approached, the new man turned. The newcomer was of nearly Kerin's age, clad in a red-and-yellow turban, a white many-buttoned jacket, slim-legged crimson trousers, and turned-up shoes. As Kerin took a closer look, he was surprised to see that the other young man, save that his hair, beard, and skin were darker, looked much like Kerin himself.

"Ah, Master Kerin!" said Huvraka. "You are meeting your new shipmate, Master Rao. Like you, he is going to Kwatna and thence, gods willing, on to Kuromon. He is taking the other passenger cabin."

"I am pleased to meet you," said Kerin in his meager Mulvanian, automatically extending a hand. Instead of clasping it, the other placed his palms together and bowed over his hands, saying:

"I, too, am pleased. You are speaking my language, I see."

"A few words only."

"Like unto my knowledge of your Novarian tongue, eh? I shall see you anon, if the seasickness lets me stir from my cabin. Already my stomach gives signs of discomposition."

Tide and wind dictated that Captain Huvraka should sail before that day's sunset. As the setting sun shot slanting scarlet rays from behind a bank of cloud, the *Dragonet* cleared the harbor and headed east across the darkling blue of the sea.

When Kerin entered the captain's cabin, he found Rao already there. The steward came in with his water and towels. When this chore was over, the steward reappeared with four cups instead of three and another bottle. Rao looked doubtfully at his cup, saying:

"I know not—it is against the rules of my master's sect. . . ."

"Oh, come on!" cried Huvraka heartily. "So small a sin will never affect your lot in your next incarnation. Besides, an adventuresome youth like yourself needs worldly knowledge to make his way."

Huvraka urged Rao some more; Kerin missed some of the speech, the language being still unfamiliar. But at last Rao held out his mug. He took a sip, coughed, and said:

"Whew!"

"Oft the first taste doth that," said the captain. "Try some more."

At length Rao got his cupful down. Kerin asked: "And what, Master Rao, sends you all the way to fabled Kuromon?"

Rao looked sly. "Aha, would I could tell you! It is a mission of utmost secrecy for my guru—my master."

"And who is your master, pray?"

"The mighty wizard and holy ascetic Ghulam. I am his chela, as he was once the chela of the great guru Ajendra. Surely you have heard of him, even in your backward land?"

Kerin had a sharp retort on the tip of his tongue; but remembering Jorian's lectures on diplomacy, he forbore. Instead he said:

"I fear the report of the great Doctor Ghulam has not reached my rustic village. Pray, tell me more about him."

While the steward refilled the cups, Rao launched into a colorful tale of the mighty Ghulam's feats of controlling the winds, healing the sick, foretelling the future, and driving his foes to destruction by sending deadly demons against them. During this recital he drank two more cups of *tari*. At last Kerin said:

"If this mission of yours be a matter of such import and stealth, I wonder your master sent you not forth with a bodyguard."

"In his wisdom he decided that an escort would only draw attention; that the safest course were for me to go alone, slipping quietly along like any ordinary traveler." Rao winked. "Betwixt thee and me, methinks he begrudged the cost of hiring guards; he's a fearful pinchpenny."

"Is it a mission to a Kuromonian colleague?"

"Nay, Master Kerin; it is weightier than that. I am to deliver the precious document to His Imperial Majesty, Emperor Dzuchen of Kuromon, and furthermore to pick up that which Kuromon is sending in return to the King of Kings, the mighty Lajpat of Mulvan."

"Good gods!" said Kerin. "I should think these rulers would have sent whole embassies, complete with ambassadors, secretaries, attendants, and soldiers."

"Indeed, indeed, some might so think," said Rao, his speech becoming a little slurred. "But the mighty Ghulam told them his scheme was best; he had foreseen its success in the stars. Of course," he added looking owlish, "you know nought of these things. It is a matter of utmost secrecy; my lips are sealed."

Kerin thought that either the wizard Ghulam or the King of Kings must be out of his mind, to entrust such a mission to one rattlebrained youth, whom a couple of drinks opened up as a fishmonger opens an oyster. But then he remembered how indiscreet he himself had been on his first night aboard. He said nothing of these thoughts, and the talk wandered off into other matters, such as the proper garb for the colder parts of the Kuromonian Empire. The steward brought dinner.

The *Dragonet* had been rolling gently; but the motion increased. Halfway through his repast, Rao, looking paler than his usual nut-brown wont, clapped a hand to his mouth, scrambled up, and bolted out the door.

"Use the lee rail!" Captain Huvraka shouted after him.

Before retiring, Kerin looked in on his fellow passenger. He found the young Mulvani lying pale and wan in his bunk. When he asked Rao how he was feeling, the Mulvani groaned and replied:

"I shall die on this accursed ship."

"Hast never been to sea before?"

"Nay. Amongst the stricter sectarians, seagoing is deemed immoral because the mariner inevitably befouls the waters with his waste. That angers the sea gods. If I survive, I will never, never . . ."

A spell of retching shook him, but Rao had nothing left to bring up. When the spell passed, Rao seized Kerin's hand, saying:

"My mission is of great moment and must be completed; the fate of nations may hinge upon it."

"Yes?" said Kerin.

"Aye, I mean that. So, if I perish of this damnable seasickness, I beseech you to make me a promise."

Kerin sympathized, but he was wary. "What promise?"

"If I die, you shall carry out my mission. It will not take you out of your way, since you, too, are bound for Kuromon."

Kerin made an impatient gesture. "Yes, yes, but what *is* it? What would you that I did?"

Rao thrust back the bedclothes, revealing that next to his skin he wore, hung round his neck by a slender chain, a package of oiled silk. He broke the waxen seal, unwrapped the package, and produced a long strip of paper of a notably thin, silky texture. The strip was covered with lines of tiny writing in the script of Mulvan, wherein all the letters hung down from a row of short horizontal lines. Rao refolded the paper and gathered a taper, a stick of wax, and a brazen seal to replace the original waxen seal. He said:

"Here is that which I am charged to give the Emperor's officials. If I perish, promise you will essay to deliver it!"

"But I have no introductions to the Imperial Court. . . ."

"Oh, you will find a way. Besides, he who turns in this precious document will be lavishly rewarded."

"Well," said Kerin hesitantly, "all right. I promise at least to try. But this will never happen. I know a bit of seagoing, and never have I heard of anyone's dying of seasickness. You may wish yourself dead; but as soon as you're back on land you'll feel as fit as ever."

"I hope so," said Rao lugubriously.

When Kerin returned to his own cabin and prepared for bed, Belinka appeared, gossiping:

"The witch's bir hints that his mistress have some subtle plan anent you, but he will not tell me more."

"What sort of plan? I like not for others unbeknownst to make plans for me."

"He will not say; but I fear she means you no good."

"Couldst wheedle it out of him?" Kerin slid beneath the blanket.

"Belike. He takes more than a passing fancy to me."

"What looks he like? I've not seen him."

"He favors invisibility; but he can take a form like unto mine, albeit male."

"Well, report aught interesting you can get. Good-night!"

They stopped at Halgir, on the Mulvanian side of the strait called the Fangs of Halgir. Kerin found the slatternly little town hardly worth going ashore for. It consisted of rotting houses and streets of black mud, peopled by underfed-looking Mulvanians clad in lengths of dirty cotton. Eventually Kerin tired of saying "No" in Mulvani to small brown locals, trying to sell him crude, unattractive wares, and fled back to the *Dragonet*.

The wind held, so that the transit of the Sea of Sikhon took less than four full days. On the second night out, Kerin stood after sunset with his elbows on the rail, looking at the ship's wake and the brilliant stars overhead; the crescent moon had not yet risen. A light touch made him turn, to see that Janji had come up silently and was leaning on the rail beside him.

"Are you enjoying the voyage?" she asked.

"Aye; though betimes it waxes tedious, with every day like the last."

He felt her smile in the darkness. "You are glad it is monotonous. When a storm comes, you will be glad to go back to monotony of fair weather."

"Do you expect a storm?" asked Kerin.

She shrugged. "One never knows. But, Master Kerin, tell me, why are you becoming so secretive? At dinner you hardly say a word about yourself. The first night you talked freely, but since then you shut up like tortoise pulling head into shell. Young Master Rao was much more forthcoming than you."

"I daresay," said Kerin. "In fact, the night he came aboard I thought him a blabbermouth, telling us things that would disturb his master if he knew. But since then we've hardly seen him."

"The poor lad is one of those who gets seasick while the vessel lies still in its dock. You seem to be adapting well to life on a deck, even though you and Master Rao look much alike. If you were darker of skin or he lighter, the twain of you could pass for brothers. But you are much more secretive."

Kerin almost launched into an account of the training through which his brother Jorian had put him. But he checked himself, saying merely: "I didn't wish to bore you and the captain with my petty personal affairs."

"Oh, we are not bored! For example, I see you wash yourself on deck today. We hear silly stories about Novarians. Some say their male members are an ell in length and writhe like serpents; but you look like normal man."

Kerin gulped, feeling himself flush in the darkness. "Thank-ee."

"Are you using it in the normal way?"

"As far as I know." Kerin thought that if his embarrassment became much hotter, he would burst into flame like the fabled phoenix.

"Another thing," said Janji. "They say that the sight of a woman's teats inflames Novarians with insensate lust, so they cannot control selves but leap upon any woman like wild beasts. Is true?" She moved closer, gently rubbing against him. Kerin became aware of perfume.

"Well—ah—that's an exaggeration. We are not used to seeing those parts exposed so freely, save in bathhouses. 'Tis a difference in customs."

Kerin felt his blood pound. In the starlight, looking up at him, the fleshy, middle-aging Janji looked almost beautiful. His heart pounding, he cleared his throat. "Would you—I mean—do you . . ."

He felt an exploratory hand. She exclaimed: "By Kradha the Preserver! What they say must be true. We must take care of that. Come, but very quietly! Huvraka is a fierce and jealous man."

She led him towards the door of his cabin. When he reached out to open the door, however, she planted herself before it, saying:

"First you are telling me truth about your secret mission."

"*What?* What secret mission are you talking about?"

"If I know, I do not ask. Tell me!"

"I told you about the clock escapement—"

"Oh, you think I believe that? I am not so simple. You are telling me real reason, or no lovemaking tonight!"

Kerin spread his hands. "I know nought whereof you speak! There's no secret mission, unless you count the search for the escapement mechanism."

"You must hush your voice, fool, or you are waking Huvraka, and he comes with sword! If you will not tell, there is no more to say. Good-night!"

She marched off into the darkness. Kerin, whose passion had been cooled by the inquisition, stood looking after her and wondering if he had been made a fool of. If he could have thought up a plausible story, about an objective like those his brother

Jorian had gone after before retiring into respectable domesticity. . . .

But Janji might trip him up with searching questions. He shuddered at the thought of the embarrassment that exposure of his little fiction would cause. No, he had better resign himself to his virginal state a while longer.

Belinka spoke in his ear: "That must have been a quick one, Master Kerin. I saw you start for the cabin; then the bir—or hantu, in his language—began chasing me round the ship. He wants my all, as you Prime Planers quaintly put it. And now, but a moment later, off she goes to her own quarters."

"Neither slow nor quick," grumbled Kerin. "She wanted some damned secret, which I have not. When I failed to satisfy, she withdrew her offer."

"But otherwise you would have accepted, would you not? I was commanded to keep you away from wanton women, and the instant I take my eyes off you, you're off seeking a bout in the bedding with this witch. I warned you she is the focus of evil! She can turn you into a codfish for all I care! I shall have a fine tale to tell Adeliza!"

"Tell her what you like!" said Kerin hotly. "I was never fain to espouse the strumpet, and for her to engraft a familiar spirit on me is an outrage!" He thought he heard a fairylike sniffle. "Now, now, cry not, Belinka! 'Tis not your fault; you but do your duty. But if you tell Adeliza that I futtered a strange woman every day of the journey, that's fine with me."

The sniffle died away. At length she said: "I am sorry, Master Kerin. I am constrained to give my mistress a truthful account upon my return."

"At least, tell her not of this failed seduction! It is too embarrassing."

"I cannot altogether hide it; but I'll strive to soften the tale."

"Good!" said Kerin. "And whilst you're about it, wilt try to pry out of this amorous bir the deadly secret whereafter Janji lusts?"

"I'll try; but in return you must remain faithful to me!"

"I—I'll do my best," said Kerin. It occurred to him that the mercurial Belinka's flare of temper might be a case of simple jealousy. He and Belinka could hardly enjoy an amour in the usual sense; but her emotions might resemble those of a mortal. He wished that Jorian, with his wide experience, were there to advise him.

The next two days passed uneventfully. Kerin and Janji treated each other with formal reserve. Huvraka did not appear to have noticed any change.

On a hot morning, the *Dragonet* put into her home port of Akkander. This was a larger town than Halgir. The streets were still of mud, flanked by many tumbledown shacks; but there were some well-constructed buildings.

The *Dragonet* berthed at a quay of red sandstone, near a small shipyard. Therein lay a half-built ship with bare ribs curving skyward, like the skeleton of a whale. The quay was a little higher than the deck of the *Dragonet*, so that the gangplank had to slope up.

While sailors shinnied down the sloping yards after brailing the sails, others wound the mooring lines around the bollards on the quay. Then the yards were swung to the centerline and lowered by jerks into their crutches. Huvraka bellowed commands, and grunting sailors hauled and pushed bulky bundles up from the hold, since Akkander had no such cranes as Vindium and Janareth boasted.

The discharge of goods for Akkander was quick, for it was but a minor part of the cargo. When Huvraka blew a whistle, sailors swarmed up the gangplank or leaped directly from ship to quay, to disappear at a run into town. The burly Huvraka strode up the gangplank, his tulwar thrust through his sash and white teeth flashing in his sable bush of beard. Mota, the lean, taciturn mate, followed. Soon Kerin found himself alone on the ship save for Rao, who had not yet appeared, and Janji. The witch-navigator said:

"Are you not going ashore, Master Kerin?"

"I thought thus to spend a few hours. What has Akkander to see?"

She ticked off the town's temples and monuments. Kerin asked: "What does one for dinner? Are there taverns? There seemed to be none in Halgir."

"Yea, there are. But a foreigner who eats in one may catch a flux; so beware of food not cooked. Or you can come back to ship."

"Doesn't the cook get shore leave?"

"Aye; Chinda is already going. But I stay here on watch. Someone must be guarding the ship, and it is my turn."

"If I come back for dinner, 'twill be early enough for you to cook for two—"

"Master Kerin!" said a male voice. Resplendent in his best white turban and a crimson jacket with buttons of semiprecious stones, Rao appeared. "Go you ashore? May I come, too?"

The young Mulvani moved unsteadily. He had lost some weight, and isolation from sunlight had lightened his skin; but he seemed to be cheerful and ripe for adventure.

"Certes," said Kerin. "Art ready?"

"Aye, verily. Let's forth!"

Kerin said: "I really must practice my Mulvanian more. Promise to correct me whenever I err!"

The town possessed more interesting features than Kerin had thought. There was, for instance, a little museum containing relics of its past, such as the turban of its founding father and the ax he had cut down trees with. Since the captions on the labels were in Mulvani, Kerin was glad that Rao could interpret them. Rao eagerly explained the Mulvanian system of writing; by the end of the visit Kerin could sometimes decipher a word in a caption.

At the city hall, Kerin noticed a clock in the tower. Wondering if this were one of the clocks installed by his father, he asked the guard at the door:

"May we go up the tower to look at your clock? I am in the business."

"You may not go up without me," said the guard, "and I . . . Wait! 'Tis almost time to refill the tank. I will escort you two gentlemen up to the clock, if you will haul the buckets."

The guard picked up two buckets and filled them at the nearby well. Rao looked puzzled. "Does he expect me to carry a bucket? That's no proper kind of work for one of my caste."

"Oh, futter your caste!" said Kerin. "I was brought up to do whatever job had to be done and not fuss about it. Do you want me to tote both buckets?"

"Well—ah—all right, if you'll not tell my compatriots. They would scorn me if they knew."

While Kerin caught his breath after the climb to the top of the tower, the guard emptied both buckets into the tank of a large water clock. Evidently the travels of Evor the Clockmaker had not carried him to Akkander, or he would have sold them a mechanical clock.

The sun had been near the meridian when they set forth and was low in the west by the time they had done with the sights of Akkander. When they passed a drink shop with a space behind the bar for four tables, at which a couple of locals sat on cushions on the floor eating, Kerin and Rao exchanged glances. Without discussion, they made their way in and were presently seated enjoying the local liquor, another variety of *tari*.

Kerin expected a long delay for their dinners; smaller eateries seldom carried a reserve of perishables. Therefore someone had to go out and buy the items ordered before they could be cooked.

Kerin was into his second mug, and Rao was expounding the mighty magical feats of his master, when a young woman glided up, saying: "You gentlemen look lonesome. May I join you?"

She spoke the local dialect of Mulvani, which Kerin could follow with some difficulty. Small and dark, she was clad in Mulvanian fashion in a length of filmy, peach-colored material wound round and round to make an ankle-length skirt. She also wore multiple strings of beads around her neck, earrings, bracelets, and a jeweled nose ornament.

Kerin had become so used to Janji's bare breasts that the sight no longer roused his lust. He said: "Certes, mistress. Pull up a cushion; the table is big enough. Who are you?"

"Call me Yakshi. Tell me of yourselves, you big, beautiful strangers!"

Rao continued the tale of his guru's magical prowess. The girl hung on his every word. After a while she raised her eyes and said: "Oh, there is my friend Surya. Wouldst mind if she, too, joined us?"

"The more the merrier!" cried Rao. "As I was saying, when the demon escaped from the pentacle, the mighty Ghulam . . ."

The second young woman, similarly clad but in a skirt of turquoise blue, glided up. Soon both were hanging on Rao's words. The latter was into his third mug, so that the words became a trifle slurred. But his narrative aptitude was not affected, and the floodgates of his natural garrulity were opened.

"And then," he said, "there was the time when the mighty Ghulam and I were prospecting for gems along the banks of the Shrindola, near the site of ancient Culbagarh. We had

stopped in a little glade to eat our midday meal, when a tiger
came out of the jungle and started towards us, slinking along
with its belly dragging the ground.

"I said to my guru: 'Master, cast a spell, yarely, ere we be
devoured!' So he made passes and muttered formulae. The tiger
kept right on, aiming for me. When it sprang up in its final
rush, I awaited not the order of my going but leaped into the
branches of a big banyan tree, which, praise Kradha, grew at
the edge of the glade. I never climbed so fast in my life. At
that, the brute's claws scored the bark a finger's breadth below
my feet.

"The tiger slid back to earth, roaring with vexation. Then it
sat at the foot of the tree, looking hungrily up. Meanwhile
Ghulam squatted quietly nearby, eating; the tiger ignored him.

" 'Master!' I cried. 'What betides here?'

"Ghulam looked placidly up, saying: 'My boy, I did but cast
upon myself a spell of aphanasis, so that the tiger fails to notice
me. I lacked time for a more comprehensive spell to protect
us both. Find thyself a comfortable seat, and in time the beast
will tire of waiting and depart.'

"That was all very well for Ghulam to say, but after I had
waited for over an hour, whilst the tiger showed no inclination
to leave, I waxed impatient. I had, moreover, been so busy preparing Ghulam's lunch that I had not had time for mine own.

"So I complained, louder and louder. Having finished his own
repast, my master wiped his mouth and said: 'Oh, very well.'
He dug powders out of his knapsack and tossed them on our
dying fire, and muttered and gesticulated. Presently there came
a crashing, whereat the tiger looked around. Out into the glade
stepped a buffalo heifer. This beast took one look at the tiger,
uttered a bawl of terror, and fled away into the jungle with the
tiger bounding after.

"Ghulam called up: 'Thou mayst come down now, Rao. Yon

simulacrum of a heifer will dance ahead of the tiger for twenty or thirty leagues, or until the tiger run out of breath and quit. We shall see no more of that fellow today, I'll warrant!'

"And speaking of buffaloes, there was the time we happened upon a herd of wild buffalo unawares. They lined up before us, and some of the bulls snorted, pawed the earth, and lowered their heads. Plainly they were about to charge. I said:

" 'Cast a spell quickly, Master!'

" 'No time for that,' quoth he. 'Run at them shouting and waving thine arms!'

" 'Art mad?' I said.

" 'Nay; do as I say, and thou shalt see.'

"So, with much trepidation, I charged the buffalo, shouting and waving. To my surprise, one turned away, and in a trice all were fleeing into the forest.

"Returning to Ghulam, I asked how he knew this outcome beforehand. He replied: 'In any sizable group, there will be at least one faint of heart, who will flee any wight who rushes upon him. When this one flees, the sight strikes the others with fear; and they, too, run. But attempt not this jape with a single bull. He may not be a coward, in which case thou wilt await thy next incarnation!'

"And then there was that crocodile that proved immune to spells and illusions. . . ."

Kerin felt his nose a little out of joint, since both Akkandrines gave their attention to Rao while ignoring Kerin. He blamed this partiality on Rao's richer appearance, since Kerin had not donned his best clothes.

His twinge of resentment in turn aroused in Kerin a twitch of suspicion. The girls, he was sure, were local whores. Perhaps this was a good chance to get rid of his long-resented virginity. But again, Jorian had warned him that taking up with chance-met locals might get the traveler more than he bargained for.

Besides, Kerin was too embarrassable to ask right out: How much? Still, if either girl turned her charm upon him. . . .

Surya asked: "Have you handsome gentlemen ordered yet?"

"Nay," said Rao. "The hosh—host told us the cook be off on an errand but will soon return. Then the mighty Ghulam—"

"Then," continued Surya, "why go we not to my little house, where we can eat, drink, and amuse ourselves without the presence of others?"

"Very kind of you," began Kerin, "but—"

"A splendid idea!" crowed Rao. "Lesh go, Kerin old boy!"

"We shall have a wonderful party!" said Yakshi. "Surya shall sing whilst I play the *plong*."

"Beware, Master Kerin!" buzzed Belinka in Kerin's ear.

"Now wait!" said Kerin. He eyed Surya and said in careful Mulvani: "How much will this party cost?" When the girl looked blank, he repeated the sentence to Surya, who said in her own dialect—Kerin thought exaggerated—"I am sorry, but I understand not."

Kerin then spoke in Novarian to Rao: "Look, we know these damsels not. They may have their pimp waiting to knife us."

"Oh, nonsense!" said Rao. "They're jush a couple of shweet little whores who wouldn't hurt a fly. Besides, I hate going back to that damnable ship, which bounces me about like a cork—"

"Well, I'm not going with them, and that's that. You do as you wish."

"Scared?"

"Being careful, that's all. You wouldn't want to risk that thing around your neck, would you?"

"Oh. Now that you mention it. . . ." Rao fumbled inside his jacket, pulled out the little sack of oiled silk, and hoisted the chain over his head. He had to doff his turban to get it off. Handing the package to Kerin and replacing the turban, he said:

"All right, you go back to the ship whilsh I make merry with these little lovelies. Take good care of that document! Here's where I prove my manhood—with both, shee if I don't!"

They rose. Rao slapped down on the counter a gold piece worth, Kerin guessed, many times the value of the drinks they had drunk. Rao's penurious master, Kerin thought, would have been horrified. Without asking for change, Rao wavered out between the two girls, one supporting his staggering steps on either side.

Kerin turned back towards the waterfront. As he walked, he wondered if he had not, through timidity, lost out on a pleasurable experience. If only he had some magical device to tell him how far it was safe to go in such situations. . . .

As, under a twilit sky, Kerin walked down the gangplank of the *Dragonet*, Belinka buzzed: "Well done, Master Kerin! I was watching. Had you not refused that invitation, I should have made someone smart for it! Now beware the witch Janji, who hath nefarious plans!"

"I'll try to govern my evil passions."

Janji appeared from the deckhouse. "Master Kerin, where is your shipmate Rao?"

"Still ashore, trying to prove his manhood on a couple of harlots."

"Akkander is not the safest town for such adventures. He may be knocked on the head and robbed."

"I tried to warn him, but . . ." Kerin spread his hands.

"Hast dined?"

"Nay; the party broke up ere we reached that stage. Couldst—ah . . ."

"Certes; I'll put another portion on the stove. When you're cleaned up, I shall see you in the captain's cabin."

When Janji had cleared away the monotonously vegetarian repast, she said: "I am pouring you another, yes?"

"Thankee, but nay," said Kerin, remembering how liquor had loosened his tongue before.

"Oh, pray do take one more!"

"Nay!" said Kerin emphatically, placing his hand over the goblet.

She put away the bottle. "Captain Huvraka will not come aboard again until morn. He is busy proving his love for both his wives. He says he can prove it all night long, but I have not the wives' side of the story. Anyway, he is sleeping late." She gave Kerin a level stare. "So, if you will tell me of your secret mission . . ."

Kerin thought frantically. "I—the fact is—'tis nought much; merely a commission from my brothers' general practitioner of iatric magic, Doctor Uller. He would fain discover the Kuromonians' spell for smiting one's foe with emerods."

"Forsooth?" said Janji in a skeptical tone. She leaned to one side as if listening, then said: "That is not true, Master Kerin. I can tell."

In Kerin's ear he heard a tiny voice: "Her bir hath told her the tale be a lie."

"I do assure you—" began Kerin.

"Oh, go futter yourself!" cried Janji, rising. "You think to deceive me, foolish boy? You are spending your next incarnation as earthworm!" She marched out.

Kerin sighed. "Belinka, if you Second Plane sprites are so skilled at detecting Prime Planers' lies, why do we Kortolians not employ you in our courts, to tell which defender or accuser is telling the truth?"

Belinka gave a silvery laugh. "That hath been proposed, Master Kerin. But all the lawyers opposed it so vehemently that the idea was abandoned. They feared it would reduce them to beggary."

• • •

Rao did not return to the *Dragonet* that night, nor did he appear next morning. Captain Huvraka snorted: "The young fool should have known better."

Kerin asked: "Is there no authority in this town to trace down the missing man and, if he's been murdered, bring his slayers to justice?"

"As well try to spit on the moon as bring any local to justice here," said Huvraka. "If by some remote chance they caught the miscreant, he'd divide his loot with the magistrate and be let off with a scolding."

Nonetheless, the captain sent two of his sailors ashore to look for the missing passenger. Hours later they returned, saying the man seemed to have utterly vanished. Huvraka said:

"Belike the turtles and crabs in the swamps are devouring his corpse. We should have sailed at midday, since Akkander gives us no very bulky cargo. I'll hold the ship for a couple of hours more; but if he appear not, off we go."

Still without Rao, the *Dragonet* sailed in midafternoon and plowed into the Eastern Ocean. For several days, Kerin resumed his shipboard routine. He smote the rats and cockroaches that invaded his cabin; he watched Huvraka and Mota flog a sailor for some nautical malfeasance. He and Janji exchanged a few amenities but otherwise ignored each other.

The third day out, a storm blew up. Kerin, who had been preening himself on being a much better sailor than Rao, learned the pains of seasickness. Gripping the weather rail, barefoot and breechclouted like the sailors, he miserably looked up at the crest of a wave bearing down upon the *Dragonet* and, as the ship climbed, down into the watery valley yawning precipitously below. From the lowering, leaden sky, lukewarm rainwater sluiced over his body. As Huvraka, for once without his turban, hurried past, Kerin shouted over the roar of wind and wave:

"Is this a bad storm?"

"Ha!" the captain shouted back. "This is *good* weather! This is no storm at all! We are sailing through some that make this look like a flat calm! And next time you are puking, you are please using lee rail!"

Kerin started for his cabin when an exceptionally violent lurch sent him spinning down the sloping deck to the lee rail and into the net that had been rigged along it. Without the net, he was sure he would have gone over the side. When he finally struggled back to his cabin, he took off his money belt and hid it in his bag. He feared that, if he slipped on the rain-lashed decks and fell overboard, the weight of the coins would speedily drown him.

By the next morning the rain had ceased, though the ship still leaped and lurched like a stallion with a burr beneath its saddle. Kerin's healthy young frame adapted quickly, so that by noon he was able to eat and keep it down.

Ten days after leaving Akkander, Kerin was leaning on the port rail, enjoying the hypnotic effect of the endless procession of wave crests. He watched the occasional silvery flash of a flying fish as it sculled along the surface until it reached airborne speed and skimmed away over the crests on glassy wing-fins. He had learned to walk with a nautical roll, to forestall a loss of balance when the deck abruptly changed its slant.

He looked sharply at the horizon. Yes, unless he was suffering hallucinations, there was a stretch of land. A touch on his arm made him start; Janji had glided up beside him.

"Is that land?" He pointed.

"Yea; that is first of the islands we call the Peppercorns."

"Means it we near Salimor?"

"Nay, not yet. The Salimor Archipelago is farther east; but

we are more than halfway from Akkander. I must be taking ship south of the Peppercorns, to stay away from rocks. If this westerly holds, this will be our fastest passage. Coming back is harder; we must tack against the westerlies or sail much farther south to pick up easterly trades."

She pressed her bare arm against Kerin, then turned to bring a breast in contact. Kerin felt a familiar surge. Down, dog! he sternly told himself.

"Are you still keeping secret of mission?" she purred.

"Aye, you st—" he began but choked off the word "strumpet." "I'm under a vow."

"Oh," said Janji. "People are all the time taking such vows in Mulvan; but I am thinking all Novarians are monsters of lust."

Kerin shrugged. "Tales grow in telling. Isn't that another island?" He pointed.

"Aye; it is the biggest of the Peppercorns. It takes half the night to sail past. We call it Kinungung."

"Does anyone live there?"

She shrugged. "They say there be a holy hermit, clept Pwana; but no tribes or villages." She glanced back at the wake, which the setting sun had turned into a furnace of molten gold. "Time for dinner is coming. I shall see you soon!"

At dinner, the normally jovial Huvraka seemed dour and preoccupied. Later Kerin, preparing for bed, was roused by angry voices through the bulkhead between his cabin and the captain's. He put his ear against the planking but could catch no more than an occasional word.

"Belinka!" he called softly.

"Aye, Master Kerin?" The little blue light twinkled round the compartment.

"Couldst eavesdrop on what goes on there?"

"Drop an eave—is not that part of a roof? How can one?"

"I mean, listen in and report back to me."

"I will try, but her bir may chase me out."

The uproar continued for another quarter-hour. Then Belinka's light flickered into view, and her voice buzzed: "Oh, Master Kerin, you must leave the ship ere Captain Huvraka kills you!"

"What? How? Why should—"

"They quarreled, and the bir took a pull at the *tari* and now lies drunk in a corner. The captain is jealous of the navigator, whom he accuses of granting you her favors, as you Prime Planers say. He says he watched you and her on deck. She says, she will futter whomsoever she wishes; and Huvraka like it not, he can get another navigator. He says he will cut you in pieces for fish bait, and methinks he mean it."

"I fear him not. My brother taught me how to oppose those curved swords with my straight one."

"But he will bring sailors to help him, and they will seize you from behind. So please, please go like a man of sense! I am supposed to keep you safe, and I cannot let you get into a fight where you would have no chance. So go!"

"How? I cannot walk on waves."

"Use that little boat atop the deckhouse. Hasten, and be as quiet as you can!"

"Oh, very well." Kerin crammed his belongings into his bag, donned his sword, and stepped out into velvety darkness. He looked aft and was relieved to see that the man at the tiller was out of sight behind the deckhouse. By getting a toehold on his cabin porthole, he climbed to the roof and examined the boat. With his dagger he cut the lashings.

The boat took all his strength to move, but he managed to slew it around so that one end overhung the deck between the deckhouse and the rail. He feared that any instant Captain Huvraka, aroused by the noise, would come boiling out of his cabin, scimitar in hand.

Kerin inspected the boat more closely. A pair of oars were lashed down lengthwise in the hull. One more good heave would send the boat tobogganing down to the rail and into the Eastern Ocean. But the *Dragonet*'s speed would leave the boat behind before Kerin could board the little craft.

As his eyes adjusted to the starlit dark, Kerin examined the painter, coiled in the bow and eye-spliced to a ring at the top of the stem. In the stern lay a small bucket. Could he slide the boat overboard stern-first and seize the painter before it went? That would probably not work. Unless he released the boat and grabbed the line in one lightning-swift motion, the craft would get away, leaving him without means of escape.

Could he grip the end of the rope in his teeth, freeing his hands to wrestle with the weight? Perhaps; but then the boat would come to the end of its tether and either jerk the painter out of Kerin's mouth or pull him overboard. Kerin did not much mind a ducking; but what then? Would he capsize the little boat in trying to climb aboard? That would leave him in another hopeless predicament, clinging to an overturned hull with his gear at the bottom of the sea.

"Tie the rope to the ship, stupid!" squeaked the tiny voice.

Half grateful and half resentful, Kerin climbed down from the deckhouse and belayed the painter to a shroud. Moving quietly, he ascended again and heaved on the hull until the outboard end overbalanced the rest and the hull tipped down. Another heave, and the keel struck the rail. Then the hull slid down off the deckhouse, off the rail, and into the sea.

The splash aroused the helmsman, who appeared around the deckhouse corner. "Ho!" cried this man. "What do you? Who— ah, 'tis the passenger! What—"

Kerin grabbed the painter and hauled the line forward. When the boat stood abreast of the *Dragonet* and directly below Kerin, he tossed in his duffel bag with his free hand. The money belt clanked as the bag struck the floorboards.

"Hold!" cried the helmsman, starting towards Kerin. "You are not making off with the boat! It is the captain's property!"

"Keep clear!" grated Kerin, drawing his sword. "Stand back!"

The helmsman checked but cried: "Captain! We are being robbed! The foreigner is stealing the boat! Help! All hands on deck!"

The door of the captain's cabin banged open and Huvraka emerged, tulwar in hand. "By Ashaka the Destroyer!" he shouted. "What are you doing, miscreant?"

Kerin dropped into the boat, making the vessel rock and bounce. The bilgewater that the boat had shipped sloshed about the hull.

With one hand on the ship's gunwale to steady himself and to keep the boat from drifting astern, Kerin sawed through the painter with his sword where he had tied the line to the shroud. Huvraka loomed above him, leaning over the rail and raising his scimitar, when the line parted. Kerin fell back into the boat, and the sword swished harmlessly past his head.

The speed of the *Dragonet* took the ship swiftly away. Kerin gathered himself up, his rump sore from his tumble and his trews soaked with bilgewater. Sitting on the middle thwart, he worked on the knots that secured the oars.

Aboard the *Dragonet*, now receding into the dark, sounds of furious argument wafted. From a few shouted words Kerin, straining at knots, gathered that they were debating whether to bring the ship about to try to recover their boat. Tacking properly with lateen sails, Kerin had learned, was a laborious business, involving shifting the long, heavy yards and their triangular sails from one side of the masts to the other.

As he finally freed the oars and placed them in the oarlocks, a glance towards the *Dragonet* disturbed him. The ship was barely visible save for her stern light bobbing above the waves like a fading star. But Kerin could see that the striped sails were luffing, showing that the ship was coming about. In such an emergency they might do a "bastard tack"—that is, tack without shifting the yards around the masts. Huvraka had explained to him that this would make for slower, less efficient sailing; but if they took the time to shift the yards, Kerin might be out of sight when they took up the search again.

"Are you there, Belinka?" he asked the starlit night.

"Here, Master Kerin!" The blue light twinkled on the after thwart.

"Steady on," he said, and bent his back to the oars. Although the sea was moderate, with a slight swell, Kerin found ocean rowing quite different from that on a lake or pond. He caught crabs, and the butt of an oar hit him under the chin and almost knocked him off the thwart.

"I think," said Belinka, "that you must needs take short, quick strokes, lifting the oars on high on each return stroke."

With a grunt, Kerin yielded to her advice and found the going easier if more fatiguing than the rowing he was used to. He paid no heed to direction, reasoning that his best chance of escaping the *Dragonet* lay in a random, unpredictable path. The main point was to get as far as possible from where he had left the ship before the moon, then in its first quarter, rose. He expected this in an hour or two. When he paused for breath, he asked:

"Belinka, how didst know about rowing?"

"I watched the sailors at the ports we stopped at."

"Clever little girl," said Kerin.

"I do but my duty, to return you intact to Adeliza."

Kerin grunted and bent to the oars again. The *Dragonet* was still afar. As Kerin continued rowing, he glimpsed the ship's stern light less and less and finally not at all. He supposed they were sailing back and forth in the area where he had absconded.

Kerin located the pole star, swung the boat thither, and said: "Belinka! Pray keep me headed towards that island we saw at sunset."

"Then give an extra stroke on your right oar—no, no, I meant the boat's right oar!"

Kerin chuckled. "Shame on you! A month at sea, and you haven't learned that the proper word is 'starboard.' "

"Nasty young man! And who told you how to row in the ocean?"

"Just getting even. Tell me, learned you aught about the quest whereof Janji suspects me?"

"Yea, I did; but I have not had a chance to tell you. It seems they have a navigating device in Kuromon—some sort of iron pin, impaled on a piece of cork to make it float. They treat the pin by some means that, when it floats, causes it to veer to point north and south of its own accord, without a spell or the help of a familiar. Since it works without supervision, Janji and her guild fear it will put them out of business."

"And she suspects me of seeking this device?"

"Aye. She thinks that, on your return, you will offer the secret to the Sophi for money."

"A thing I hadn't thought of; but it's an idea. How came you by this knowledge?"

She giggled. "I offered the bir my all if he would disclose the tale, and he did. Then I refused what you call my 'favors.' Enraged, he chased me out of the captain's cabin!" A tinkly laugh sounded from the stern. "Master Kerin, if you pull not harder on your left oar—your left, not the boat's—we shall go in circles till dawn."

The half moon crept above the horizon. Kerin strained his

eyes. He thought he glimpsed the peaks of the *Dragonet's* sails—a pair of little black triangles, like saw teeth, showing betimes above the curve of the earth—but he could not be sure. In any case, the ship must be too far for its people to sight him.

When Kerin tired of rowing, he shipped the oars and rested while bailing bilgewater. He dug his money belt out of his bag, put it on, and asked: "Belinka, about you and the amorous bir: Do you sprites—ah—I mean, is it the same as with us? That is—ah. . ."

She laughed. "We Second Planers' habits and customs are too complicated to explain, Master Kerin, our boat hath drifted until it points away from our goal. You had better start rowing again."

·III·
The Isle of Kinungung

The sun was well up when the
Dragonet's boat approached the pale-buff beach of Kinungung,
backed by slanting palms with fronds like gigantic emerald
feathers. Kerin's blistered hands were bandaged with strips of
cloth from the hem of an extra shirt. Craning shoreward, he
said:

"Belinka, methinks there's enough surf to run in on an incoming wave. Keep me headed exactly shoreward. If the boat
slews, the wave could roll us over."

"Aye, aye, Master Kerin. A little more on your right oar!"

As the waves grew steeper with shoaling, Kerin took easy
strokes. When a big one towered greenly over the stern, he dug
in his oars, heedless of the pain of his blisters, and sent the
boat shooting shoreward. Up and up went the stern as the craft
gathered speed.

"More on your left!" squeaked Belinka, dancing above the after thwart.

The wave curled and broke, hurling foam and spray into the boat. The broken crest raced by on either side; and the bow of the vessel crunched on the ivory sand.

Kerin threw himself out in knee-deep water and seized the bow to keep the boat from being carried away by the backwash. When the water had fallen to ankle depth, he dragged the boat up the beach. The next upwash boosted the boat a few feet more, and Kerin wrestled the craft to above high-tide mark. As he hauled, huge yellow crabs, with bodies the size of a human head, scuttled away.

Sitting down to catch his breath, Kerin called: "Belinka!"

"Here, Master Kerin!"

"It's hard to see you in the sunshine. Where is that smoke you spake of?"

"Yonder, to your left where you sit."

"Thankee. Methinks that's where the hermit, whereof Janji told me, can be found."

"Then rise and march, Master Kerin!"

"I'm spent from that all-night row. Let me sit quietly, will you?"

"Master Kerin!" she squeaked. "The day waxes hotter, and you lack food and shelter. We are much nearer the equator of your world than we were in Vindium. The sooner you seek those of your kind, the better your chances. Up!"

"You remind me of a onetime schoolteacher of mine," grumbled Kerin.

"I do but do my duty, to save you whole for Adeliza. So on your feet!"

"This talk of Adeliza begins to make death seem like a welcome relief." With a grunt, Kerin heaved himself up. As he lifted his sword and bag from the boat, Belinka said:

"Master Kerin, this sun is too bright for the likes of you. You must don more garments, lest you incur a fearful sunburn."

Kerin, clad in his trews and the loincloth beneath them, growled: "I suppose you are right, curse it!" He fumbled for a shirt.

"You will need hat and shoon, too," Belinka persisted.

"I have no hat; only that little cap. And it's easier to walk in sand with bare feet."

She started to argue further; but defiantly Kerin slung his sword and bag over his shoulders and set out along the beach.

As Kerin trudged, gulls flew screeching up from the beach ahead, while giant crabs rustled out of the way. Some defensively raised gaping chelae. Belinka asked:

"Master Kerin, would this isle harbor dangerous beasts?"

Kerin shrugged beneath the weight on his shoulders. "Unlikely, unless the island be larger than I think."

"Well," said the tiny voice from above, "something lies upon the beach ahead, which looks formidable. It is one of those crawly things you Prime Planers call lizards, but large."

"Oh, oh," said Kerin. "That sounds like one of those dragons of the Marshes of Moru, whereof my brother has told me. I must not blunder into it unawares!"

Kerin dropped his bag, drew his sword, and stole ahead. When the curve of the beach afforded him a view, he saw a long, slate-gray shape sprawled out upon the sand. He said:

"It looks to be either dead or asleep. Couldst go closer and tell me what you see?"

The sprite flitted away and returned to report: "Its ribs move with breathing. You must go no closer!"

Kerin grunted. "I'll not wait all day for the creature to digest its previous meal, ere it awaken and go about its business."

"Be sensible, Master Kerin! You are fatigued from your row and your walk, and 'tis time to rest!"

"And who wouldn't let me rest when we got ashore from the boat?" said Kerin. "Besides, I fear it not. It's but a little longer than I; and I could outrun it, as my brother outran one in Moru. If we move quietly, we can skirt the creature."

"You shall not!" shrilled Belinka. "I cannot let you risk your precious person. . . ."

Kerin shouldered his bag and, sword in hand, set out cautiously. As he neared the lizard, he saw that the space between it and the water was wider than that between it and the vegetation—at least twenty feet.

On the other hand, the lizard proved larger than he had thought. It was as big as a mature crocodile, ten or twelve feet long.

He hesitated; but fear of seeming timid before a female—even a non-human female—drove him on. He angled into the wet sand, so that the final upwash of each wave curled around his ankles. The lizard slumbered.

As Kerin came abreast of the reptile, the lizard opened its eyes, looked around, and rose on stumpy legs. It swiveled about to face Kerin, scattering sand; it opened fangful jaws and hissed like a kettle.

"Master Kerin!" cried Belinka. "Flee! Drop your burdens and run!"

Kerin stood still watching the lizard. For a score of breaths, man and reptile confronted each other, neither moving. Then the lizard turned away and walked deliberately towards the shrubbery beyond the beach, each leg sweeping out in a semicircle with every step. Once it paused to stare back at Kerin, as if daring him to start something. With a crackle and rustle, it disappeared into the vegetation.

Kerin drew a long breath. Grinning, he said: "See, Belinka? It decided I was too large to swallow."

"Bad boy!" squeaked Belinka. "Some day you will take one chance too many, and I shall be blamed by Madame Erwina for losing you, you great fool!"

"That, my dear, is your problem." Keep cool and don't argue, he told himself. "I did not invite you on this journey."

Kerin heard the ghost of a sniffle. "By Imbal's brazen balls, stop blubbering! If you wish to give advice, I will listen; but I shall make the final decisions."

Kerin felt weak from his reaction to the reptilian stand-off but tried not to show it. Belinka's advice was often sound, but her dictatorial manner made him contrary. He might do something foolish just to spite her. Jorian, he reminded himself, had warned him to judge each incident on its merits without letting petty irritations cloud his judgment.

Making sure that the lizard had disappeared, Kerin resumed his march. Another quarter-hour brought him in sight of the source of the smoke. On the edge of the beach, a fire smoldered in a circular hearth of stones and lumps of coral. As Kerin approached, he espied a small clearing in the vegetation, laid out as a vegetable garden. On the edge of this clearing, a hut of bamboo and palm fronds arose. Before the hut, seated on the ground and leaning back against one of the corner poles with his eyes closed, sat a naked, brown-skinned oldster. The man was scrawny, wrinkled, and egg-bald, with a fringe of white hair and white whiskers.

"Belinka," murmured Kerin, "dost remember the name of the hermit who, Janji said, dwells on Kinungung?"

"Methinks 'twas 'Pwana' or the like."

"Thankee." As Kerin approached the old man, doubtful whether the hermit was alive, Belinka tinkled:

THE HONORABLE BARBARIAN

"Have a care, Master Kerin! Trust not this so-called hermit until you know him better!"

"I'll try," muttered Kerin, suppressing a flash of irritation. Aloud he said: "Master Pwana, I presume?"

The man's eyes snapped open. "Aye, I am the Balimpawang Pwana. And who might you be?"

"You speak Novarian?" said Kerin in surprise.

"Aye; and all other civilized tongues as well. And you, young sir?"

"A castaway hight Kerin of Ardamai. How knew you I hailed from Novaria?"

Pwana chuckled. "It is evident from your garb, your cast of feature, your complexion, and the accent wherewith you spake Salimorese. I might be wrong on one of those inferences, but hardly on all four. I must explain my theory of probability. Meanwhile, art hungry?"

"Now that you speak thereof, I am ravenous."

"Then enter my hut and make yourself at home. On the right you shall see, dependent from the peg, a weighty club. Take it to the beach, strike a crab with force enough to break its shell, and fetch it hither."

Kerin found the hut well organized. Pwana had brought ample equipment to his hermitage. There were cooking utensils, an ax, a shovel, a spear, and a big brush knife that could serve as a sword. He set forth with the club.

A half-hour later, Kerin returned to the hut, gingerly bearing the crab by one leg. Although his blow had smashed the shell, the creature's limbs still twitched. Kerin did not intend to let a pincer get a grip on him.

He found Pwana stirring a pot, which hung from a tripod over a fire. The hermit set down the long-handled spoon and took the crab, which he deftly dismembered.

"Watch!" he said, bending back the flap on the underside of

64

the body until it broke. "Now you must peel back these parts, which we call 'dead man's fingers,' since they are not edible." He glanced sharply at Kerin. "Doth the sight revolt you, young sir? If so, you will never survive in the wilderness."

Gulping, Kerin mastered an impulse to gag. "N-nay, Doctor. Pray proceed."

Piece by piece, crab meat went into the pot, wherein vegetables already bobbed. Pwana chattered on, telling of the properties of each kind of green and ways of cooking it.

At last the hermit set aside the pot to cool. "We bother not with plates; and since I have but one spoon, you must needs use the fork from the hut." When Kerin returned with the fork, Pwana continued: "It is a pity you came not yesterday. I still had some smoked wild pig, but I finished it."

"How did you get it?"

"I set a snare. The time before, my trap caught a megalan."

"A what?"

"A megalan, one of those monstrous lizards. Hast seen any?"

"Aye; I passed one on my way hither. Are they dangerous?"

Pwana chewed and swallowed a mouthful of stew. "Not usually. But pirates marooned a man on Kinungung a few months past, and the lizards ate him. Methinks he lay down to sleep on the beach, and they seized him ere he could flee. And now, young sir, tell me how you come to be cast adrift on Kinungung?"

Kerin paused in trying to spear a bobbing piece of crab with the fork. "I was journeying to Salimor. The navigator, a witch, made advances, and the captain waxed jealous. To save my gore, I borrowed the ship's boat and fled. Now tell me how you come to dwell alone here."

Pwana gave a deep sigh. "I atone for my sins."

"Were they so great?"

"Ah, yea! Didst ever hear of the Temple of Bautong?"

"I fear not. Do tell me!"

"I was a simple practitioner of magic and wizardry, a member in good standing of the guild. But I was not satisfied with the decent living I earned from my profession. I lusted for more wealth, power, and glory. So I started a religious cult, of an obscure god, worshiped on one of the lesser isles, clept Bautong.

"To bedazzle my followers, I told a tale of the evil Emperor Ajunya, who lived during the previous cycle of Vurnu, twenty-six billion years ago."

"Your pardon, Doctor," said Kerin. "Vurnu, I am told, is a god of Mulvan; one of the holy trinity of Vurnu the Creator, Kradha the Preserver, and Ashaka the Destroyer. Do they, then, worship Mulvanian gods in Salimor?"

"Aye. Centuries ago, the Salimorese had no higher worship than that of nature spirits, of whom Bautong was one. But missionaries came from Mulvan to reveal their facets of the truth. To continue: By a mighty spell, I preached, Ajunya imprisoned the souls of all the previous mankind in a single gem, the Cosmic Diamond, which he wore as a pendant.

"There these souls remained whilst the universe, at the end of the cycle, shrank to a single atom in the mind of Vurnu. When Vurnu conceived a new universe, these souls remained imprisoned in the diamond. I told people that, therefore, in this cycle human beings were born without souls. Only I could release captive souls from the Cosmic Diamond, which I possessed, and assign them to bodies. Naturally, I gave my own followers preference in thus ensouling mortals.

"This was nonsense, which I made up out of mine own vagrant fancies. But my followers loved it. They flocked to my temple, and soon my subordinates began setting up more Temples of Bautong.

"I said that Bautong, my patron god, had guided me in this holy work; and the treasure rolled in. So vast became my wealth that I could command obedience from the Lord Sophi. My spies in the households of the great, from the Sophi down, kept me apprised of their malfeasances and scandalous doings. This knowledge proved useful in persuading them to contribute to Bautong.

"Then one night, Bautong himself visited me, a fanged and fiery presence. To prove that this was no dream, he laid his hand on the wall and left a black, scorched handprint still to be seen. If any further proof were needed, the aspirant temple girl who shared my bed awoke and fled screaming.

"Bautong complained that my methods were giving him a bad name amongst his fellow deities. I must, therefore, close the temples, give my hoarded wealth to the poor, and go into exile, on pain of punishments too ghastly to repeat. So here I am, striving by prayer, austerity, and doing such good as I can to enhance my lot in my next incarnation."

"Was the Cosmic Diamond a pure fiction, or didst pass off some bauble as the true gem?"

Pwana chuckled. "A shrewd guess! At first I told my worshipers the diamond was too precious to expose to their mundane gaze. Then my activities brought me a gem as big as an egg of one of yon gulls. So I caused it to be set in the forehead of the statue of Bautong; but covetous wights persisted in trying to steal it. Every few mornings, my temple attendants had to remove the corpse of some would-be burglar, slain by one of my familiars, and to clean up the blood and scorched flesh.

"When I went into exile, methought it unwise to leave this bauble where it would tempt weak mortals to sin. So I pried it from its setting and put it safely away, in case the gods should call me back to my spiritual duties. And now, Master Kerin, methinks we can enjoy our frugal repast."

They ate, washed out the pot in the surf, and returned to the hut. Kerin's eyelids sagged.

"And now," said Pwana, "I shall explain my theory of probability. It is that, for a sequence of events to occur, the chance of the whole series taking place is the product of the chances of the individual events in the series. Take your nationality for example. If the chance that you, with your complexion, were *not* a Novarian were one in four, and with your features were one in four, and with your accent . . ."

Looking around, Pwana found that Kerin had fallen asleep, curled up against the wall of the hut.

When Kerin awoke, the sun was near to setting. It took him an instant to orient himself. Then he found Pwana hoeing his garden. The hermit said:

"Aha there, Master Kerin! On the morrow, you can bear a hand with the weeding."

"Glad to, if my blisters permit."

"I shall speed their healing with a minor spell."

"But tell me," asked Kerin, "how can I get hence to Salimor?"

Pwana leaned on his hoe. "Kinungung is not an established stop for ships, albeit I often see them sailing past. That is one reason for my choice of this retreat."

"Could one build a signal fire?"

"One could, but then one might draw the attention of pirates, who are not too proud to snap up a single castaway to sell in the slave marts. Whereas I fear not death at their hands, it were wrong to expose you, with many years ahead, to that fate.

"There is another possibility. An old sea captain, a friend of long standing named Bakattan, stops by here on his way to the Inner Sea. He brings news and such articles as I have asked him to buy for me."

"How often comes this to pass?"

"Belike once a year. His last visit was but three months past, so expect him not for a long time hence. Look not so stricken, boy; I shall find plenty of chores to keep you occupied."

"A good, healthy existence, I doubt not; but it is not my ambition to pass my life thus," mused Kerin. "Could I build mine own boat, think you?"

"I doubt that. With palm trunks and bamboo stalks you could assemble nought better than a raft, which one good blow would demolish. Nor could you, alone, conn such a craft out of sight of land, or in contrary winds, or whilst asleep.

"Nay, my son, give up that fancy. You will be safe and comfortable here, and free of worldly temptations. I shall make you my holy disciple, or chela as they say in Mulvan. And now let me explain my theory of the variations in sea level. . . ."

Kerin listened with the best grace he could muster. When the old man ran down, Kerin asked: "Sir, if you were a genuine wizard, why brought you not some of your powers and instruments with you, to defend yourself?"

Pwana shrugged. "One or two nicknacks, such as a tarncap. But I have forsworn the serious practice of magic during my penance. I have dismissed my familiars, albeit I perceive that you have one."

"That was—" Kerin began to explain Belinka's presence but thought he had better not. Instead, he asked: "Your pardon, but what's a tarncap?"

"A cap of invisibility. It loses its charge and after a number of usages must needs be recharged with an extensive spell.

"Now, young man, take this bag and this pole and go along the beach, knocking ripe coconuts off their palms and gathering them. Be sure to return ere dark."

He handed Kerin an eight-foot length of bamboo and a large string bag.

When Kerin was out of hearing of the hut, he murmured: "Belinka!"

"Aye, Master Kerin?" The dancing blue light flickered into view against the evening sky.

"What in the seven frigid hells shall we do now? We must not linger here for months, awaiting Captain Bakattan's arrival."

"Couldst not lay a signal fire away from Doctor Pwana's demesne and, when you see a ship upon the horizon, touch it off?"

"How about pirates?"

"Canst tell a pirate ship from that of an honest merchant?"

"I might, if I could see it close. Pirates, my brother tells me, are a disorderly lot. Their ships are filthy, and their garb mingles dirty rags and looted finery. But if I were near enough to discern the difference, they would also see me and add me to their plunder."

Belinka: "Methinks in Pwana's hut I witnessed one of those brazen tubes you Westerners use to peer at distant things."

"A spyglass, like those they make in Iraz? How is it that I saw it not?"

"You were looking for certain things and ignored the rest. If Pwana hath this instrument, you could climb one of these slanting trees and sight your ship through the glass."

"That's an idea," said Kerin dubiously. "All I need do is borrow the glass without the good Doctor's knowledge. Methinks it more expedient to use you as my eyes, to fly out over the water for a closer look."

For several days, Kerin was busy with chores for Pwana. Not that the old man was idle; he kept busy, with rests few and far between. To survive alone, even in this mild climate, Kerin found, required constant activity: gathering food and firewood, fetching fresh water from a distant spring, tending the fire, patching the house, mending equipment, and cultivating the garden. When Kerin's nose became painfully sunburned, Pwana lent him a large straw hat, which the exile had woven of grass stems. Kerin also began a calendar by cutting notches in a length of driftwood.

Evenings he had to listen to Pwana's monologues. The hermit had theories on everything, including the origin of the planets, the movement of continents, the evolution of life, the rise of civilization, and the growth of mankind's morals and ethics. Although Kerin's brother Jorian intermittently journeyed to the University of Othomae to work as an instructor, Kerin had not been exposed to higher education. Hence he could not judge whether Pwana's ideas were sound or insubstantial moonbeams like his tale of the wicked Emperor Ajunya.

Kerin was sure that some at least of Pwana's theories were mere wind, because they often seemed to contradict what Pwana had maintained a few nights previously. Kerin resolved, if he returned whole to Kortoli, to remedy this lack in his training, in hopes of being able to sort out the true from the false.

Kerin found Pwana a mercurial character, one day gloomily speculating on the punishments for his sins awaiting him in his next life; the next, irascible and arrogantly dictatorial; or again, amiable and slyly charming. He told endless tales of his adventures; although, as with his theories, some stories flatly contradicted others. He even told alternative versions of how he came to go into exile. Kerin noticed that whatever tale Pwana told, no matter how flagrantly inconsistent with his other stories, the hermit spoke with such intense conviction and sincerity that it was all Kerin could do to keep from believing him.

Kerin thought long and hard about escaping from the island and from its dubious overlord. Recovered from his sunburn, he was more careful about exposing his skin to sunlight.

One hot, sticky day, when he was chopping firewood, he shed his everyday shirt, thinking himself now brown enough to withstand the tropical sun for a while. As he resumed his chopping, Pwana tottered up, saying:

"What is that, Master Kerin?"

"What's what?"

"That thing hung from your neck."

"Oh, that." Kerin pulled off the chain holding the package of oiled silk. "A paper of some sort, borne by a young fellow who started the voyage with me. He fell into misfortune and begged me to carry out his mission."

"Hm. And this mission?"

"To give it to the authorities of Kuromon, if I ever get there."

"What is in this paper?"

"I know not; it's sealed and in Mulvani, which I read not. My erstwhile shipmate opened it, showed it to me, and resealed it."

"I read all civilized tongues. May I see this package?"

Kerin handed Pwana the package. The hermit turned it over, saying: "It is some sort of paper, folded many times in a silken envelope and secured by a waxen seal. Pray, fetch my sewing kit and reading glass from the hut."

"What mean you to do?"

"I shall remove the seal and read the document."

"But—but that was given to me confidentially. . . ."

"Oh, trouble not your little head! I shall replace the seal so that none shall know."

"Well—ah . . ."

"Come now, young man, art not curious? Suppose it hold the message to slay the messenger forthwith? Such things have happened. Therefore it behooves you to know what the paper contain."

"Oh, very well," said Kerin doubtfully. But he fetched the articles from the hut. Pwana got a needle from the kit, heated it in the smoldering fire, and adroitly pried off the seal. He unfolded the long strip of paper.

With the magnifier, Pwana frowned at the tiny writing. "It seems to be some sort of spell. 'Before thou enter the circle, perfume it with musk, amber, aloes-wood, and incense. Take care that thou have fire whenever thou make invocation, and fumigate only in the name of the spirit whom thou wouldst call. When placing perfume on the fire, thou sayest: I burn this—' I know not the name that follows; something like unto 'Silichar.' Then it goes on: '. . . and in the name and to the honor of—' That name again; doubtless some demon. 'When thou invoke, thou holdest the invocation in thy left hand, having the rod of elder in thy right, whilst the ladle and the knife should be at thy feet. . . .'

"It goes on interminably like that. Wouldst that I read all? I know not that my aged voice will hold out."

"Nay, Doctor; but could you give me some idea of what it's about?"

Grumbling, Pwana ran his glass down the lines. He said: "Meseems it be a formula for making a kind of magical fan."

"What were the use for a magical fan?"

Pwana shrugged. "I know not. I am told that in Kuromon, they make fans with outer ribs in the form of iron blades, for cutting an enemy's throat."

Kerin laughed. "I see. One is invited to a grand feast. One sees one's foe across the room, swilling wine or whatever they drink there. One approaches, fanning oneself against the heat. One hails one's victim with a pleasant greeting, and when he looks up, *khlt*!" Kerin drew a finger across his throat.

"I doubt the host were pleased," said Pwana. "More likely the fan be used as a parrying device for the left hand, whilst the right wields a sword. How comes the firewood?"

While patrolling the beach for edibles, Kerin came upon the *Dragonet*'s boat, sitting above the high-tide mark. It struck him that someone might make off with the boat, so he hauled it back among the palms. Knowing somewhat of the ways of boats, he took the bucket, which still reposed in the bottom, filled it with water, and emptied it into the hull.

"What dost, Master Kerin?" asked Belinka. "When we fled the *Dragonet*, you had much ado to scoop water out of this craft; but now you put water in. Wherefore?"

"If the boat dry out here in the sun, the boards will shrink. Then, when I launch it again, 'twill leak."

Kerin poured several more bucketfuls into the hull and resumed his trek. He came to where he had been building a hearth on the edge of the beach and paused to add a few more lumps of coral to the hearth and pieces of dead palm frond to his fuel supply. Belinka said:

"Master Kerin, you have not yet obtained Doctor Pwana's spyglass. If you see a ship, how couldst run to the hut, procure the glass without the old man's knowledge, and get back here in time to accomplish aught?"

"I know not. Belike I can persuade him to let me carry the instrument, to have it ever ready."

"Meseems—oh, oh, Master Kerin! It looks as if the time for such stratagems were past!"

"Eh? What meanst?"

The tiny voice came from overhead. "Here comes a ship now!"

"What!" Kerin dashed to the water's edge. Around a bend in

the shore came a vessel of a size and rig much like those of Captain Huvraka's *Dragonet*, two or three bowshots from shore.

"Belinka!" said Kerin. "Canst flit out yonder and see what manner of ship it be? I must warn Pwana!"

Kerin ran back towards the hut. He arrived out of breath, to find the hermit sitting with his back to the hut and his eyes closed.

"Master Kerin!" squeaked Belinka above him. "I have visited the ship; but I cannot say what sort of persons man it. You said that pirates were clad in rags and looted finery, but all these men are naked, with no garb to judge by."

"'Tis this heat," muttered Kerin. "I must rouse the Doctor—"

"I am awake," drawled Pwana, opening his eyes and stretching. "I did but meditate. I infer from your aura that something has stirred you?"

Kerin told of the ship. With a groan, Pwana climbed to his feet. He ducked into the hut and emerged in a wrap-around skirt or sarong. Then he hobbled across the beach, shading his eyes with a hand as the ship dropped anchor and launched its ship's boat. Following him, Kerin said:

"Hadn't we better flee into the brush?"

"That were wise for you, since you are just the sort of hale young man they are fain to capture for sale. But I shall remain. I can convince them by logic that they have nought to gain by seizing me. Imprimus, I have no property worth stealing; secundus, no sane slave buyer would give a clipped copper for such a scrawny oldster. So get you hence! Run, ere they sight you!"

With a last glance at the approaching boat, Kerin dashed to the hut, retrieved his sword, and made off into the brush. But he did not go far. He hovered just beyond the line of scrub that formed a barrier between the beach and the more open palm forest beyond. Crouching behind this screen, he watched through chinks in the fronds as the boat rowed in and beached. This boat was much larger than the *Dragonet*'s; it must, he thought, hold nearly a score.

These men debarked in the shallows and hauled the boat up from the surf. All now wore a sarong or a loincloth of some sort. All were armed, either with tulwars like Huvraka's or with straight blades of a curious wavy-edged pattern, which Kerin had never seen.

Kerin blinked as he realized that one of those disembarking was a woman. Like many of the men, she wore only a wrap-around skirt. At the distance Kerin could not discern her age or comeliness; but she had the same deep-brown Salimorese skin as the men. A cord was tied around her wrist, with the other end in the fist of a man; she was patently a captive.

The men approached Pwana, who stood like a mahogany statue waiting. For a while the hermit engaged three pirates, for Kerin was now sure that so they were, in a low-voiced dialogue. Then one of the trio, a big, stout, scarfaced man with more beard than most Salimorese, shouted in accented Salimorese:

"Seize him! He denies he has hidden treasure, but I know better. This is Pwana, the wizard and prophet of some god, who fled Salimor when his thieveries became too great to be hidden!"

Several pirates sprang upon Pwana, who did not resist as they bound his wrists, pushed him roughly to where the others were setting up camp and building a fire, and threw him down upon the sand. The boat, manned by two men, was on its way back to the ship.

Kerin heard a buzz of conversation, much of which he missed through unfamiliarity with the language. The sun was subsiding when the boat returned with bags of food and a couple of casks. An argument raged on how best to persuade Pwana to reveal the place of his hoard. The fire crackled and sent a pillar of blue-gray smoke aloft to the banded sky. At last the stout man, evidently the leader, roared:

"Nay, I say his feet shall be pushed into the fire, little by little! I have always found that effective."

A pirate said: "Captain Malgo, can we bugger him first?"

"Forget it," said the captain. "Business before pleasure."

"We had better start soon," said another. "If he be a wizard, he may have magic to counter pain or extinguish the fire."

The name "Malgo" stirred a buried memory in Kerin's mind. He was sure he had heard it but knew not when or where. Moreover, the man looked like a Novarian. He was bigger than any of his crew, and the rugged features on his scar-crossed visage distinguished him from the glabrous faces and almond eyes of the Salimorese.

"Right!" said Captain Malgo. "Tubanko, you and Bantal haul him to the fire."

Two pirates seized Pwana's ankles and pulled until his feet were close to the crimson blaze. Malgo stood over him, growling: "Now, my fine wizard, wilt talk?"

"I have told you I have no such treasure," came the thin, high voice of the hermit. "Burn me, flay me, or slay me, it makes no difference. I cannot give what I possess not."

Kerin gathered his feet beneath him, preparatory to rising. "Master Kerin!" said Belinka's voice. "What folly is this? Keep out of sight!"

Kerin knew the advice was sound. Even his intrepid brother, who had survived such desperate adventures, would have told Kerin to stay under cover, at least until dark. But Kerin could not help himself. Even as he sternly told himself not to be a fool, an irresistible urge impelled him to rise and draw his sword. He pushed through the fringe of scrub and walked, with an air of more confidence than he felt, to where the pirates were clustered around Pwana. He said:

"Captain Malgo!"

The massive pirate spun around. "Whence in the seven hells came you? Who art, and what would you?"

"Kerin of Ardamai, at your service. Are you brave?"

"Some have thought so. Why?"

"Then I will fight you for the lives of Doctor Pwana and the young woman. If I kill you, your men shall depart, leaving us unmolested. If you slay me, then of course you will do as you list."

"Of all the crazy—" began Malgo. But one of his men cried out:

"Take him up, Captain! You'll chop him into gobbets, giving us rare sport." Others took up the cry.

"Novarian, aren't you?" said Malgo.

"Aye, sir. Will you fight?"

"Anon. What's this nonsense about leaving Princess Nogiri and the hermit with you? Think you we're daft, to give up a handsome ransom and a chance at his treasure, on a whim? My men will let you go if you win, agreed; but forget the princess and the hermit. They're ours."

"But Captain, consider—"

"Enough chatter!" shouted Malgo. "Have at you, silly boy!"

The captain had drawn a scabbarded sword from his sash. Now he whipped out the sword, a long weapon with a wavy, serpentine blade like those of some of the other pirates. He held the scabbard in his left hand against his forearm and raised the arm to guard with. Then he rushed upon Kerin, who had barely time to get his guard up when the pirate leader caught his blade in a *prise*, whirled it around, and sent it spinning out of Kerin's grasp into the scrub.

Malgo roared with laughter. "Anyone can see you're a tyro at swordplay, youngling. Seize him! He shall give us rare pleasure ere we let him die."

Kerin turned to run. But a pirate tripped him, another landed on his back, and others bound his wrists and ankles.

"Good!" cried a pirate. "A real man would rather bugger a well-thewed youth than futter a mere woman any day!"

Captain Malgo stood over the recumbent Kerin, saying: "What said you your name was?"

"Kerin of Ardamai, or Kerin Evor's son."

"Ha! Hast a brother named Jorian?"

"Aye." Then it occurred to Kerin that he had been disastrously indiscreet. This Malgo must be he who had once been Jorian's fellow recruit in the Othomaean army and later his jailer. Jorian had told how, wrongly blaming Jorian for loss of his post, Malgo had tried to murder Jorian. The man had been subdued and, with the help of Jorian's friend the sorceress Goania, Jorian had put upon Malgo a geas to take ship for the Far East. To reveal himself as kin to one whom Malgo viewed as a mortal foe was the abyssal depth of folly.

A pirate said: "When we are done with him, we'll hang his head from the bowsprit, to show what happens to those who vex us!"

"Nay!" said Malgo. "I have mine own plans for this head. His kin are mine enemies; so I will pack the head in a cask of salt and send it to them. I only regret I shan't be there when they open the cask." He kicked Kerin.

"We could hang it from the bowsprit for a while and then dispatch it as you say, Captain," said another.

"Nay; the sea birds would damage it beyond recognition." Malgo kicked Kerin again.

Struggling for breath from the last kick, which had battered his ribs, Kerin said: "You should have more consideration for a fellow Novarian, Captain."

Malgo kicked Kerin again and spoke in the Othomaean city dialect of Novarian: "And ye should have better sense than meddle in things that concern you not."

"Couldn't I join your crew?"

"I have a full crew and no need for rash boys; nor am I fain to give up the pleasure of your slow death." He kicked Kerin again.

"But listen! Since you left Novaria, you've risen to chief of this band, with your own ship. So my brother really did you a favor, didn't he?"

"Oh, hold thy tongue!" Malgo roared, kicking Kerin again. "I'm a man of deeds, not words, and I'll not let you turn me from my course by fine talk!"

Sunk in misery, Kerin fell silent. Facing death was bad enough, but this death promised to be in a peculiarly disgraceful, degrading form. If others had not been present, he would have wept.

"Fool! Ninnyhammer!" squeaked Belinka from the air above him. Kerin had already come to that conclusion himself; but what else could he have done?

The sun sank below the sea rim, leaving bands of red, yellow, and green below the deepening blue, mottled by meager clouds, of the sky. Overhead the half-moon brightened. Several pirates strolled past, pausing to kick Kerin and to boast of the heroic feats of sodomy they would perform. Since all but the captain were barefoot, their kicks were ineffectual compared to Malgo's.

"Now," said Captain Malgo, "let's get on with the old wizard—why, where in the seven hells is he?"

Kerin struggled into a sitting position and looked towards the fire, where Pwana had lain. The space was empty. Shadows cast by the flickering firelight indicated the hollows in the sand made by Pwana's body, but of the retired wizard and cult leader there was no sign.

·IV·
The Pirate Ship

"The old *garantola* must have slipped his bonds!" roared Captain Malgo. "Search! Search! You, look in his hut! You, west along the beach! . . ."

Kerin did not know the word *garantola* but assumed it to be a pejorative. Malgo continued shouting until he ran out of breath. A pirate said:

"Captain, he is a wizard. To tie up one such, you need another wizard to bespell his bonds."

"Too late for that!" yelled Malgo. He continued issuing orders until most of the pirates had gone off in search of their prisoner. Kerin could hear them thrashing about in the brush. After a while they straggled in, baffled. One ran up limping, crying:

"I stepped on one of those god-detested lizards, and the damned thing bit me! Somebody tie up my leg, for Vurnu's sake!"

As another pirate improvised a bandage for the lacerated limb, Malgo said: "That is all right, Krui. We will give you the first go at Kerin here. Is dinner ready yet?"

Racking his brains, Kerin remembered Pwana's tale of having a cap of invisibility. If the hermit had hidden such a thing beneath his sarong, he might have slipped it on when the pirates' attention was elsewhere. As for his bonds, making them tighten or loosen on command was elementary magic.

Would Pwana take advantage of darkness to rescue Kerin, and perhaps the princess as well? The thought gave him hope; but he did not much count upon it. Before his exile, by his own admission, Pwana had been a ruthless, unscrupulous adventurer. It was all very well to prate of his reformation; but Kerin would believe in Pwana's new-found virtue when he had a demonstration. Of one thing Kerin was sure, namely, that Pwana remained an incorrigible liar, from the mutually contradictory stories that he told of himself.

The pirates squatted or sat in a circle round the fire, while one of them passed out mugs, which he filled from the smaller cask. They thrust swords and daggers into the stew pot to spear their food. Captain Malgo stood grinning over Kerin, with a piece of meat impaled on the end of a dagger.

"Hungry?" he said.

"Aye, Captain, I am," replied Kerin.

"Isn't that too bad?" said Malgo, pulling the gobbet off the blade with his teeth. Having chewed and swallowed, he kicked Kerin. "I know not how ye did it, but ye maun have had to do with the wizard's vanishment." He gulped from his mug.

"If I knew how, I should have done likewise," said Kerin. "Now hold, Captain! Instead of kicking me again, wouldst rather not have a story? I know some good ones."

Kerin hoped to postpone the treatment the pirates meant to give him as long as possible. He recalled that his brother Jorian had often entertained others in his adventures by telling stories.

"Very well," grunted Malgo. "Gather round, boys. If ye please us, we will as a special favor give you a speedy death—" Malgo brought the edge of his hand sharply against his neck "—instead of the fancier one I'd planned. Say on!"

Kerin: "Know you the tale of the frog god of Tarxia?" When all professed ignorance, Kerin started the story. Thinking it tactful to omit the part his brother had played in the original transformation, he said:

"Tarxia City stands on the river Spherdar, which winds through the great Swamp of Spraa on its way to the sea. In the city, the Temple of Gorgolor is one of the finest structures in Novaria, with its gleaming corner towers and enormous central dome, which soars at least 350 feet into the air, all bedight inside and out with gold leaf and semiprecious stones.

"The central figure of the interior was a statue of Gorgolor in the form of a frog the size of a bear or lion, carved from a single emerald. No other emerald in the world, I'm told, compares with this in size. If some thief were to steal it, 'twere worth more than all the other gems in the world combined. Purloining it would, however, present a problem; besides being closely guarded, the statue must have weighed nigh unto a ton.

"At any rate, the Theocrat of Tarxia, Kylo of Anneia, was at outs with a leading local magician, a Doctor Valdonius. The wizard found the rule of the priesthood irksome and blamed it for holding progress back in the magical and other sciences in Tarxia. Plotting an uprising to overthrow priestly rule, he decided to steal the statue. By a mighty spell, he thought he could shrink it down to a size that could be carried on one's person, say that of a cat."

"Hey!" said a pirate, one of those who had gathered in a circle to listen. "I know about shrinking spells; but the weight of the thing stays the same. So your emerald frog would still weigh a ton."

"Valdonius thought of that," continued Kerin. "This spell lessened the weight of the statue whilst leaving the mass unchanged."

"What is the difference?"

"It is a technical matter involving the science of physics, which I am not qualified to explain and whereof I am a little uncertain myself. But let me continue the story. Valdonius reckoned he could pick up the shrunken statue and carry it, though it would take a much greater push to get it moving and more effort to stop it than a normal object of its size.

"He took some confederates to confer with the Theocrat on conditions in distant lands, whither the priesthood considered sending missionaries. Whilst these allies distracted old Kylo at the temple entrance, Valdonius wrought his spell at the central altar.

"The spell did not work quite as planned. Instead of shrinking the statue to a convenient size, it turned it into a living frog the size of the statue. With thunderous croaks of *gloop! gloop!* this superfrog went leaping and bounding out the temple, knocked down the Theocrat and Valdonius' accomplices, and vanished into the night.

"The Theocrat raised an alarm, and soon the folk of the city were running pell-mell after the frog, hoping to head it off; for they had little hope of catching it once it reached the Swamp of Spraa. And reach the swamp the monster did, and vanished into the stagnant waters.

"Meanwhile Valdonius sent some of his followers into the streets to raise a revolution. But they had no success whatever. When they mounted stands on corners to harangue the multitude, they found no multitude, only a few too old or too young to go haring after the holy frog. When the returning temple guards appeared, the agitators fled. Doctor Valdonius fled likewise to Govannian, where he was a distant cousin of the Hereditary Usurper.

"When the priesthood recovered from the shock of losing their runaway god, they sought to get Gorgolor back, albeit they were a little vague as to what they should do with the creature when they had it. Should they build a pool to keep it in? A frog of such size could not live on flies as normal frogs do, by shooting out a long, sticky tongue to ensnare insect prey. Live fowls might serve the purpose.

"Whilst the pool on the temple grounds and the massive fence around it were a building, the priests attempted schemes to capture Gorgolor. The holy frog seemed quite happy in Spraa, where it subsisted on prey like muskrats, voles, and herons. The priests spread nets and essayed to lasso the frog; they tried to herd it with drums, horns, and other noise makers. But Gorgolor evaded their efforts with ease. It was even proposed to harpoon it; but this plan was rejected on the ground that, resenting the injury, the divine batrachian would surely visit disaster on Tarxia.

"After months without results, the Theocrat received a secret message from Doctor Valdonius. Through his partisans, the wizard had kept in touch with events in Tarxia and knew of the failure of the priests to recapture Gorgolor. For a modest fee and a guarantee of his own safety, Valdonius offered to come back and cast a counterspell.

"After some bickering and dickering, it was arranged that a brace of temple officials should go to Govannian and present themselves to the Hereditary Usurper as hostages for the Usurper's kinsman Valdonius, who would then return to Tarxia to perform his spell. And so it was done.

"On a propitious day Valdonius, the Theocrat, and other in-
terested parties assembled on the margins of the swamp, and
the wizard cast his spell. Gorgolor warily watched the pro-
ceedings from a patch of open water, in which he floated with
only his eyes and nostrils showing. The sky darkened, lightning
flashed, the earth shook, and the air came alive with the rustle
of wings of unseen presences. And Gorgolor turned instantly
back into a lion-sized frog of solid emerald.

"That was all very well, but neither Valdonius nor Kylo had
considered the physical properties of swamps, since neither
was familiar with nature in the wild. When the giant frog
turned to emerald, it recovered the weight it had possessed
when it squatted on its plinth in the temple. Hence it sank at
once to the bottom and kept right on sinking into the ooze and
soft mud beneath the water. None knows how deeply it sank
ere coming to rest. The priests tried sounding for it with poles
without result. For all anyone knows, it may be buried half a
league below the surface of the swamp.

"The Theocrat, a kindly and rather simple old man, was
vastly vexed. Some of those present had to remind him of the
hostages in Govannian to dissuade him from commanding his
guards to seize Valdonius and do him to death in some ingenious way. The wizard was suffered to depart without his fee,
and the priests returned sorrowfully to their temple.

"Without their emerald god, however, the cult of Gorgolor
lost its hold upon the masses. Within a year, its rule was over-
thrown by another revolution, wherein Valdonius played no
part. The last I heard, the factions were still quarreling and
fighting over the form the new state should have: a republic
like Vindium, a limited monarchy like Kortoli, a dictatorship
like Boaktis, or an archonship like Solymbria with the Archon
chosen by lot. And that is the tale of the holy frog of Tarxia."

"Pretty good," growled Captain Malgo. "How about another?"

"Captain!" came a voice from the darkness. "Cannot we bugger him now?" But others cried: "Story! Story!"

"One thing at a time," said Malgo. "It will be time enough to have at him when he runs out of stories. Go on, Kerin."

So, as the half-moon sank towards the horizon, Kerin told the tales of King Fusinian the Fox and the Teeth of Grimnor, and Fusinian and the troll Vuum, and Fusinian and the Boar of Chinioc, and King Filoman the Well-Meaning and the golem general, and Filoman and his ghostly prime minister, and King Forimar the Esthete and the waxen wife, and such other stories as he could call to mind.

For a while, as he finished each tale, some pirates cried out for more, whereas others demanded that the grand sodomy begin forthwith. With each tale the voices of the lechers, though still in a minority, waxed louder, and Kerin was sure that after the next story they would become a majority. But then the voices at the end of each account began to die away, so that each time there were fewer shouts either to stop or to continue.

Although it was hard to be sure by the fading firelight, Kerin saw that the pirates were, one by one, dropping off to sleep. He did not know whether to allow himself a spark of hope, that they would all go to sleep instead of using him in the revolting manner indicated, or to be affronted that they found his storytelling too boring to keep them awake. When he finished the tale of how King Forbonian had nearly drowned in trying to consummate the union with his mermaid bride,* not

---

* For these stories told by Jorian, see my novels *The Goblin Tower*, *The Clocks of Iraz*, and *The Unbeheaded King*.

a sound of approval or otherwise came from the sprawling mass of pirates. When Kerin fell silent, he heard instead a chorus of snores.

Kerin jerked as something touched his arm. Peering through the moonlight, he saw a knife come out of nowhere and cut the lashing on his wrists.

"Be quiet!" whispered the invisible Pwana. The knife went to work on the cords around his ankles.

"What's toward?" murmured Kerin.

"What think you? I am not fain to let them roast me without protest."

"Why not release the girl, too? She's a captive."

"A good idea; one cannot have too many folk under obligation. Then we must needs cut the throats of these rascals, for they will not remain insensible for aye. I had but little of the drug I put in their beer."

"Slay sleeping men? That were—were—"

"Try not your silly Western notions of chivalry on me, youngling! Wouldst live or die? These scoundrels do far worse; for sport they gouge eyes and burn off private parts. Besides, they defied my well-reasoned logic. The only good enemy is a dead enemy!"

"But—but—"

Pwana snapped into full but naked visibility in the moonlight as he peeled off the tarncap. Kerin leaned forward to examine the object. It seemed a cap made of metallic mesh, like chain mail but of much slenderer links, such as might make a lady's purse or ornamental coif.

Pwana picked up and did on his sarong. Wadding the cap into a ball and tucking it into the garment, he snarled: "Then watch whilst I do the deed, milksop!"

The hermit first cut the young woman free. The twain spoke in low voices; then Kerin was shocked to see the girl step to

89

the nearest pirate, pull out the man's knife, and go to work. She and Pwana went from man to man, seized the hair of each, tipped back his head, and drew the knife firmly across his throat. Then the throat cutter stepped quickly back from the widening pool of blood.

"That, my dear, is that," said Pwana in his everyday voice as, having cut the last throat, he wiped his blade on the corpse's kilt. "What is the late news from Salimor?"

"Sophi Dimbakan died," said the girl, "being succeeded by his brother Vurkai."

Kerin said: "That name is familiar. Is it not the name of the man who overthrew the previous dynasty, when the reigning Sophi was slain in the riots that followed the fall of his great tower? I've heard tales of that."

"Aye, Master Kerin," said Pwana. "The late ruler was the third of that name. The revolution came about from meddling in our affairs by an exiled Novarian king named Porimar, or Forimar in your tongue; just as you call our ruler the Sophi whilst we call him the Sohpi. I believe this Forimar hailed from your own Kortoli. He persuaded the Sophi to build a lofty tower in Kwatna, ignoring Salimor's many earthquakes. At the next severe quake, down came the tower.

"During the disorders that followed this catastrophe, this first Dimbakan, a sea captain, gathered a following. He announced that he would set up a government of the Western kind, a republic, with officers chosen by the votes of the masses. But for all his talk, he never brought this strange system into being. Instead, he declared himself the new Sophi, and his line has ruled Salimor for above a century."

For an instant Pwana stood silently, absently pulling his whiskers and fiddling with his knife. Then he said: "Kerin, send your sprite out to the ship, to report how many now man it."

"Belinka!" called Kerin.

"Aye, Master Kerin?"

Kerin passed on the order from Pwana, and the little blue light danced out to sea. While Pwana asked more questions about affairs in Salimor, Kerin recovered his sword from among the dwarf palms. Belinka returned saying:

"I could find but one man aboard, and he asleep in the stern."

"Kerin!" said Pwana. "The fools have left but one lookout. If we take the ship, canst sail us to Salimor?"

"If weather stay fair, methinks I can manage the craft somewhat, having sailed small boats and watched Huvraka's men. For foul weather, I should need more crew. For direction, I know only that Salimor lie south of east."

"Good enough," said Pwana. "Gather your gear and lead me to your boat."

"Mean you to return to Kwatna?"

"Aye. The gods have laid upon me the duty to spread my message of enlightenment. First, help me to strip these losels of such articles as might prove useful, or at least salable. This fellow's hat might save you the need to borrow mine."

"We cannot carry all our gear and a pile of loot as well," said Kerin. "Let me fetch my boat whilst you strip the bodies."

"Why not use the pirates' boat?"

"Too large for one man to handle."

"I will go with you," said the girl.

"Humph," grunted Pwana. "Ever the fair prefer the young and callow to the old and wise. Well, go your way; and I hope you can handle that sword more featly than you did with the late Captain Malgo!"

Kerin and the girl set out along the beach, silvered by the low half-moon. Little ghost crabs scuttled away. Kerin said: "Your pardon, madam; but did I hear the pirates call you 'Princess Nogiri'?"

"You heard aright; but the 'Princess' means little. I am only a distant cousin of the Sophi; his sisters and daughters are called 'Exalted Princess.' And you, sir?"

Kerin introduced himself, adding: "I never expected to see a person like you calmly cutting throats. Had you no qualms?"

"I might have had, had they not used me as they did."

"You mean—ah . . ."

"Aye, they raped me to a fare-thee-well, more times than I can count. Luckily I know a good contraceptive spell. I am so sore that the mere thought of love-making horrifies me."

"You poor thing!" said Kerin. "You're safe with me."

"Who is the other, the old man?"

"A hermit hight Pwana."

"He who created the cult of Bautong and later vanished? I might have guessed. I can tell much of his deeds in Kwatna—"

"Here's the boat. Help me launch it and then take a seat in the stern."

As the half-moon neared the horizon, the *Dragonet*'s boat cautiously approached the stern of the pirate craft, with Kerin at the oars, Pwana in the bow, Nogiri in the stern, and between the occupants two piles of loot—swords, knives, purses, jewelry, and a few choice garments. Belinka tinkled:

"He sleeps, Master Kerin. But do take care! Is there nought I can say to turn you from this peril?"

"Nought," murmured Kerin. He twisted about to view Pwana, who said:

"Go ahead, youngling, unless you be frightened!"

"Methinks it wiser to wait for full dark," said Kerin, suppressing an urge to make an angry retort. He would need all his wits on the next step, without letting personal irritations distract him.

Pwana had been especially irascible ever since Kerin and No-giri had gone off to fetch back the boat; the idea struck Kerin that the old codger might be jealous. It was hard to believe, but Pwana must once have been young also, with his head full of images of desirable females.

At last the moon subsided below the horizon. Kerin said: "Doctor, may I borrow your tarncap?"

"If the lookout sleep, you need it not."

Kerin persisted: "But he may awaken. If he caught me climbing the rail, he'd let out my gore were I never so prow a swordsman."

"Nay, nay," grumbled Pwana. "I trust my bauble to none other. Go on, board! If you encounter trouble, I will climb aboard to render aid. I am spry enough for that!"

Kerin became stubborn. "No tarncap, no boarding. If you persist, I'll return us to Kinungung."

"And have us subsist on smoked pirate, eh? But hold: Hast a protective counterspell on your person? My spiritual senses tell me you have; that is why my healing spell failed to cure your blisters so quickly as it should have."

"Yea," said Kerin. "Doctor Uller put it on me ere I left home. Is it still effective?"

"I cannot be sure here; but I think it valid. If you did on the cap, either the cap or your counterspell would lose its charge, and belike both at once. Besides, you would have to strip naked."

"Eh? Why?"

"Because it would not affect your garments. The sight of your clothes mounting the rail by themselves were quite as arresting as of you yourself. You would have to climb holding your sword in your teeth."

"Then I suppose I must do without." Kerin gave a final pull on the oars, whispering: "Ward us from bumping the ship!"

A reverse stroke swung the boat broadside to the stern, so that its gunwale lined up parallel to the ship's transom. Kerin saw that he could reach the rail when he stood. Taking a deep breath, he rose and grabbed for the rail, hoisting a leg to put a foot on the transom. . . .

Kerin never knew just what went wrong; but his foot slipped off the ship's planking. He fell back into the boat, came down unbalanced and, arms flailing, fell backward into the sea. Water closed over him.

Though his sword and garments weighed him down, Kerin struggled to the surface, blinking water out of his eyes. Overhead a hoarse voice shouted:

"Who is there?"

The lookout's visage appeared above the rail, and his weapon glimmered in the starlight. Nogiri sat in the stern, apparently alone in the boat. Looking up, she cooed:

"Master Bakai? When your shipmates had taken their pleasure of me, they thought it only fair that I should come out to give you your turn. Wilt help me aboard?"

"That is a kindly thought!" said the lookout. "Come on up, lass; take my hand. You are too good for those *embarpos* ashore. Here, let me spread my cloak on the deck. . . . *Unhh!*"

The lookout disappeared from Kerin's view, and he heard the sound of a body's striking the deck. Then Pwana's voice:

"Kerin, hand me my sarong, which you will find in the bow!"

Kerin coughed up water. "Doctor, I must—*cough*—needs get into the boat without upsetting it."

Rope snaked down through the darkness, striking Kerin's head. He caught it, worked his way around the bow of the boat, and pulled himself up on the ship's stern, standing outside the rail. The boat drifted away.

"Pox on it!" said Pwana, who had taken off the tarncap and stood naked in the starlight. Nogiri stood near him, while the body of Bakai the lookout sprawled across the deck with a knife in his back. "Doff your garments, Kerin, and swim after it! You swim, do you not?"

"Aye," grumbled Kerin. "But—ah—if the princess would step away. . . ."

"Rubbish! We Salimorese make nought of the body," snapped Pwana. "So hop to it, ere the boat drift too far to recover. It holds all our gear."

With a sigh Kerin began to strip. "I see you made yourself invisible and climbed aboard whilst the princess distracted the man."

Pwana snorted. "Good there be at least two level heads amongst us! The shortcoming of the tarncap is that one must use it bare-arsed, rendering it impractical in colder climes. Hasten!"

As Kerin shed his last garment, Nogiri exclaimed: "By Vurnu's timeless turban, you're bruised all over!"

"Malgo's boots," grunted Kerin, squaring his shoulders and thrusting out his chest.

"Enough of displaying your manly form to the incony wench," growled Pwana. "Speed you to the boat. On returning, hand me that rope in the bow, lest it escape again. Hasten!"

"Master Kerin!" squeaked Belinka, dancing luminously about. "I forfend this deed! The water swarms with sharks!"

Ignoring the sprite, Kerin told Pwana: "We seamen call that rope the painter." He dove, feeling some small satisfaction in having for once set the omniscient hermit right.

When Kerin climbed aboard again, Pwana said: "Bear a hand with this carrion." He indicated the pirate, whose body he had already stripped of anything useful.

Bakai's body went overboard with a splash. As Kerin dried

himself on such parts of the pirate's cloak as were not sticky with blood, Pwana announced:

"I shall take Malgo's cabin in the forward part of the deckhouse. You and the princess may use the two small cabins further aft. The rest of the deckhouse is full of verminous old pallets, whereon the pirates were wont to sleep." The hermit yawned. "Forsooth, this has been a taxing night for one of my years; so I shall retire. You twain should stand watch alternately till morn, when we shall sail."

Nogiri began: "But if the pirates be all dead—"

"He's right," said Kerin. "A blow might come up, or another ship, or we might spring a leak. I'll take the first watch, if you like, and wake you when yon bright star—" He pointed. "—sets."

Pwana walked off forward with a bundle of his belongings. "I am not sleepy," said Nogiri, standing with her elbows on the rail.

"Then you can keep me company," said Kerin beside her. "My conscience is still uneasy over those throat-cuttings, but I ween they'd have done the same to us. Tell me more about Pwana!"

"What thought you of him after dwelling with him on Kinungung?"

"He confessed many frauds and fakeries in his former life but insisted he was now reformed; that he had become a saintly altruist. He said his god, Bautong, had commanded him to give up evil ways and go into exile."

"Ha! He fled Kwatna because too many of those he had cozened hatched a plot to kill him, and he got wind thereof. Didst believe his fine talk?"

"Well, he is very persuasive, albeit what he persuades one of today may be the opposite of what he persuaded one of yesterday. And I noted how ruthlessly he cut all those throats and stabbed the lookout in the back."

She gave a little sniff. "But you intended an assault upon Bakai whilst invisible, didst not? That were hardly a fair fight, either."

"I suppose not. Pwana did treat me well on the island, albeit he kept me running with his chores. He released me when Malgo had me tied and stood by us in taking this ship. Is he then so great a villain?"

"Forsooth he is. He befriended you on Kinungung because, being old, he needed a lusty youth to help with the toil. And he cut your bonds because he needed you. He aided in taking the ship because he could not conn the craft alone. But trust a venomous serpent ere you trust him! Even his doctor's degree comes from some institution none ever heard of; I suspect it be self-conferred.

"His deeds were the talk of Kwatna: his harem of captive women whom he abused; and the experimental spell supposed to make his followers into demigods, instead of which it drove them mad. Then there was the trapdoor through which he dropped rebellious followers, never to be seen again. The more his crimes were exposed, the more fanatical in his defense became his followers, until at last he got one of the Sophi's wives in his grasp.

"That was too much for the Sophi who, taken in by Pwana's pretensions, had protected him. Some of Pwana's former followers, disillusioned, tipped off the ruler, and Pwana fled from Kwatna one leap ahead of the Sophi's guards, who had orders to bring back his head."

"Very enlightening," said Kerin. "If ever I have occasion into a river to leap to pull out a drowning man, I will not hand Doctor Pwana my purse to hold whilst I do so. I suppose your news of the former ruler's death led to Pwana's decision to return to Salimor?"

"Assuredly! But hark ye, Master Kerin! Would there not be a hoard of stolen money and jewels aboard? Chests of treasure in the hold, awaiting burial ashore?"

Kerin shook his head. "We'll search. But my brother Jorian has had to do with pirates—"

"Meanst he has been a pirate?"

"Nay, nay. When he was King of Xylar, he commanded their navy in hunting down the rascals—"

"Your brother a king? Be this a tall tale, Master Kerin?"

"Nay again. They had a curious custom in Xylar. When a king had reigned for five years, they cut off his head and threw it up for grabs. My brother unwittingly caught the late king's head and found himself in that foredoomed post. With the help of a wizard, he escaped.

"But about pirate treasure, Jorian assures me that there is no such thing, whatever folk may dream. The reason, quotha, is that when they have taken a prize, pirates forthwith divide the loot amongst officers and crew. When the ship stops at a port where corrupted officials permit, each pirate spends his share in one grand debauch. And now, my girl, methinks you had better get some sleep ere yonder star below the horizon slinks."

Kerin let Nogiri sleep through her watch as well as his. Before dawn, Pwana and Nogiri prepared breakfast from supplies in the galley; Kerin ate while woozy and unsteady with fatigue. His companions told him they need not fear for lack of food or drink, since the hold held ample supplies.

After breakfast, Kerin wanted to hoist the anchor forthwith; but he let his companions argue him down. Pwana said:

"If you try to sail us half asleep, lad, you will run us on a rock for certain. Take your ease whilst the princess and I essay to clean up this filthy ship."

When the sun was high, Kerin awoke. Moving painfully from his bruises, he found Pwana at the rail, staring shoreward through his spyglass. The old man chuckled, saying:

"The megalans feast. Carrion those lizards detect a league downwind and a bowshot up. What next?"

"I shall hoist the mizzen," said Kerin, "and shall need your help."

"What is the mizzen?"

Kerin pointed to one of the two yards over their heads, both of which lay lengthwise of the ship in a pair of crutches rising from the deck. "This is the after sail, the smaller. I don't intend to hoist the other."

"Wherefore not?"

"Because I am not sure we three can handle the ship with so large a spread. If all go well with the mizzen and we are becalmed, we may try the main."

"Oh, fiddle-faddle! In these light breezes we need all the sail we can spread to get to Salimor, which I mean to do in haste."

"I won't, for the reason I gave."

"We shall hoist both, I tell you! If the blow strengthen, it will be time enough to haul them in."

Nogiri, attracted by the men's rising voices, approached and stood silently. Kerin put on his firmest face. He knew that he faced a critical test. Inwardly he quaked, his knees seemed ready to fold, and his bladder sent a call for relief. But with shoulders squared and chin up, he said:

"Let's understand something, Doctor Pwana. At sea, the captain is absolute ruler. Whilst I'm no barnacled old salt—"

"A clown like you, who let Malgo disarm him and could not even climb aboard without falling into the sea, you captain? Be not absurd, boy! A tame ape were abler—"

Kerin raised his voice to a shout: "And who tried to tame the pirates with logic? I still know more about sailing than you twain together! That makes me captain; and if I say we shall sail on the mizzen alone, so shall it be."

"Insolent young princox!" screamed Pwana. "Know you not that, as a wizard, I can cast upon you a spell of impotence or a disorder of the bowels?"

"And then how would you, old, frail, and ignorant of seamanship, manage the craft? If you contest my authority, I'll toss you back in the boat and cast you adrift. You can row back to the company of crabs and lizards."

"You would not dare!"

"Try me and see!"

Pwana grumbled something under his breath, of which Kerin caught only ". . . shall rue your impudence!" Aloud he said: "Aye, aye, sir, Captain, Admiral, Great Lord of the Oceans! What commands Your Divinity of this humble deckhand?"

Kerin grinned. "I hadn't expected such rapid promotion. First, I want you and the princess to climb to the roof of the deckhouse and cast loose the stops from the mizzen yard."

"What are stops?" said Pwana.

"Those short lengths of line tied around the sail. Nogiri, find a bag or a basket wherein to gather the stops."

"But, Admiral," said Pwana, "how shall we untie the ropes on the back half of the yard, over our heads?"

"You shall do as sailors do: straddle the yard and bump along it on your arses. Be glad the sea is calm."

While Kerin identified the halyard by which the yard was hoisted and the winch to raise it, he murmured: "Belinka!"

"Aye, Master Kerin? What idiotic nonsense are you up to now, scorning my prudent advice?"

"I cannot go without sleep all the time. So I want you to watch Doctor Pwana, whose feelings for me are less than adoration. Warn me if you see him doing aught suspicious, such as putting poison in my food or creeping with dagger upon me asleep."

"Oh. I understand, Captain. Pray forgive my outburst. Adeliza will be proud of you when I report how you mastered this arrogant trickster!"

"Humph!" snorted Kerin. He leaned heavily on the rail, without the support of which he feared he would collapse on deck from sheer funk.

· V ·

The Coasts of Ambok

Day followed day as the former pirate vessel plodded eastward. Pwana named the ship the *Benduan* after an island of the archipelago on which he had been born. When they passed another ship, the other always turned away and ran for it. The third time this happened, it occurred to Kerin that the other probably recognized Malgo's vessel and fled in fear of attack.

As Kerin had predicted, a search of the hull turned up no treasure. In the hold they discovered a pile of oddments of clothing behind the jars and casks of provisions: wine, oil, rice, dried chick-peas, salted meats, and so on. The only worthwhile loot was that which they had already taken from the bodies of pirates killed on Kinungung.

Betimes they passed other islands, some mere atolls and sand spits, supporting no life but sea birds. Kerin insisted, despite

Pwana's fretting over the delay, on anchoring at night whenever the water was shallow enough for the anchor to bite.

Then the islands waxed larger. Sometimes these forested
bodies of land showed signs of human life. Once, when Nogiri
was at the tiller and Kerin and Pwana were leaning on the rail,
Kerin pointed, saying:

"Look yonder, Doctor. Do I see people putting out in a boat?"

Pwana stared through his spyglass. "You do indeed, Captain.
If I mistake not, that island is Siau, whose folk have unpleasant
habits. You had better raise the larger sail, unless you wish our
heads to adorn their village gate posts whilst our bodies are
roasted for dinner."

"Oh? Give me a look, pray."

Kerin saw through the glass that the craft was a dugout
canoe, manned by a score of brown-skinned paddlers. They
drove it ahead with powerful strokes, timed by a barking chant.

"Master Kerin!" squealed Belinka. "You must speed the
ship!"

"I will," said Kerin. "I shall need help with the sail, Pwana."
He tried to keep his voice level, but it rose with tension. "Help
me to take off the stops."

When this was done, Kerin needed the oldster's help on the
winch to hoist the yard. This buff-colored sail was twice as
heavy as the mizzen on which they had leisurely been sailing.
A glance showed the canoe to be gaining fast.

"Nogiri!" Kerin shouted. "Crouch down!"

He and Pwana strained at the crank handles. But the winch
was meant to be raised by two well-muscled men, and Pwana
lacked the needed strength. Digit by digit the sail arose, flapping its folds in the gentle breeze.

"Harder!" Kerin gasped.

"I am working—as hard—as I can!" panted Pwana.

Astern, the canoe grew larger. The paddlers were muscular

men even darker than Pwana, naked but wearing headdresses of bright-hued feathers. Closer they came, until the shouts of one in the bow came clearly across the water.

"It's only—half up!" said Kerin. "Come on!"

"I can do—no more!" sighed Pwana.

The man in the bow of the craft drew a bow to the ear and aimed up at an angle. The arrow whistled down into the sea a few yards astern of the *Benduan*.

"Nogiri!" Kerin called. "Lash the tiller and come up here!"

The girl's modest strength provided the extra force needed to raise the sail the remaining distance. Kerin sent Nogiri back to the tiller, since the *Benduan* had begun to fall far off course. Then he busied himself with securing the lines. The sail, which had been flapping and booming, at last filled properly. The ship heeled a little more and sent out a larger wake.

"I think we gain," said Kerin at last, staring aft.

The Siauese veered off, to double back and shrink away towards their village. Pwana said:

"With the Captain's permission, I will go to my cabin and lie down. Cranking that thing was a little too much for mine aged heart."

"Go ahead," said Kerin. "I'll take the conn, Nogiri."

When Pwana was out of sight, Kerin, now at the tiller, said: "Princess, have you noticed how obedient and respectful our hermit has become?"

"Aye, I have."

"Think you he's had a change of heart, or that he merely bides his time to take revenge?"

"From what I know of him," the girl replied, "I should guess the latter."

"I could have ranked him out of the captain's cabin. What would then have ensued?"

She shrugged. "I know of no way to test these surmises, save to put us back on Kinungung and start over, pursuing the other course."

"Nogiri," said Kerin, "you can always be counted upon for common sense."

"Thank you. Mine uncle complains I have too much sense for a woman. He will probably say that picnicking with my sister and no attendants and being seized by pirates proves I am nought but a woman after all."

"Your uncle?" said Kerin.

"Aye; I dwell in his household with a swarm of cousins, my parents being dead. I shall leave that house when I wed next month."

"You are betrothed?" said Kerin, feeling an obscure pang. He had been true to his promise that Nogiri would have nothing to fear, but his lusts had begun to fever him. He had been working up the courage to make a discreet advance, at least to ascertain if she were willing. If she were, what harm? But now even that prospect went glimmering.

"Aye," she said, "to a young man mine uncle chose."

"Are you and this lucky youth in love?"

"Great Vurnu, what a barbarous notion! My family wants an alliance with his, and we shall doubtless come to like each other well enough. As far as I can judge from seeing him twice, he seems a man of parts. Mine uncle would not, I am sure, betroth me to a scoundrel or wastrel. I trust you'll escort me to's house in Kwatna, where they will reward you."

"I shall be glad to," said Kerin a little stiffly, "and not merely in hope of reward."

As sunset neared, Kerin routed out Pwana to help him lower and furl the mainsail. The hermit grumbled: "At this rate, I shall be dead of old age ere we raise Ambok!"

"I dare not sail fast in strange waters," said Kerin firmly.

"Even with the moon, 'tis mainly by luck that we haven't struck a rock or a shoal."

Since the water was too deep for anchoring, Kerin sailed through the night. When this happened, he took the tiller for most of the night, posting someone in the bow for a lookout. This night, with Nogiri in the bow and Kerin at the tiller, Belinka danced before him, twinkling:

"Master Kerin, I warn you! Cease lallygagging after that brown barbarian maid! Adeliza will be furious!"

"Let her rage," said Kerin. "I'll pick my own mate. Not this one, however. She's betrothed."

"But I know you Prime Planers! Put a pair of healthy young of opposite sex together, and neither laws nor customs nor promises will thwart their lusts."

"Were you of sensible size," grinned Kerin, "I'm sure I could lust after you."

"Oh, you beast! You unnatural monster! You vile lecher! You are impossible, and I will have nought more to do with you!"

Kerin chuckled. "Just be on hand the next time danger threatens, Belinka, and all will be well."

The journey from Kinungung took twice as long as it would have with an experienced crew. When not otherwise busy with the ship, Kerin practiced his Salimorese on Nogiri, who also taught him the few words of Kuromonian she knew.

Nineteen days after leaving Kinungung, the *Benduan* sighted a stretch of forested land. Pwana said this was Ambok, the main island of Salimor and the site of the capital of Kwatna. Kerin wondered how he knew, since one stretch of beach, fenced by a line of coconut palms and backed by a towering hardwood forest, looked much like another. They had passed several such shores in recent days. To each Pwana had said:

"Nay, that is not Ambok. That is either Pola or Jambiang, or Waiku or Sakudina."

As they neared the new coast, Kerin said: "Kwatna must be elsewhere, since I see no signs of habitation. Should we turn north or south?"

Pwana frowned, staring through his spyglass. "Methinks Kwatna lies a dozen leagues to northward. First, I pray, let us anchor. Our water is turning foul, and we must find fresh."

"What sort of folk live hereabouts?"

"Mostly simple peasants. The Sophis have turned the head-hunters into taxpaying farmers. That cannot be said of some of the smaller isles, as we have seen."

An hour later, the *Benduan* anchored a bowshot from shore. Leaving Nogiri on watch, Kerin and Pwana rowed the ship's boat, laden with empty casks, to the beach. They agreed that Kerin should walk to northward seeking a stream, while Pwana trudged to the south. Each, if nothing he found, should turn back after half a league's hike.

After a quarter-hour, Kerin came to the mouth of a rivulet, winding sluggishly out of the shadowy green of the jungle. He dipped a finger and tested; it was fresh.

Kerin whooped and trotted back along the strand to where the boat was beached. Pwana was not to be seen; so Kerin sat down to wait. If Pwana, too, had found a water source, they would take the boat to the nearer.

Kerin sat and watched an occasional crab beachcombing for carrion. Then he glanced out at the *Benduan*. He saw the small figure of Nogiri in the bow, holding a stay and waving her free arm. Her mouth worked, but the distance was too great to hear.

"Belinka!" Kerin called.

"Aye, you lascivious monster?" The sprite materialized.

"The princess seems agitated. Pray, flit out and find the cause."

Belinka soon returned, saying: "She demands speech forthwith, Master Kerin! She thinks that Pwana hath absconded."

Kerin rowed back to the *Benduan*. When he had climbed aboard and secured the boat, Nogiri told him:

"I suspected some such scheme. When you set off northward, he bent his steps south; but after a few paces, he looked about, pulled something from his garment, and vanished! I could still see the garment, which fell to the sand. It lies where he dropped it."

"He must have donned the tarncap," said Kerin. "Now why should he do such a thing?"

"I can but guess. Would he walk boldly into Kwatna, counting upon the new Sophi's good will? As he counted upon his logic to tame the pirates? Perchance. But suppose he wished to take a new name, change his appearance by magic, and resume his magical practice?"

"If that were his plan," mused Kerin, "he would not wish us to see him change; we could threaten to expose him. It would seem riskier, though, to set out naked on a barefoot hike through the jungle. What is the danger from wild beasts?"

"Not great. Tigers are few near Kwatna; from being hunted, they are seldom seen. A leopard will not attack a grown man; and the only elephants hereabouts are tame ones. The prime hazard is that of venomous serpents. So, shall we go for water or sail for Kwatna?"

"The latter, methinks," said Kerin. "With Pwana absent, I'm sure we have enough water to get us thither. He said it lies a day's sail northward."

"But if he wished to assure our arrival after his—or not at all—would he not give false directions?"

Kerin smote his palm with his fist. "My clever, suspicious princess! Certes he would; so let's sail south for at least a day or two. If we find neither the city nor any wight who can direct us, then we'll turn north."

Since the sun was already far down, the *Benduan* remained at anchor for the night. Kerin examined the scanty belongings that Pwana had brought aboard. He helped himself, not without a twinge of conscience, to such useful articles as the spyglass.

The next morning they sailed. At the mouth of another creek, they passed two fishermen standing immobile on stilts in the shallows, poising spears for a deadly thrust at some unwary fish. Nogiri hailed these watchers and asked if they were headed aright for Kwatna. She reported:

"As nearly as I could grasp their dialect, this is the right direction; but Kwatna is twenty or thirty leagues."

Later that day, Kerin did what he had so far avoided by cautious sailing and anchoring every night when the depth of water permitted. He ran the *Benduan* aground on a sand bar. There the little ship remained despite Kerin's sweat-streaming efforts to tow it off with the *Dragonet*'s boat.

Kerin and Nogiri had to set out in the boat to hunt for fresh water after all. They found another rivulet, with a ten-foot crocodile asleep on its bank. Having driven the reptile away by throwing stones, they filled their casks. While they were at work, a bloodcurdling scream resounded from the forest. Startled, Kerin asked:

"Means it that some jungle beast is slaying Pwana?"

Nogiri laughed. "No such luck! That is the cry of the long-tailed fowl we call a peacock."

"According to those fishermen," said Kerin back on the *Benduan*, "Kwatna is still too far for us to row. But we cannot stay here for ay."

"Do not give up hope of getting free," said Nogiri. "See how the moon does dwindle nightly."

"What has that to do with freeing the ship?"

"Know you not that high tides are higher at full moon and at new moon than in between? We ran aground at low tide with the moon just past half full. Any day now, a high tide should float us."

Kerin smiled. "My clever princéss! I was reared inland, and there were no tides on the lake where I learned boating."

So it proved. Two days later, the *Benduan* sailed into the harbor of Kwatna, the capital of Salimor.

Kwatna harbor was cluttered with ships of all sizes, having hulls painted in every hue—crimson, emerald, buff, and black—anchored or moored to quays. The Salimorese lacked piers. Other craft moved in or out of the harbor; small boats bustled about, proffering merchandise or offers to tow.

These ships bore an exotic look. There was not a true square-rigger in sight; most of the local craft bore triangular sails like those of the *Benduan*, although those moored or at anchor had their sails furled. Others had sails of curious horned or trape-zoidal shapes. Kerin saw a couple of big, square-ended, three- and four-masted ocean-goers with lugsails stiffened by bamboo battens. He supposed these last to be from Kuromon.

Some smaller vessels were little more than dugouts, with outriggers to keep them upright. There were also two ships that Kerin supposed to be galleys of war. They were long, low, and lean, designed to be paddled rather than rowed, with seats along the gunwales for paddlers. In addition, each had a pair of outriggers, one on each side, and the outriggers also had seats for paddlers. At the moment these anchored craft appeared to have but skeleton crews aboard.

Kerin knew that maneuvering the *Benduan* through the crowded harbor and bringing the ship up neatly against a quay, single-handed, were beyond his strength and skill. With Nogiri at the tiller, he dropped the mizzen sail into its crutches. The ship slowed to a gradual halt. Soon a tug, propelled by eight naked brown paddlers, approached. A man in the stern shouted up.

"What say they?" Kerin asked the girl.

"They ask if you wish a tow."

"How much?"

A brief chaffer between Nogiri and the tugboat captain brought agreement. The *Benduan* was creeping towards a vacant quay when another craft, a galley bearing a score of paddlers, approached with swift strokes. With disciplined precision, it swung broadside to the *Benduan*, the paddlers on that side all lifting their paddles out of the way. When the two vessels gently bumped, a dozen Salimorese in fancy skirts and turbans scrambled aboard with swords of the serpentine, wavy-edged form that Kerin had seen on some of the pirates. Nogiri had told him it was called a *kris*.

Unarmed, Kerin found himself backed against the deckhouse facing a semicircle of swords. The leader barked a command; a couple of boarders hauled Kerin forward. Others forced him to his knees; still others dug fingers into his hair, grown long since leaving home, and pulled his head forward.

Still another stood beside Kerin, kris in hand. Sighting on Kerin's neck, he raised his blade. Struggling, Kerin shouted in rudimentary Salimorese: "What do? I friend! I peaceful traveler!"

Nogiri was pulling at the arm of the man in command. At last that officer, distinguished by a golden medallion suspended by a chain against his bare chest, turned. The two argued, but the rush of words was too fast for Kerin.

At last the leader barked another command. The men holding Kerin let go; the headsman, looking disappointed, put away his sword. Nogiri explained:

"The harbor guard recognized this ship as Malgo's *Maneater*, which they have long pursued. They thought you a survivor of that crew."

The officer said: "A simple misunderstanding, foreigner; nought to get excited about. What befell Malgo?"

"I slew him in a duel," said Kerin, mentally thanking Jorian for training him in lying. "We wagered my life against freedom for me and the princess, and I won."

The leader looked quizzical. "It sounds not like that gang of cutthroats to let a captive depart, oaths or no oaths."

"He speaks the flawless truth," said Nogiri. "I was there."

The officer shrugged. "If Lord Vunambai's niece says so, it must be so. I am glad now that I did not summarily cut off your head."

"I am even gladder," growled Kerin.

Hours later, the *Benduan* was berthed and the customs and harbor dues paid. At Nogiri's suggestion, Kerin hired an off-duty harbor guard to watch the ship when he was away from it, to guard against pilferage.

"Now," said Nogiri, "let us forth to Lord Vunambai's house, as soon as we make ourselves presentable. Mine uncle is a fussy man."

An hour later, Kerin and Nogiri, dodging around water-buffalo carts and an elephant ridden by two Salimorese, approached the estate of Nogiri's uncle. Kerin wore his best trousers and shirt but no jacket in this steamy, muggy climate. He insisted on stopping at a barber's for a haircut and a beard trim; his beard was at last reaching respectable proportions.

Nogiri had donned an embroidered sarong that she found in the hold.

A porter sat half asleep against the outer gate of the grounds; a spear was leaning against the surrounding wall. Through the grillwork Kerin could see a fountain and colorful plantings, with a glimpse of a big house behind the palms. Flowers of scarlet, magenta, and purple blazed in the beds. The house looked to be a solid structure of stone and timber, whereas most dwellings in Kwatna were flimsy affairs of bamboo and palm fronds, larger versions of the hut that Pwana had built on Kinungung. Nogiri explained that earthquakes favored this construction.

The porter leaped to his feet and seized the spear, crying: "Mistress Nogiri! We all thought you slain!"

Kerin could not follow the ensuing rush of talk. At last Nogiri said: "Wait here, Master Kerin. Trojung has orders to admit no person unannounced. I will go in and explain."

The porter opened the gate, bowed Nogiri in, and followed her. Kerin waited outside, strolling up and down. Passers-by stared at him; naked children pointed and giggled.

Time passed; the sun declined until it touched the roofs among the palms. Kerin wondered what had gone wrong, when a cry of "Master Kerin!" from the street brought him about.

Nearby stood Janji, Captain Huvraka's witch-navigator. She was barefoot and clad as usual in nothing but the short Salimorese sarong. "How come you here?" she rasped.

"That's a long story," said Kerin. "I cannot tell you now, because I have an appointment within."

"Indeed? Know you Lord Vunambai?"

"In a manner of speaking."

Janji looked piercingly at Kerin. "Art still on your way to Kuromon?"

"Aye, if my Western gods permit."

"Novarian gods have no power in these purlieus," she said in a tone of menace. "You will never get to Kuromon. My powers tell me that if you try, you will surely perish. Better you should return forthwith to your own barbarian land!" Abruptly she turned and walked away.

"Watch out for that one!" tinkled Belinka from the air above Kerin's head. "Remember what her hantu told me on the other ship! She and her guild will do aught in their power to keep out knowledge of that new navigating device."

"Thankee, Belinka," said Kerin. "I'll try to be careful." An idea struck him. "Couldst follow the witch to see where she goes and report the tale to me?"

"But I cannot leave you unguarded—"

"We must take that chance. Her guild may try to make trouble. If you find out where they meet and pay them a visit unseen from time to time, you could give me timely warning."

"Nay, Master Kerin; that would leave you for too long helpless—"

It irked Kerin that she supposed him so incapable of taking care of himself. But, remembering his brother's admonition that "flattery will get you everywhere," he said:

"But Belinka darling, think! I cannot flit about the city awing and unseen with the speed of the wind, as you can. A timely warning were the surest precaution against a blade in the back. With your ease of movement and nimble wit, your scouting will make me safer than an Othomaean knight's defense of iron plate."

"Oh, very well," said Belinka. "Where will you be, so I can find you again?"

"I await reception by Lord Vunambai, who may load me with gold and honors. If he ask me to remain, I shall have to return to the ship for my gear. So after the witch, Belinka!"

"I go," said the sprite.

. . .

Kerin resumed his wait with growing unease. Surely, he thought, it should not take so long for Nogiri to tell her tale and for Lord Vunambai to arrange to receive her rescuer; unless, Kerin wondered, the uncle planned some grand reception, with feasting and dancing. That would be nice, but Kerin did not really expect it.

He turned at the sound of motion. The porter stepped out of the gate, gripping his spear. After him came a pair of Salimorese wearing a livery of spangled vests above their skirts and armed with krises.

"Well?" said Kerin. "Am I to be escorted in?"

"Nay!" said the porter. "Lord Vunambai says: Go away!"

"*What?*" Kerin's jaw sagged with astonishment.

"Go away! Get hence! Get out of sight!"

"What is matter?" asked Kerin. "I rescued his niece—"

"That is nought. He wants you not. So go!" The two behind Trojung the porter drew their swords.

Kerin looked the trio over. To try to force this issue would probably get him killed, even if he succeeded in taking one of the three with him. This was the sort of situation that Jorian had warned him to avoid at whatever cost to his pride. Kerin had traveled enough to have an idea of the troubles arising from getting into a fray in a foreign city, regardless of rights and wrongs. He fought down his anger and asked, in as level a voice as he could:

"Very well; could you gentlemen name me a place to eat?"

"What meanst?" said Trojung. "People eat in their houses."

By much repetition and fumbling with the language, Kerin learned that Kwatna had no such thing as a place serving ready-cooked meals for travelers. There were drink shops along the waterfront. If he made arrangements at one of these and bought the food himself, he might persuade the shopkeeper's wife to cook it for him.

An hour later, Kerin was sitting in a room behind the liquor counter of a dramshop, gingerly sampling the unfamiliar foods—a fish, a small bowl of rice, and some strange greens—that he had procured at the goodwife's direction. Belinka returned, saying:

"Oh, there you are, Master Kerin! I have searched all over."

"I'm sorry; I knew not how to get word to you. What didst learn?"

"But little. I followed Mistress Janji to her home, one of those little houses of bamboo and leaves of the palm. She shares it with a timid-seeming little man; but whether he be husband, lover, or servant I could not ascertain."

"Belike all three at once," said Kerin.

"We must be more careful to let each of us know where the other will be found. How fared you with the barbarian lord?"

"Alas!" Kerin told of his repulse. "Now will you please go back to Vunambai's house and see what has become of Princess Nogiri? You will find me, when I finish this much-needed repast, back at the ship."

An hour later, when Kerin was dozing on the deck of the *Benduan*, Belinka returned saying: "I searched that big house from roof to crypt but found no trace of your brown barbarian maid. Nor is she on the grounds. It is as if she had vanished from the earth."

"Crypt, eh?" responded Kerin. "Has the place underground chambers, as we often have in Novaria?"

"Aye. One such chamber seems a prison cell for disobedient servants. It held but one occupant, chained to the wall; but he was a burly man of middle years."

"Too cursed many mysteries," grumbled Kerin. "Could I but find an all-knowing seer or soothsayer. . . ."

"Master Kerin! Let yourself not be distracted from your proper goal! These Easterners do all sorts of ghastly things to one another, and 'tis not our business to interfere. You must get to Kuromon!"

Kerin bridled, then sighed resignedly. "I fear you are right, Belinka. But the day is gone, and our next step must await the morrow."

Next day, Kerin hunted down the harbor master. Yes, said this official, the two batten-sailed ships were from Kuromon. Yes, they would soon return thither. How soon? The harbor master shrugged and spread his hands.

"They will sail when the gods will, *tuan*."

Kerin controlled his impatience. "Have you any idea of when that will be?"

Another shrug. "What mortal knows the thoughts of the gods?"

Kerin gave up and walked to the nearer of the two ships, of a kind that the Salimorese called a *jong*. The ship was even larger than he had expected, with four masts and a hull painted grass-green. A swarm of short, yellow-skinned, flat-faced men crewed it. At first he seemed unable to communicate at all, and he had to fight down the rush of embarrassment that accosting strangers always gave him. At last they directed him by gestures to a ship's officer in a thin silken robe whereon scarlet flowers were embroidered, who identified himself as Second Mate Togaru. This man told Kerin in strangely accented Salimorese that they expected to sail in seven or eight days.

On the other jong they told him that they would not sail for at least a fortnight; so he returned to the first ship to engage passage to Koteiki, the main southern port of the Kuromon Empire. He accosted the first officer he saw and was referred to another who, Kerin learned, was Zummo the purser. Zummo quoted fares and said:

"Alone, or bringing a woman?"

"Alone, sir."

"Then I can put you in Number Eighteen. Your cabin mate will be the Reverend Tsemben."

"What kind of reverend is he?" asked Kerin.

"A priest of the goddess Jinterasa, returning from a tour of missionary duty to Salimor. You will find him a quiet room-mate."

"I should like to see the cabin, please."

The officer summoned a deckhand to show Kerin the way. The sailor bowed to the officer, bowed again to Kerin, and led his passenger to the forward hatch and down the ladder.

On either side of the cabin deck were a score of cabins opening on a central corridor. Kerin tried out the rudimentary Kuromonian he had learned from Nogiri on the sailor. He learned that most of these cabins were occupied by Kuromonian merchants, each of whom had brought a stock of goods to Salimor to sell. Most of the merchants were then ashore; only a couple of flat yellow faces peered out of cabin doors as Kerin passed.

The sailor opened the door of one cabin, which proved already lit within. The sailor bowed to Kerin and stood in the anticipatory stance of a man expecting a tip. Kerin gave him one of the smallest Salimorese copper coins and turned to the cabin. Failing to stoop low enough, he banged his head on the door lintel. While he was of but little over average height for Novarians, most Kuromonians were substantially shorter than he, and the spaces on the ship were proportioned accordingly.

Kerin found that shipboard spaces were compact to the point of being cramped, and those of the *Tukara Mora* were even more so than those he had already seen. The cabin had just room for two pallets, one taking up half the floor and the other, of the same size, on a shelf directly above it. Otherwise the furnishings consisted of a single stool, a small shelf jutting from the wall at one end of the pallets, pegs driven into the wall at an angle for hanging clothes, and a small bronze lamp suspended from above.

The cabin also had an inhabitant, a small, wrinkled, yellow-skinned, black-robed man, who sat cross-legged on the edge of the lower pallet with a scroll in his lap. The man looked up.

"Good-day, sir," said Kerin in hesitant Kuromonian. "The Reverend Tsemben?"

"Good-day to you," said the priest, and rattled off a string of unintelligible syllables. Seeing Kerin's blank look, he changed to Salimorese, saying: "Are you my cabin mate?"

"Aye. You are, I understand, a missionary?"

"Aye, young sir. And whence come you? Your aspect is of one of those Western barbarians of whom I have heard."

"From Kortoli, in the Twelve Cities of Novaria. And you? . . ."

Kerin and the Reverend Tsemben cautiously felt each other out. Kerin said: "Are you happy to return to your homeland?"

The priest sighed. "Alas, nay! It means that this wretched worm has failed."

"How, failed?"

"This inferior one came to enlighten these barbarians in the true religion, but I made no converts. They stubbornly adhere to their heathenish little gods, Bautong and Luar and the false deities of Mulvan. Mere demons, betimes useful if captured and coerced into worthy labor, but otherwise useless or hostile.

"So, when my superiors learned that the worship of the Queen of Heaven was getting nowhere, they ordered me home. Had I been a man of honor, I should have cut mine own throat; but I lacked the courage even for that. Forsooth, this person is the lowest of the low."

Kerin saw a tear, highlighted by the lantern beams, trickle down the wrinkled yellow cheek. He felt silly consoling a man at least twice his age, but he said: "Come, Reverend Sir! If you have done the best you could, nobody can expect more. Would it comfort you to do me a service on the way to Koteiki? I can pay a modest fee."

"What would that be, young man?"

"I need lessons in the Kuromonian language, starting forthwith. I have never gotten beyond a few simple sentences, such as 'Good-morning,' and 'How much does this cost?' and 'Where is the latrine?' " They agreed on a figure, and Kerin departed to pay his fare.

Returning to the *Benduan*, Kerin sought out the proprietor of the grogshop where he had been taking his meals. He explained: "Master Natar, I need a good wizard or soothsayer. Can you recommend one?"

"As to that, since the Balimpawang Pwana returned, none in Kwatna rivals him."

Kerin winced. "Pwana back?"

"Aye; he came in a fortnight past and resumed the rule of his old Temple of Bautong as if he had never been exiled."

"I thought he was at outs with the Sophis."

"With the late Sophi, aye; but the new one, Vurkai—may whose virility never flag—was also at outs with his brother. Hence he welcomed Doctor Pwana's return."

Kerin frowned. "I know of Doctor Pwana; but I fear his charges are out of reach. Canst recommend one of less—ah—exalted repute?"

"Let me think," said Natar, stamping on a foot-long centipede that rippled across his dirt floor. "I know of Pawang Klung, who seems a good enough sort. You reach his house thus. . . ." The shopkeeper squatted and scratched a street map with his finger in the earthen floor.

"Thankee!" said Kerin. "How is business?"

"Good, did not the Sophi's publicans skim off any profit for taxes. It is his mad scheme to pave the whole city, as if yon cobblestones along the waterfront were not good enough."

Kerin went in search of Pawang Klung. The magician occupied a stone-and-timber house of moderately prosperous aspect, behind a fenced courtyard in which several Kwatnites lounged. At the door, a burly guard blocked Kerin's way.

"May I see Pawang Klung?" Kerin asked.

"In your turn, after these folk," said the guard, indicating the loungers.

Kerin found a place in the courtyard and sat on the grass with his back to a tree. He was hungry and tired after a morning of juggling the tones of the Kuromonian tongue. Then he heard Belinka's tinkly voice:

"Master Kerin, I like this place not! I feel other supernatural presences within. I trust no magician or soothsayer save my mistress, the good Madame Erwina."

"We must take that chance," grumbled Kerin.

A man issued from the house, followed by a large, stout Salimorese carrying a yard-long dowel with a silver star on the end. The stout one pointed his stick at a woman among the loungers, saying:

"You next, madam!"

The woman scrambled to her feet, then dropped to her knees and bowed until her straight black hair swept the ground. She rose and followed the stout one into the house. Kerin asked a fellow lounger:

"Is that Pawang Klung?"

The man looked surprised. "Certes," he sneered. "You must come from a distant land indeed, to be so ignorant. But you should call him the Balimpawang."

"Thankee," said Kerin, returning to his doze.

The next he knew, the door guard was shaking him awake, saying: "Wouldst see the Balimpawang or not?"

Kerin blinked the sleep out of his eyes, discovering that he was the last of Klung's clients. All the others had departed. "I—ah—where—of course I am fain to see him," he mumbled. Then he sighted the wizard nearby and gave him his best Novarian bow.

"You!" barked the guard. "Why show you not due reverence to my great master?"

"Let him be," rumbled the fat wizard. "He is from a land where customs differ from ours. We will consider the obeisance as given." The stout man turned to Kerin; his dark slanting eyes flickered right and left, up and down. "Aha! I see you have a familiar spirit in tow."

"Forsooth," said Kerin, "you could say she has me in tow. Her witch-mistress commanded her to ward my welfare."

"Well, I cannot allow her into my house. She must wait without."

"Indeed!" squeaked Belinka, dancing about in full visibility. "And what is so obnoxious about me, O great and mighty wizard?"

Klung chuckled. "Nought with you, my winsome sprite. But I dare not admit a strange familiar, lest strife erupt betwixt the stranger and my established stable of spirits. They wax ferociously jealous of outsiders' influence."

"Master Kerin!" cried Belinka. "Wilt put up with such shabby treatment of one who hath faithfully served your behalf for lo these many months? I demand—"

Kerin, his anger rising, barked: "Belinka you may go—" He

was about to add "jump in the Eastern Ocean" but thought better of it. Jorian had cautioned him against unnecessarily forcing issues. He changed his words:

"Pray, go spy on Janji and find out what her Navigators' Guild be up to. That's the most useful thing you can do just now. Then join me back on the *Benduan*, will you?"

Belinka uttered a sound that could have been called a grunt, if so tiny and ethereal a being could be said to grunt. Kerin watched her zip out of the courtyard and turned back to Klung, who said:

"Come along, young man."

·VI·
Kwatna City

Following Klung down a hall, Kerin glimpsed through an open door a spacious chamber cluttered with apparatus, softly glowing with highlights of steel and brass and copper. Klung led him to a smaller room and waved him to cushions on the floor before a kind of stunted, crimson-lacquered desk, rising little more than a foot above the floor. The wizard plumped himself down on other cushions behind this furnishing.

"Well, younker," he said in passable if old-fashioned Novarian, "What wouldst?"

"Sir," began Kerin circumspectly, "first, I would fain not commit more discourtesies than I can help in a strange land. So pray explain the difference betwixt a pawang and a balimpawang."

The wizard made a steeple of his fingers. "A pawang is simply our word for 'magician' or 'wizard.' But we also have guilds, and a balimpawang is the chosen arch of such a supernaturalists' guild."

"And you are the leader of the Magicians' Guild of Kwatna?"

"Aye, and of all of Salimor. Practically speaking, that means Ambok; the pawangs on the other islands are for the most part mere primitive witch doctors, ignorant of the higher branches of the magical sciences."

"Then enlighten me, pray. Know you the wizard Pwana?"

Klung gave a low growl. "Aye, I ken the scoundrel. What of him?"

"I know him, too. When I met him, a month or so ago, he named himself a balimpawang."

"Oh!" said Klung, his slant eyes rounding. "So ye must be he who brought the rascal back to Ambok! Better had ye left him on his isle till the crabs had picked his bones. Now he is up to his old quillets, reviving his Cosmic Diamond cult; the gullible flock to's temple."

"I meant no trouble," said Kerin. "But he helped me and another captive to turn the tables on Malgo's pirates."

"I heard something of that; another time ye must read me the tale entire." Klung paused. "This villain's rescue hardly prejudices me in your favor; still, I essay to weigh the issues fairly."

"But about the title, sir?"

"Oh. After Pwana was driven forth by exposure of his villainies, the Guild held an interim election and chose me by an overwhelming show of hands to succeed him. Then all went well until this losel reappeared, claiming he had never resigned his office, which still had two years to run; and that he, therefore, was rightful balimpawang. There will be a special election to settle the matter when the members can agree upon a date. By then I shall have my great invention in working order, so I fear not the outcome.

"But I must not while away the day in superfluous chatter. It is one of my besetting faults. Who be ye, and what your especial desire?"

Kerin gave a brief account of himself, adding: "Now I wish to learn the fate of the Princess Nogiri. I last saw her entering Lord Vunambai's grounds; but anon, when I sent Belinka to find out what had befallen her, the sprite declared she was nowhere to be found. From the curious way her uncle used me, I fear that he, too, may be up to no good."

"What is your interest in this damsel? Be ye lovers?"

"Nay," said Kerin. "First, she is already betrothed; and second, as a result of her evil treatment by the pirates, she was averse to such intimacies. But she has been a true and helpful friend."

"And ye would fain discover whither she have gone? Canst pay?"

"Up to a point. How much?"

Klung mused: "For this task, I fear my familiars be not up to the mark. I shall have to send my spirit through the astral plane to search. It will take an hour at least and cost you a hundred royals Salimorese, or the equivalent in foreign coin."

They chaffered over rates of exchange until a bargain was struck. Kerin was losing his former embarrassment over haggling; he fished several gold pieces from a pocket in his money belt.

"Ye may look about whilst my spirit be away," said Klung. "But touch ye nought, lest ye be turned to a crocodile or blasted to atoms. Here goeth!"

The magician sat back, closed his eyes, and muttered a cantrip over and over. After a while he fell silent; then his body shuddered and stiffened.

• • •

During the wait, Kerin got up, stretched cramped limbs, and prowled the building. At the door to the magician's sanctum he found the guard, who said:

"Ye can look but not go in!"

Kerin peered past the man's shoulder into the darkening chamber. Of the pieces of apparatus within, the dominant object was a kind of man-sized cage in the center, containing a congeries of hoops and wheels.

"What's that?" Kerin asked, pointing.

The guard shrugged. "The Balimpawang calls it his transporter. With it he once transported my pet mongoose to a place outside the city; frightened the poor creature half to death." The guard paused. "Be it true, Master Kerin, that ye come from the mysterious West?"

"I suppose so," said Kerin, "though it seems not so mysterious to me. But then, any land seems mysterious until one becomes used to it."

"Hm! I never thought of it that way. I have read of the West in books." The guard stuck out his chest proudly. "I can read, which few amongst persons of my class can do!"

"Congratulations! One cannot have too many skills to get through life."

Back in the chamber of audience, Kerin still found Klung in his trance. After another tedious wait, the magician shook himself and opened his eyes. For a time he breathed in deep gasps, as if he had been running. At last he spoke:

"I found your princess, Master Kerin; albeit it took a mort of searching."

"Where is she?"

"She is a prisoner in the Temple of Bautong."

"But how—" began Kerin. His voice commenced to rise with excitement until he controlled it.

"Her uncle hath sold her to Pwana, who means to use her in some rite involving human sacrifice."

"Why in the name of all the gods should he do that?"

Klung spread his plump hands. "It took a deal of nosing about and eavesdropping, in Vunambai's palace and again at the temple, to piece the tale together. When Vunambai heard her story, he became convinced that she was no more a virgin, which with brides of her class is a weighty matter. Even if she were, her betrothed would never believe it, what of her having been a captive of pirates and having dwelt unescorted with you on the voyage hither. When he asked her, she foolishly told of the gang rape. That young woman is too honest for her own good, meseems."

"Did he ask the young man's intentions?"

"I know not. In view of their class, I am sure the youth would have renounced the bargain, citing damaged goods. It is not as if she were a wench of low degree, amongst which class the questions of lineage and pedigree are of lesser moment."

"It seems to me that Nogiri has done nought amiss, save perhaps to go on that picnic. Be that the Salimorese idea of justice?"

"Nay; but lords do as they list. When a young lord reach his majority, his sire gives him a fancy kris, bedight with jewels, the wearing of which by one of lower class would earn the wearer a hundred stripes. Then the youngling sallies forth and often tries his edge, with impunity, on the first wight of lower class he encounter.

"Furthermore, of all that crew, Vunambai is the most punctilious in matters of rank and procedure. Had he admitted you and ye failed to offer the full obeisance, belike he would have commanded off with your head."

"Perhaps it's well I saw him not," mused Kerin. "Methinks I must essay to rescue this princess. Where in the temple is she immured? In an underground crypt?"

"Nay; in a locked room at the top of the tower. But what ye

propose is impossible, young man. The tower is lofty, the temple well-guarded. Ye have done your duty in fetching her to Kwatna."

"I still feel responsible for her, and she's a friend."

"But ye will accomplish nought, save belike to be thrown to the crocodiles the Sophi keep in the moat around his palace!"

"Still, I should be ashamed of myself if I didn't try at least. I was brought up not to abandon a comrade."

Klung shrugged. "Well, I know not how to rede you. I regret the young woman's death; but it is not my affair, and I should mislike to see a likely youth like you come to untimely cease in a foredoomed adventure."

Kerin persisted: "What's this deadly spell that Pwana concocts?"

Klung smiled slyly. "All I know is what rumor doth waft about or is garnered by my familiars. The burden of these bruits is that our noble Sophi—may his virility never flag—find that selfsame virility not up to the tasks he demand thereof."

"Keeps he a harem?"

"Aye; and that is the trouble. Since his recent accession— ye will note I use not the word 'usurpation,' the breathing of which hath cost more than one subject his life—he hath become the foremost ruler in the archipelago, largely by espousing the female kin of all the lesser rulers. Hence he now rejoices—if that be the word I seek—in a harem of one thousand, two hundred and forty-six wives, at least at last count. Now, a thousand wives may gratify the vanity of a potentate, but where wilt find a potentate who can gratify a thousand wives?" Klung suppressed a snort of laughter. "They say some women have sent out smuggled messages to their royal kin, complaining that Vurkai never performs his husbandly duties with them. Enough of this, and he will find the throne a-rock beneath his

royal arse. So Pwana hath undertaken to stiffen the royal—
ah—sinews by this goëtic operation."

The wizard looked sharply at Kerin. "Another matter, howsomever, doth concern me. Said ye not ye were on your way
to Kuromon?"

"Aye, sir."

"How would ye like to make the journey in the wink of an
eye instead of a hazardous fortnightly voyage?"

"What's this, some magical transport?"

"Aye." Klung lurched to his feet. "Come hither, lad."

The wizard led the way to the oratory and pointed to the
cage. "Behold my magical triumph! It shall redound to mine
eternal fame in magical science; it is the unsurpassed advance
of the century."

"How does it work?" asked Kerin.

"I place the subject therein, close the door, and perform certain incantations, fumigations, and passes, and presto! The
wight is translated to his destination with the speed of light,
whatever that be. As ye doubtless ken, philosophers dispute
about whither the passage of light be instantaneous or whether
it occupy an interval, however brief, of time."

"But how—"

"I employ that which none of my predecessors hath succeeded in doing, namely: to harness the entities of the Fourth
Plane. These beings are not exactly spirits, albeit sentient non-
material organisms. They are not very intelligent; nor can they
manifest themselves on the Prime Plane as doth your little
familiar. But I have found how to make them seize the creature
within the cage and move it instanter to the destination I have
chosen, via the Fourth Plane, which permits them to remove
it from the cage despite the bars."

"Does it work?"

"Doth it work! My boy, I have sent a mouse hence out into

the courtyard, and then a mongoose half a league away, to the beach to northward of the city."

"How know you the beast arrived safely?"

"I had stationed Wejo—" Klung nodded towards the guard. "—there on the beach. When the mongoose appeared, it galloped up to its master to be petted and fetched home. Now, could I but send you to Kuromon, my triumph at the forthcoming vote for balimpawang were assured. Thus shall I receive the honor that be rightfully mine!"

Kerin looked doubtful. "Dost mean it would send me and all my gear—clothes, weapons, money, and so forth?"

Klung frowned. "A few trifling adjustments are needed ere it will send inanimate objects. Attempts to transport things like a bowl or a knife have not yet succeeded. Certes this is but a temporary check; I shall soon have made the requisite improvements. By the way, art wearing a counterspell against others' magic?"

"Yea, sir. Is it still effective after all these months?"

"I could not be sure without tests; but my spiritual senses tell me it be. Of course, I should have to cancel it for my transporter to become effective."

Kerin thoughtfully replied: "I think not that I care to chance arriving in Kuromon naked, penniless, and without even Doctor Uller's protective spell. That might not bother Wejo's mongoose, but it's not my idea of an auspicious arrival in a strange land. My ship does sail a few days hence. Since I have already paid a deposit, methinks it wiser to adhere to my previous plan."

"Humph! Are ye sure ye be not simply affrighted by the prospect?"

Kerin grinned. "Not at all sure, sir."

Klung sighed. "Ye were a fine subject; but all the lusty youths to whom I have made the offer find reasons why they cannot.

At your age, I should have seized the chance. The younger generation are a spineless lot!"

Outside the balimpawang's house, dusk was falling. Kerin called: "Belinka!"

"Here!" said the little blue light, dancing against the darkling sky.

"Didst learn much?"

"Somewhat, but not so much as I should have had I remained for tonight's meeting of the Navigator's Guild. I had to return hither to meet you."

"You know where this guild meets, then?"

"Aye; I followed the witch. They foregather in an abandoned temple, half fallen down from earthquakes."

"Well, go back and report to me when the meeting be over. You'll find me aboard the ship."

The moon, now a narrow crescent, had not yet set when Belinka returned. She found Kerin in the captain's cabin, poring over a booklet of Kuromonian phrases by the light of a candle. He put the book away, saying:

"I'm glad of an excuse not to wear out mine eyes on these damned scribbles by this feckless light. It gives me a headache. Now tell me all."

"The navigators were enjoying a supper when I arrived, sitting in a circle on cushions and served by Twelfth Plane demons."

"How many navigators were there?"

"Seventeen when I arrived, and one more came in later. Then they called the meeting to order. After the tedious preliminaries—minutes of the last meeting, report of the treasury, and so on—Janji, who is treasurer, brought up your visit to Kuromon. The thought of that navigating device did stir them deeply. They spake of giving you a mortal thrust in the tripes; others favored hiring a pawang to blast you by magic. Janji said a maleficent spell might not penetrate your counterspell. Another objected that to attack you were unethical; another, that it might get the guild in trouble, and so on. One progressive wight proposed that they embrace the new device and learn to use it instead of their spells, but they howled him down.

"An aged member argued to move cautiously. After all, you might never reach Kuromon, the hazards of sea travel being what they are. If you did get there, the Kuromonians might thwart your efforts to filch their secret or punish you for trying. Some of their punishments are most unpleasant, such as staking you out and causing one of the Emperor's elephants to tread upon you. If you got the instrument despite all odds and survived the voyage back to Kwatna, that were time to lay an ambuscade. They ought to assign the members in rotation to keep a watch on Kuromonian ships and to scout such ships by their familiars whilst they be still at sea."

"What was the outcome?" Kerin asked.

"I know not, for I was compelled to flee. Janji's bir, or hantu as they call them here, returned from a tour of the drink shops, where he had been stealing a few drops from each drinking vessel. Still furious over my broken promise, he chased me forth. Had he not been so drunk, I could not have lost him."

"Let's hope the cautious elder's advice prevails," muttered Kerin. "And now, another task. I wish you to examine the Temple of Bautong from capstone to crypt, taking careful note of its structure so I can draw an accurate plan."

"But Master Kerin!" protested Belinka. "The balimpa-wang—the other one, that is—will have familiars at his command! They will assail me, or at least alert the wizard to my presence."

"Not necessarily. He said he had dismissed his spirits when

exiled, and belike he hasn't yet replaced his spooks. In any case we must chance it; so go!"

"But wherefore this sudden interest in temple architecture?"

Kerin sighed. A familiar spirit might be handy to have, but not one who argued every step. "My princess is imprisoned in the Temple of Bautong, where Pwana means to sacrifice her in some abominable rite. I'm told Nogiri is in a chamber atop the tower. To get her out, I must know the structure's plan."

"Master Kerin, you are mad! I'll not permit it! If you succeed, you will have been untrue to Adeliza; if you fail, you will have thrown away your life!"

"Belinka," said Kerin sternly, "I have made up my mind. So go study the temple!"

"I will not! You cannot compel me!"

"If you don't, I'll go myself and try to break in. I shall probably be slain; whereas with knowledge in advance, I shall at least have a better chance. Which shall it be?"

"I said I won't—"

"Then here goes." Kerin rose, strapped on his sword, and fumbled in his bag.

"Oh, you pig-headed monster!" cried Belinka. "I'll go, since you force me. But you shall rue your contumacy! If I suffer scathe, it will be all your fault!" She zipped away into the darkness.

Kerin settled himself to think. Jorian had warned him: Ere you begin any perilous emprise, take time to think. Imagine what every step along the way will entail and formulate a plan to cope therewith. Then imagine what could go wrong at every step, and make alternate plans for such events. The only thing worse than entering upon an adventure with no plan is to go in with a plan you have become so fond of that you cannot bear to change it, even if it leads you to destruction.

Fortunately for Kerin, he was not one whom such advice

repelled. While not altogether free of youthful impulsiveness and recklessness, his character leaned more towards the prudent and judicious.

First he had to gain access to Nogiri's room. Locked doors and windows offered no great obstacle, thanks to Jorian's picklocks, whose use he had practiced. But first he had to get to the chamber. If he went up inside, that meant evading the guards and priests, or somehow rendering them harmless, as by a drug or spell. If that would not work, he would have to ascend outside. Having no wings or flying broomstick . . .

Then, supposing he got the princess out of the temple, they must needs flee to the *Tukara Mora*. So he would have to make sure that, first, the gangplank was out and the crew warned of his arrival; and second, that his possessions were already aboard, since he would have no chance to go back for them. And Nogiri would need accomodations. . . .

Next day, Kerin came to Balimpawang Klung's door with a roll of paper. It had taken him hours to locate a source of paper, since the Salimorese were not a highly literate folk and there was little demand. When he located a source, it turned out not to be the familiar rag paper but a brown local product made from palm fronds cut and glued together in a press. As before, Belinka remained outside when Kerin entered the house.

"Here," Kerin told Klung, "are the plans of the Temple of Bautong. Here is the chamber wherein Nogiri is immured, over thirty feet above ground."

"Interesting," said Klung, "but why bringst these plans to me?"

"Because I shall want your help in getting her out ere Pwana slay her."

"My dear young man! I mind not helping a worthy youth in

everyday matters, but ye ask me to interfere with one of the deadliest sorcerers our fair land hath produced. Why should I endanger myself for you or Princess Nogiri? It is not as if ye had put me in your debt. If anyone owes you a favor, it is Pwana, for fetching him from his isle. But ye ken how much succor to expect from that source. Certes, for a Sophi's ransom I might consider it; but I misdoubt ye have enough wealth to tempt me from the path of prudence."

Kerin pondered. "I doubt if the money I fetched from home will last me out the journey, be I ever so thrifty. But perchance I could be useful to you in other ways."

"How so?"

After another pause, Kerin said: "Belike I could help you at the forthcoming election in your guild. I've seen how such things are done in the Republic of Vindium, and in mine own Kingdom of Kortoli we elect a House of Burgesses to control public expenditures. My father served a term as a burgess."

Klung shook his head. "Salimor is no republic, like those I hear of in the Far West, where candidates for office harangue the rabble from street corners. Ye would only antagonize the members by exhortations, being not only a nonmember but, in their eyes, a mannerless foreigner to boot."

Kerin pondered. "Know you of the Kuromonian navigation device, which the Navigators' Guild so fears?"

"I ken somewhat thereof. What is your connection therewith?"

Kerin told of his troubles with Janji. "Come to think, those Kuromonian ships in harbor must bear the device. Has none sought to buy or steal it?"

"Yea; but the Kuromonians keep it locked up in a secure part of the ship, whereto only the captain and a few trusted officers have access. Well?"

"If I smuggled such a device to Salimor, wouldn't it be of
value to you?"

"Why? No sailor, I."

"But if the navigators so fear it, wouldn't it augment your
power amongst the guilds?"

Klung took time to answer. "Now that ye mention it, belike
it would. It hath been proposed to choose a single super-
balimpawang over all the guilds affiliated with mine own: the
Navigators', the Diviners', and the Healers'. The guilds' bal-
impawangs oppose the change, fearing diminution of their
power. Had I this device, methinks I could swing at least the
navigators; or belike get the navigators and Irapat, the head of
the Merchants' Guild, bidding against each other for it. . . . I'll
do it! Present the device on your return from Kuromon, and
ye shall have mine unstinted aid in rescuing your lass."

"But sir!" cried Kerin. "I may not be able to return thence
until long after the lady have been offered to Pwana's dark
deities!"

Klung sighed. "Ever some fribbling difficulty! Had ye some
vasty treasure to leave as security. . . ."

After an hour's haggling, they agreed that Kerin should sign
an agreement making him Klung's bondservant for one year in
case he returned from Kuromon without the navigating device.
Klung wrote the contract in both Salimorese and Novarian.
Knowing that Wejo the guard was literate, Kerin insisted that
Wejo read off the Salimorese version, while Kerin followed the
Novarian version to make sure that they were equivalents.

"Now for details," said Kerin. He spread out the sheets of
palm-leaf paper on which he had drawn plans of the temple.
"Here's the princess. Inside, Belinka tells me, all corridors are
guarded, especially the stair that winds up the tower. Could
you cast a spell of immobility upon these men, or drug them?"

"Nay; the temple is shielded by potent counterspells."

"Could you then make me invisible, as Pwana did to himself when he left us?"

"I could; but then ye were bounden to strip naked lest your garments seem to enter the temple by themselves; and for the same reason ye could not bear any weapon. Besides, the counterspell would cancel your invisibility as ye neared the temple. Furthermore, I could not so ensorcel the princess whilst she were in her chamber and I on the ground outside."

"Then, methinks, I must invade Nogiri's chamber from the outside, if I can get up there."

Klung pursed his lips. "It would take a monstrous ladder to reach the third story. I warned Pwana that so tall a building invited the wrath of the underground dragon whose twitchings, they say, cause earthquakes. But Pwana scoffed; his vanity insisted upon the tallest structure in Kwatna. The setting up of the ladder would surely arouse those within. Couldst climb the wall, using the decorations as handholds?"

"I might, if the decorations were ornate enough all the way up; though I haven't seen such intricate masonry on Salimorese buildings. But even if I could, I doubt if Nogiri could clamber down by the same route."

"She could cling to your back."

"I doubt that even more. Not sure am I that I could find holds for hands and feet, and a hundred-odd pounds on my back would render the task hopeless. Hast no flying broomsticks, such as the mightiest Western magicians use, like Sir Fendix of Othomae?"

Klung shuddered. "I have heard of such utensilabes, but we have none in the archipelago to my knowledge. I am told their use be most exhausting, leaving the flier fordone for days."

"Not so bad as that—"

"Besides," said Klung firmly, "I am not fain to risk my aging, gorbellied self by swooping through the empyraean astride a slender stick. The mere thought fills me with horror."

"Well then, have you one of those magical ropes, animated by a Second Plane entity to spring upright on command? My brother once escaped execution by such means."

Klung pondered. "Aye, now that ye remind me, methinks such a device doth indeed lie amid the clutter in my storage room. I have not used it for many years. For one thing, only a handful of houses in Kwatna have more than one story; for another, I am not the lithe young athlete I was forty years ago." The balimpawang smiled reminiscently. "When I was a lusty, lecherous youth, I employed the rope to offer my—ah—services to ladies fair in lofty quarters." He sighed. "But I have long been respectably wived, and . . . Master Kerin, art wed?"

"Nay, sir."

"Had ye been, ye'd understand why I would not roil domestic tranquility for amorous adventures."

"If the rope be so long unused, wouldn't you have to recharge its spell?"

"Aye; the entity would long since have leaked out and decamped. But think ye simply to march into the temple grounds, set up the rope, and climb without causing attention? If I know Pwana, he will have the grounds patrolled."

"Then," said Kerin, "let's devise a distraction. Couldst ignite a magical fire or something of the sort?"

Klung tapped his chin with his forefinger. "Methinks I can do better. My stable of spirits includes an Eighth Plane entity. I can compel it to take on your aspect and make a disturbance at the door, or as near to the door as the counterspell allows."

"A doublegoer, as we call it? What's needed to evoke such a being?"

"Evocation is easy; the hard part is teaching it to play the rôle of Kerin the Novarian convincingly. Oh, Wejo!" he called.

"Aye, Master?"

"Tomorrow I shall not be available for consultations. For the benefit of clients who can read, write a sign telling them to return anon, and turn away any who present themselves. For emergencies, refer them to my colleague Pawang Banting; I shall send him word to cover for me." He grinned slyly at Kerin. "I should never have let you lure me into this birdbrained scheme, but the chance to do the accursed Pwana one in the eye were too seductive to resist."

"One thing more," said Kerin. "I still have Malgo's little ship and some of's loot. How does one sell them at the best prices in Kwatna?"

"Why not hire your own crew and sail the ship to Kuromon and back?"

"I am not expert enough. 'Tis by the grace of Psaan, our sea god, that I sailed her hither from Kinungung with no worse disaster than a temporary stranding. So how best to dispose of her?"

"Ye need an auctioneer. In my youth, ere I entered my present profession, I apprenticed at that trade. Belike I could manage your emprise—naturally, for a commission."

"How much?"

Klung pursed his lips. "One quarter of the price."

"Oh? Back in Novaria, the going rate is ten per centum." Kerin knew something of auctions from his experience in the family clock business.

"Belike," said Klung, "but this is not Novaria. Save that I like you, I should ask half or at least a third."

Kerin did not altogether trust this genial if vain and garrulous magician, even though Klung had shown more candor than was usual in his secretive profession. On the other hand, he might run a worse risk with any other Salimorese. As a lone foreigner in a strange land, he was somewhat at the mercy of anyone with whom he did business. Besides, the *Tukara Mora* would soon sail; so he ought to take what quick profit he could and get out.

"Agreed, twenty-five per centum," he said.

Next morning, assured by Belinka that Nogiri was still in the tower chamber, Kerin remained aboard the *Benduan* long enough to examine the loot in the hold. He picked out an especially fine kris, with a jeweled hilt; probably the one Malgo had worn. Kerin, who had been warned that such a weapon was forbidden to lower-class persons, found its balance quite different from the swords he was used to. Having only a blunt point, it was intended purely for cutting.

Still, he coveted it as a souvenir of his journey. So he wrapped it in a fancy cloak and shoved the bundle into his bag. He also sequestered a gaudy silken sash with a pattern of red, green, and yellow stripes. There seemed to be no such thing in Salimor as a pair of trews with loops for a belt to hold them up. The Salimorese made do with a sarong, a wrap-around skirt or kilt held up by the friction of the rolled overlap or by a sash.

Thinking of the discomfort of his woollen trousers in this steamy, sticky climate, he took them off and donned a sarong and the sash over them. Thus clad, he hoped to be less conspicuous. Not wishing to draw attention to the package hung round his neck, he kept his shirt on instead of baring his thorax like most Salimorese.

Then he went to Klung's house and persuaded the balim-pawang to start work on the auction of his surplus properties. Klung conducted the auction with dispatch that afternoon, while Kerin moved his baggage to the *Tukara Mora*.

• • •

The following morning saw Kerin seated on a cushion in Klung's oratory, surrounded by the dull-gleaming brass of cryptic magical devices. Standing at a table laden with apparatus, Klung strove to make the Eighth Plane entity into a proper duplicate of Kerin. The entity, a manlike shape, shimmered and wavered in the pentacle. Klung said:

"Rise, Master Kerin!" Then to the undulating shape in formal Salimorese: "Behold thy model! Assume its aspect!"

The shape slowly solidified and took on Kerin's appearance from the turban, which Kerin wore to look more like a local, down to the sea boots.

"Turn!" commanded Klung.

When the shape did so, it resembled Kerin only in front. The back was a smooth, brownish surface, into which the clothing merged. It was as if someone had made a mannequin of Kerin designed to stand with its back to a wall, so that only the front could be seen.

"Idiot!" shouted Klung. "Thou shalt replicate Master Kerin all the way round. Turn, Kerin!"

Kerin thought this a little unfair to the entity, since it had seen only his front; but it was not for him to interfere. He obeyed, and gradually the entity's impersonation became more exact. When Klung was satisfied with the being's appearance, he asked Kerin:

"What think ye to say when ye confront Pwana—or rather, when your simulacrum accosts the rascal?"

Kerin thought. "Something like: 'Doctor Pwana, where is Princess Nogiri? What have you done with her? I demand to see her forthwith!' Not that I expect him to yield to my wishes."

"Good enough." Then to the entity: "Repeat after Master Kerin: 'Doctor Pwana, where is . . .' Nay, thou must needs speak with his foul foreign accent."

"That is unfair!" protested the entity in a thin, reedy voice.

"The last time I served you, ye insisted I speak your tongue like a Salimorese lord. Now ye ask that I distort it as doth this round-eyed foreigner. There be too many accents to learn them all!"

"Just do as thou art told!" shouted Klung. He fiddled with his magical apparatus, causing the entity to yelp. "And lower thy pitch!" added Klung. "Master Kerin speaketh in the middle register for males, compared to which thy speech is as the twitter of birds."

As the day wore on, the entity's imitation of Kerin became more and more convincing. Klung insisted on going over every detail of clothing, every word, and every gesture, until the entity had it just right.

"Pwana may be the biggest villain unhung," he explained, "but none hath accused him of stupidity. He will be on watch for any betraying incongruity. Dost plan your emprise for tonight?"

"I'm unsure. I must warn the folk on the *Tukara Mora*, so that when we arrive in haste there shall be no delay in boarding."

"Why all this preparation for boarding a ship?"

"Because most captains draw in their gangplanks at night, to foil the harbor thieves. Armed guards walk the deck and, if a stranger rush aboard unannounced at night, are wont to strike instanter and question anon." Kerin stood frowning. "I know! I'll ask my familiar to scout the Temple of Bautong, to see if any preparations for the great and grisly sacrifice go forward. Whilst she's about it, I shall see to quarters for Nogiri." He went out and called: "Belinka!"

"Here, Master Kerin. Hast finished your business within?"

"Not quite." Kerin gave Belinka her orders.

"Ugh!" she said. "I hate to enter that temple; it hath an evil aura, and the counterspell that envelops it makes the passage through it seem like flight through syrup. And you know what I think of your brown barbarian."

"Just go like a good sprite!"

On the *Tukara Mora*, Kerin hunted up Purser Zummo, explaining: "I shall bring a woman with me after all. What accommodations can you give her?"

The purser looked dubious. "This person sold our last double cabin today. Some of our passengers have a spare pallet, but I know not if your woman would care to sleep with a strange man."

"I'm sure she would like it not."

The officer fiddled with his thin fringe of whisker. "Unless perchance one of those who have a double cabin but occupy only one bunk would trade places with you. . . ."

"Master Zummo," said Kerin, "this woman is a princess. Have you no single cabins?"

"Oh, that is different. Aye, there are two, for persons of rank. Number Two is free for the voyage."

"How much?"

Zummo named a figure substantially higher than the total cost of a double cabin. Kerin winced at the bite it would take from his remaining funds. After hesitation he said:

"Pray, could I hold that single cabin with a deposit whilst I ask the lady for her preferences?"

"Aye, that you can do."

"May I see this splendid single cabin?"

The single was larger than any of the doubles and, moreover, had a substantial bed instead of a mere pallet on the floor. The bed was secured to the floor by wooden pins. The cabin was otherwise more impressive, also, with black and crimson dragons writhing along the walls. Kerin sighed and paid his deposit, saying:

"We may arrive in haste, pursued by ill-wishers. Could I count on your leaving your gangplank in place for most of the night, so that we can board without delay?"

"When is this furtive arrival to be?" asked Zummo.

"Tomorrow night, methinks."

"'Twill cost you extra, since we shall have to work one of the marines overtime, to guard the plank."

When Kerin returned from the *Tukara Mora*, he found the balimpawang seated at a little table bearing victuals. "Aha, Master Kerin! Sit ye down; Wejo shall fetch your repasture."

In the course of the meal, Klung said: "A rumor doth agitate the navigators of a secret compact betwixt the Emperor of Kuromon and the King of Kings of Mulvan. It is said that an envoy will travel from court to court, bearing some token—perchance a missive, perchance a gem, amulet, talisman, or other object of worth and power. For this, the Kuromonians will give the messenger something to bear back to Trimandilam. Kennest aught of this?"

"Why, there was a young Mulvani—" began Kerin. He bit off his sentence, remembering his imprudent outburst the first night on the *Dragonet*.

"Yea, ye were about to say?" probed Klung, looking keenly at Kerin.

"Nought much. There was a young Mulvani on my first ship, who boarded at Janareth; but he left us at Akkander. So I doubt he had aught to do with any secret treaty."

Klung: "Ah, well, perchance there be nought to the tale. The navigators wet their sarongs with anxiety, lest the Emperor hath sold the secret of their navigating device to the Mulvanians."

Then Klung dropped the subject. Kerin was glad that, at the moment, Klung's hantu was not scrutinizing him for veracity.

Kerin was finishing his meal when he heard Belinka's squeak: "Master Kerin! Master Kerin! Come out, pray!"

Outside, Kerin asked: "What found you?"

"N-nought; all is dark and quiet in the temple. Your giglot remains in her tower room."

Inside, Kerin reported to Klung what Belinka had said. "So, I take it she's safe for the night?"

"Think ye the sprite told the truth?" asked Klung.

Kerin frowned, pulling at his new beard. "Now that you mention it, there was something odd in her manner. She sounded excited, like a mortal out of breath; but why should finding nought excite her? Couldst visit the temple in your astral form, as you did before?"

"No need; I shall dispatch my hantu. The task were well within his modest ability. Oh, Sendu!"

"Aye, my lord?" said the voice of someone hovering invisibly above the remains of their dinner.

Klung gave his command; the sprite replied: "I hear and obey!"

In a quarter-hour the sprite was back, saying: "There is a hubbub in the temple, my lords. Pwana and his folk are robing themselves in brilliant hues, whilst others move magical furnishings about in the crypt below the altar."

"As I suspected," said Klung, "your familiar lied for jealousy. If ye go thither on the morrow, ye will find the princess already slain."

"Then we must chance it tonight!"

"We shall see," said Klung. "Sendu! Was Princess Nogiri still in her chamber?"

"Aye, my lord."

"How is her room furnished?"

"As best I can recall, a bed, a chest of drawers, two chairs, and a wash stand."

"Doth her door open inward or outward?"

The sprite hesitated. "I examined the hinges not, my lord; but methinks it open inward."

"Then return thither and tell the princess, if she value her life, to pile all the furniture against the door." Klung turned to Kerin. "Take the coil of rope. Art sure ye remember how to activate it?"

Kerin ran over the spell, moving his lips and gesturing. "Is that correct?"

"It will do. Shog along!"

·VII·
The Temple of Bautong

The silver sickle of the lunar crescent hung in the western sky, above a horizon whereon the blue-green gloam of sunset was fading, when Kerin, Klung, and Kerin's double approached the Temple of Bautong.

Kerin wore his everyday shirt and breeches, with his Salimorese turban and his scabbard, in Salimorese-style, thrust through the back of the fancy sash from the loot. This arrangement proved less comfortable than suspending the sword from his baldric. But he thought that, first, it made him less conspicuous and, second, that it was less likely to swing about and bang things as he climbed.

The temenos or sacred enclosure filled a lot in Kwatna over a bowshot across. Around the borders ran a ten-foot wall of stone with broken crockery set in mortar along the top.

The gate in the wall had been locked, but Kerin brought out his bag of picklocks and soon had the portal open. The temple, softly gleaming in the light of the quarter-moon, rose amidst the grounds. Unlike most fanes of Salimor, the temenos was rather bare of vegetation. There were flower beds and a few trees, standing well away from the temple; but nothing like the jungle of greenery crowding most temple grounds.

Klung motioned to crouch behind the scanty screen of a spray of flowers. Kerin whispered: "Why so bare?"

"Pwana fears lest some foe miche up under cover of plantings, as we do now. He lays out his grounds so there be nought for an ill-wisher to hide behind."

"Then how shall we approach unseen?"

"I shall command your simulacrum. Whilst he holds the cullions at the door in play, hasten beneath the damsel's window. . . . Quiet! There goeth the sentry."

Dim in the moonlight, a figure paced into view around a temple corner. Although Kerin could not make out its features, he could see that it wore a Salimorese jacket and skirt and bore a heavy kris, like the one that on his arrival in Kwatna had almost deprived Kerin of his head, upon its shoulder.

As the figure plodded on its circuit until it showed its back to the watchers, the balimpawang whispered to the phantom: "Carry out thine orders!"

The pseudo-Kerin rose and marched determinedly towards the temple. When, small with distance, it reached the door, Kerin heard its voice raised, though he could not discern the words. The sentry, sword in hand, bustled back around the corner. The door opened; figures appeared. Voices rose in dispute.

"Now!" breathed Klung. "Go yonder, crouching, until ye be out of sight of the front door; then cut in to the wall beneath your sweetling's window. Run!"

"Where will you be?"

"Here, unless compelled to flee. I know a little spell, from a Twelfth Plane demon, to make people overlook me. I should be useless where a clean pair of heels must be shown. Go, whilst the entity hold the priests' attention!"

Crouching, Kerin scuttled along the path inside the wall, past flower beds whose blossoms would have shown a blaze of color by day but which now displayed only shades of gray. When the corner of the temple cut off the view of the entrance, he rose and trotted towards the building, the coiled rope on his shoulder swaying and bumping against his boots.

As he neared the structure, Kerin thanked his Novarian gods he had not undertaken to climb the masonry, which provided hardly any handholds. Around the ground floor, interrupted at intervals by windows, ran a frieze of dancing girls holding arms in angular poses; but the relief was too low to afford a grip. The second story was largely occupied by shuttered windows. Above it, the window of the tower room showed yellow candlelight around the edges of the shutters.

Kerin dropped his rope on a flower bed, grinning at the thought of how his mother would carry on if someone so abused her flowers. He straightened out the coil, making sure there were no tangles. Sounds of dispute still wafted from the further side of the temple, mingled with the whine of mosquitoes. Kerin raced through the spell, muttering and making passes.

For an instant nothing happened. Kerin wondered if he had missaid a syllable or scanted a gesture. Then the upper end of the coil arose, like a monstrous serpent rearing to strike. The end went up and up.

When all but the final turn of the coil had risen, the cable halted. Kerin took deep breaths to store up energy, sprang up, seized the rope, and locked his legs about it. Foot by foot, he rose past the ground-floor frieze; his face came close to the oversized stone breasts of a dancing girl on the sculpture. He paused to slap a mosquito on his cheek and resumed his climb. The clamor from the entrance came but faintly.

Kerin rose past the shuttered second-story windows. Golden gleams from within escaped around the shutters' edges; as Kerin's position shifted, the rope beneath him swayed.

As he reached the tower-room level, he realized that the tower was smaller in plan than the lower stories. Hence, at this level, he found the window a good eight feet away.

Kerin thought. By swaying from side to side, he set up a rhythmic oscillation in the rope, as if it were the trunk of a sapling. Wider and wider he swung, but he could not bring himself within reach of the window.

He pulled out his sword and resumed his swinging. When a totter brought him close, he rapped on the shutters with the sword. He did this again on the following swing.

The shutters opened, shedding candlelight. Salimorese windows had no glass panes; only wooden shutters. A shadow occluded the light as Nogiri appeared, saying:

"Who—what—Master Kerin! What do you?"

"Keep your voice down!" snapped Kerin, edgy with tension. "I'm getting you out."

"Wherefore? Have the priests an evil intention?"

"Human sacrifice to some evil god or other, with you as the offering. As I swing towards you, catch my blade and pull me in—nay, first get a cloth to seize the blade, lest it cut you."

Nogiri disappeared; Kerin glimpsed a pile of furniture against the door before she returned with a towel. When a swing brought his blade within reach, she caught it and pulled, until Kerin could grip the edge of a shutter.

"If I could hold the rope up against your window, couldst climb down it?" he asked.

"I know not. I climbed trees a-plenty as a girl, but this . . ."

"To hold the rope in place—is there aught in your chamber

to serve as a cord?" Kerin silently berated himself for not thinking to bring such a cord with him. She said:

"With your sword or dagger, I could cut ropes from beneath the bed. Oh, oh, something is up!"

The noise from the front portal waxed in volume, and then came a trampling and a knock on Nogiri's door. "Princess!" cried a voice. "Open! Admit us!"

"Delay them!" said Kerin.

Nogiri called back: "Wait an instant, sirs. I must make myself decent."

"Never mind that!" said the voice. "Open forthwith!" The door boomed to blows of increasing force.

"No time to cut ropes now," said Kerin.

"Lower yourself as far as you can whilst holding the shutter," said Nogiri. "I shall seize the rope above you. . . . Oh, plague! I can never climb down in this skirt."

The battering increased; the door began to yield. Nogiri whipped off her sarong, wadded it into a ball, and threw it out past Kerin, who was trying to sheathe his sword with one hand. His point repeatedly missed the mouth of the scabbard, which jutted awkwardly out behind him.

"Throw your sword!" she said.

Kerin tossed away his sword and lowered himself as far as he could and still hold the shutter. Naked, Nogiri climbed to the window sill and swung out on the rope.

"Ouch!" said Kerin as her bare toe poked him in the eye.

As he released his grip on the shutter, the rope swayed dizzily outward. He lowered himself hand over hand, while above him Nogiri descended more slowly.

When Kerin's feet were a man-height from the ground, he let go and came down in a crouch, as he had in farmer Eomer's barn. He picked up his sword and sheathed it as Nogiri reached the ground and snatched up her skirt. Above, the door of No-

giri's room crashed open. Shouts and tramplings seemed to
come from all directions. When Nogiri started to wrap herself
in her skirt, Kerin said:

"Later! Run!"

Grasping her hand, he dragged her towards the gate. He saw
no sign of Klung; but as the principal portal came into view,
Kerin sighted a group of priests and temple guardsmen running
through the flower beds after the simulacrum. Keeping just
ahead of the mob, the doublegoer shouted taunts.

Pwana stood in the temple doorway, screaming: "Leave off!
Pursue not that phantom! Come back!" Sighting Kerin and
Nogiri, he pointed and shrieked: "There they go! Behold your
quarry!"

The fugitives ran through the gate, which Kerin slammed
behind them. Nogiri panted: "Whither away?"

"To the Kuromonian ship. What's the quickest way?"

"I can lose them in the alleys. Come on!"

Trailing her sarong, Nogiri ran ahead of Kerin. She led him
along a street sloping down to the waterfront as the pursuers
burst out of the gate behind them. Instead of continuing
straight on, Nogiri took Kerin into a crooked side street, then
zigzagged through a maze of alleys. The crescent moon had set,
so that Kerin stumbled through the darkness. Only Nogiri's
guidance saved him from tripping and falling or barging into
walls.

Although few roamed abroad at night in Kwatna, the Salimorese they passed regarded them with amazement. When
sounds of pursuit died out, Nogiri halted, panting:

"Pray, let me—catch—my breath."

"I could use a breath, too," gasped Kerin. "Whither lie the
Kuromonian ships? You've lost me."

She pointed. "Thither, methinks. First let me . . ."

She started to wrap the sarong again when Belinka's tiny

voice came from above: "Master Kerin! Flee instanter! They have picked up your trail with the help of a spirit!"

Sounds of pursuit rose above the general level of nocturnal urban noises. "Come on!" said Kerin.

They raced off. After several turns, they came out on the waterfront a few ship-lengths from the *Tukara Mora*'s quay. They ran towards the ship. Before they reached it, a man in the uniform of Pwana's temple guards emerged from a smaller street and approached them, waving a kris and shouting:

"Halt! Ye are my prisoners!"

"Stand aside!" said Kerin, drawing his sword.

"Foreign scum!" said the guard, advancing and winding up for a slash.

Kerin drew his feet together and extended his sword to the fullest. The simple stop-thrust, which Jorian had drilled into him, caused the onrushing guard to impale himself on Kerin's point, which entered his chest while his sword hand was still above his shoulder and his blade extended out behind him. The guardsman checked his rush, staring cross-eyed down at the blade as if he could not believe his eyes.

Kerin jerked out his blade, grabbed Nogiri's hand, and ran on to the *Tukara Mora*. To his dismay, the gangplank was not out, as the Kuromonians had promised. Instead, the ship sat in her dock with her nearer gunwale six feet from the quay. A downward glance showed dark water lapping gently; also that the ship was held away from the quay by poles lashed fore and aft.

"Canst jump it?" Kerin asked.

"Aye, methinks. Let go!"

She ran back a few paces, sprinted, and leaped from the edge of the quay. A pale shape in the darkness, she soared over the gap, came down on the rail, and sprawled on the deck. A deck guard, one of the *Tukara Mora*'s marines, shouted and pointed.

The temple guard had folded up on the cobblestones, but more pursuers poured out of a side street. Other Kwatnans issued from houses to see the cause of the disturbance.

Kerin threw his sword like a javelin, so that the point came down on the deck and the blade stood upright, swaying. He backed and ran to the ship. Like Nogiri, he took off at the edge of the masonry. But he failed by a finger's breadth to clear the rail. His boot slipped on the gunwale; he grabbed at the rail, missed, and fell fifteen feet into slimy harbor water.

Sputtering and coughing, he struggled to the surface. Weighed down by dagger, scabbard, and money belt, he found it all he could do to keep his nose out of water. Overhead a furious dispute broke out between the pursuers and the crew of the *Tukara Mora*, who had come boiling out of their quarters.

Kerin spat water and called: "Ahoy the ship! Throw a rope!"

"There he is!" yelled a pursuer from the temple. "Who has a bow?"

Another man lay down on the cobblestones at the edge of the quay and struck at Kerin with his kris but could not quite reach him.

"Throw your sword!" said a voice.

"What, lose my good sword? Be not absurd!"

"Who has something to throw?" shouted a voice.

The yammer rose. Something struck the water near Kerin with a splash; drops sprayed over him.

"Missed!" shouted another. "Pry up one more, yarely!"

They were throwing cobblestones. Thinking the further side of the ship were safer, Kerin struggled towards the ship's nearer end. More cobbles splashed. One struck his head a glancing blow, cushioned by his turban. He dizzily doubled his efforts and presently rounded the bow. When he could get his mouth above water, he shouted:

"Where is a rope?"

At last a rope splashed into the water nearby. Kerin seized it and was pulled up to the deck. He found a dozen Kuromonian sailors, directed by Second Mate Togaru, hauling on the rope. Beside the officer stood Nogiri, now wearing her sarong. Along the port rail stood a row of Kuromonian marines bearing pole arms of a Far Eastern pattern, with long, curved blades at the end of their shafts. Novarians called such a weapon a fauchard. The blades were straight enough for thrusting but broad and curved enough to slash with. These men faced shoreward and traded shouts and threats with the priests and guards from the Temple of Bautong, clustered on the quay.

"Master Kerin, is it not?" said Second Mate Togaru.

Dripping and coughing water, Kerin replied: "Aye. Methought you'd leave the gangplank out for us?"

"It was tomorrow night you said you might board in haste."

Kerin clapped a hand to his forehead. "So it was! I had no chance to tell you of the change of plan."

"I see," said Togaru. "Now tell me what betides! By the divine bureaucrats, in all my years at sea, never have I seen a naked woman leap aboard at midnight. Those ashore wish to deliver you up to justice for having stolen this woman, who they say was the temple's property, and for having wounded one of their men pursuing you."

"'Twas simple self-defense. I'm sure you can find a crewman who saw the fellow attack me. As for the Princess Nogiri, she is kin to the Sophi and they were about to kill her. Besides, you would not wish to lose two paying passengers, would you?"

Togaru bowed to Nogiri, saying: "Your Highness." He allowed himself the flicker of a smile. "I will speak to the captain. Meanwhile, you may hie yourself to your cabin to dry. Certes, we will not allow that mob on our decks, which are Kuromonian sovran territory."

The pursuers were straggling off when Togaru told a breechclouted deckhand to show the passengers to their cabins. The deckhand bowed to the officer, bowed again to Kerin, and led the passengers to the forward hatch and down the ladder. Kerin, who had recovered his sword, and Nogiri followed the sailor to the cabin deck.

The sailor disappeared into a cabin and emerged with a lighted taper. He entered one of the two larger cabins at the end of the deck, lit a small bronze lamp hanging from above, and bowed Kerin and Nogiri in.

Nogiri looked at the bed. "It seems a little narrow for two, but I can make do on the floor."

"Not at all," said Kerin. "This is your own exclusive cabin. I shall bunk with the Reverend Tsemben in Number Eighteen."

She looked amazed. "Oh, but Master Kerin! That would be entirely against custom! Why should a rankless woman like me have this grand cabin all to myself? Dost find me repulsive or stinking?"

"Good gods, no! But as a princess—"

"Oh, forget the princess!" she said with a flash of irritation. "Since mine uncle sold me, I am no more than a commoner of the lowest class—a mere thing. In Salimor, a woman's rank derives from her family. Since my family has cast me off, I have no rank. And since you have taken me from the temple, whither I would not willingly return, I am your chattel, concubine, slave, or whatever pleases you."

"Well!" said Kerin. "I never meant to—to consider you as aught but a friend. Could I restore your rank by freeing you?"

"Only my family could make me a princess again, and I expect that not. If you cast me off, any ruffian could seize me. That is the way of things."

"Well, let's not tell the Kuromonians. If they think you're a princess, 'twill get us better treatment." He sneezed.

She said: "Master Kerin, off with those sodden garments ere you catch your death of cold!"

Hardened to Salimorese indifference to nudity, Kerin began to strip, saying: "So no more of this 'I am your humble doormat' thing. Second Mate Togaru seems to take your rank at its titular worth."

"I will take care." Having vigorously scrubbed Kerin with the cabin's towel, she gathered up his dripping clothes. "I'll fasten these things up to dry." She went out, leaving Kerin sitting on the stool.

"Master Kerin!" squeaked Belinka. The little blue light danced in the lantern's beams. "Leaping aboard ships at night is evidently not your greatest skill. Remember what befell on the *Benduan*?"

"You need not remind me," growled Kerin.

"Well, I see you entertain lustful thoughts towards Mistress Nogiri."

"How know you?"

"I am not blind. You think, when she return, you'll ask her to be your concubine in fact. Then you think to test the cordage under yon bed."

"Rubbish! You know I shall sleep in Number Eighteen."

"Oh, doubtless—but after you have enjoyed Mistress Nogiri's embraces here."

"What if I did?" demanded Kerin angrily.

"You shall not! I forbid!"

"By Imbal's iron pizzle! Who are you to tell me whom to futter?"

"Madame Erwina's familiar, that's who; and I am straitly charged to save your virtue for Adeliza!"

"To the frigid hells with Adeliza! I'll do whatever—yeow!" Kerin sprang erect, clapping a hand to his bare buttock. "Curse you, that hurt!"

"And I'll hurt worse if you try to bed your brown barbarian! You'll afford a juicy target!"

"Not if I'm under a blanket!"

"I can sting through a blanket. If you believe me not, wrap yourself in yon quilt!"

Kerin seethed with turmoil. Muttering curses, he wrapped himself in the cabin's blanket. He had worked up the courage to ask, as Belinka put it, Nogiri to be his concubine in fact. To do so, he had to overcome a violent seizure of embarrassment. Belinka's opposition made him all the more determined; on the other hand he feared that the threat of being stung would cause more than his spirits to droop at a critical time. If only he could imprison this meddlesome sprite in a bottle. . . .

Nogiri reëntered, saying: "Your clothes now hang on one of those ropes that steadies the mast. But Master Kerin, wherefore have you wrapped yourself in my blanket? I thought you ready for bed. Since that bed be narrow for two, why not drag in the pallet from your other cabin?"

"Well—ah—but . . ."

"Why, wouldst fain not exercise your rights tonight? I am ready."

Kerin squirmed with embarrassment. He eyed Nogiri hungrily; but it would only have added to his shame to admit that he had let Belinka bully him out of his intentions. He did not see the dancing blue light; but Belinka could make herself completely invisible.

At last he said: "Well—ah—there are two reasons, my dear. First, as you say, it is late and I am more than a little tired, after climbing that magical rope, snatching you from the evil priests, skewering the man who tried to halt us, and swimming about that stinking harbor."

"Doubtless you know best," she said. "After witnessing your

feats tonight, I had begun to think of you as some hero of legend, immune to fatigue."

Kerin waved a deprecatory hand. "So it might seem; but I should have perished many times had not Elidora cast her mantle about me."

"What? Who is Elidora?"

"Our Novarian goddess of luck. A hero of legend would not have fallen into the harbor; nor would he have forgotten to carry the magical rope away. Klung will rue its loss."

"And the other reason?"

"If we are to bolster the Kuromonians' belief that you are in fact a princess, it follows that you must have the cabin to yourself, as any royal person would."

"True," she said with a thoughtful frown. "Kuromonians, I hear, are even fussier about rank and status than my own folk. At home they spend their time insulting their inferiors and fawning upon their superiors, trying to inch their way up the ladder of rank. They have a curious system whereby men of low birth can rise into the mandarin class of officials by passing written examinations."

"That sounds interesting," said Kerin.

"Belike; but it means that such persons, having a hope of rising, commit any sort of corruption or chicanery to enable them to do so. Amongst us the classes, being fixed, are more resigned to their lot and hence live in greater harmony."

"I can see advantages and disadvantages either way," said Kerin. "But you see why you must sleep alone. When circumstances permit, I may pay you visits; but your cabin is your sovran territory."

She shrugged. "Whatever you say, Master Kerin. I am glad 'tis not that you find me ugly. Good-night, then."

"Good-night, my lady—oh, by the way, do the Salimorese practice—I know not your word, but we call it 'kissing'?"

"I know not. What is it?"

"I'll show you," said Kerin, doing so.

She wiped her mouth with the back of her hand. "What means that? Is it an expression of affection?"

"Exactly! What do your people do?"

"We rub the nose against the other's cheek."

"Show me!"

Nogiri did. Kerin's blood pounded as they stood with arms about each other's shoulders, alternately kissing and nose-rubbing, until Nogiri uttered a shrill yelp.

"Ow! Something stung my back!"

Kerin sighed. "It's Belinka again, furiously jealous. Anon I'll explain what befell back home, which led to my getting her as my keeper. So good-night again; I'll return your blanket shortly."

"Good-night, Master Kerin. I see how Mistress Belinka will complicate our relationship."

"I fear so. And speaking of your back, we shall soon sail northward into cooler climes, where you'll want some sort of coat. I'll shop amongst the merchants for one. Till tomorrow!"

It seemed to Kerin that he had hardly fallen asleep when Belinka was buzzing in his ear and Nogiri was shaking his shoulder, crying: "Wake up, Master Kerin! Pwana's men are back!"

Sitting up and rubbing his eyes, Kerin took a while to remember where he was, who Pwana was, and what their dispute was about. By the time he had pulled on his clothes and armed himself, he was fully awake. The Reverend Tsemben slumbered through the disturbance.

On the cabin deck outside, groups of Kuromonian merchants huddled, chattering in the early morning light. As Kerin and

Nogiri passed them, they stared and broke into more excited speech.

Kerin stumbled up the ladder to the weather deck. He found a sky of gray overcast and a deck thronged with the *Tukara Mora*'s marines. Ashore, he sighted not only Pwana and some of his priests and temple guards, but also a squad of archers in the Sophi's household livery of scarlet turbans and jackets and gold-embroidered skirts. Looking further, Kerin also sighted Klung and Wejo on the edge of the crowd ashore. The gangplank was still withdrawn aboard the ship.

The wizard Pwana was arguing with a man whom Kerin took to be the vessel's captain. Although no taller than Kerin, the man had an indefinable air of authority, from his curious black lacquered hat with a chin strap and a button of some semi-precious stone on top, to the hem of his silken robe bedight with writhing dragons in golden thread. Pwana shouted in a high, cracked voice:

"But the Sophi himself hath authorized me to take that pair; the woman is the temple's property, and the foreigner stole her! And if my guardsman die, I will prosecute a charge of murder!"

"Sophi or no Sophi," said the captain, "I cannot allow you to tread the sacred soil of the Empire for any such purpose—ah," he said, turning to Kerin. He switched to Novarian: "There you are, Master Kerin! As you see, bringing your princess aboard has stirred up trouble. What reason canst give me for not putting you and the female ashore, to cope with Doctor Pwana on your own?"

Kerin groped for arguments. "For one, I've paid the passage for us."

"Your fare could be refunded—minus, naturally, a charge for bookkeeping costs. Well then?"

As Kerin racked his brain, Klung called out from the quay:

"If I may come aboard, Captain Yambang, this humble worm can explain."

"You may—" began Captain Yambang, but Pwana shouted: "Nay, glorious captain! If you let this mass of offal aboard, this insignificant one demands to come, too!"

"Oh, let the twain of you come," said Yambang. "But each alone, and none of your magical tricks! Our sorcerer has cast a counterspell upon the ship."

Sailors hoisted the gangplank off the deck and swung it over the gap between the ship and the shore. As the plank thumped into place, both Klung and Pwana started for it. Since its shoreward end had come to rest near Klung, the stout balimpawang reached it first. By a hasty scuttle, Pwana caught up with his rival, crying:

"Out of my way, charlatan!"

The plank was just wide enough for two men to walk abreast, if they moved with care. As Pwana tried to shoulder Klung aside, the latter roared:

"Out of *my* way, turd!"

Klung pushed back. For an instant the two jostled shoulder to shoulder on the plank. Since Klung was the younger and heavier, he sent Pwana staggering over the edge. With a shriek, the old wizard cartwheeled down into the slimy water below.

Captain Yambang shouted, and a pair of breechclouted sailors rushed to the rail with a rope. When the end of the rope reached him, Pwana seized it; but when the sailors heaved on the rope, the old wizard's grasp failed, dropping him back into the water.

Captain Yambang paused in giving orders to say to Kerin: "As barbarians go, you Novarians show better manners than these jungle savages. I saw your land on a voyage years ago."

The sailors brought up another rope, with a loop at the end. When the loop reached him, Pwana worked his scrawny body into it so that it encircled him below the armpits. This time the retrieval succeeded.

Reaching the deck, Pwana said to the captain: "Why didst not afford me protection from that mountebank?" He indicated Klung, who stood grinning. "I am after all the high priest of a god! As such, I merit deference."

The captain snorted. "You? To me you are nought but a horde of chattering monkeys, whom someone has caught and shaved and taught to play tricks."

Pwana glanced at one of the marines, who was moving his fauchard in a significant way and staring at Pwana's neck. He grunted and turned to the rail, wringing water from the hem of his sarong.

"Come!" said the captain sharply. "We cannot waste more time, for we load today. You two wizards and the couple over whom you dispute, follow me!"

The captain's cabin was a two-room suite, done up in a style like that of Nogiri's cabin but more ornate. Golden dragons writhed along the walls; across the overhead flitted conventional bats and cranes. The cabin boasted substantial chairs and a massive table of black-hued wood.

Captain Yambang sat at the head of this table in a thronelike chair. He motioned the rival wizards to chairs on either side of him and Kerin and Nogiri to seats at the farther end. Kerin was glad again to sit in a genuine chair instead of cross-legged on the floor.

"Now, gentlemen," said the captain, "state your cases. You first, Doctor Pwana."

"It is simple theft, my lord," said Pwana. "This wench was the lawful property of the Temple of Bautong, having been given to the temple by her uncle, Lord Vunambai, acting *in loco parentis* since her natural parents are dead. We could present a formal request for the extradition of Master Kerin as a common thief and possible murderer; but we shall be satisfied with the return of the woman Nogiri to representatives of the temple. There is no reason for you, representing His Imperial Majesty, to detain a piece of plainly stolen property—"

"Oh, yes there is!" cried Klung. "The temple was about to slay the Princess Nogiri as a sacrifice to their demonic deity. The laws of Salimor do not permit the killing of a slave or other bondperson at the whim of his or her master. There must be an official procedure to weigh whether the bondperson hath done aught to merit such treatment, such as defying a lawful command. That law dates from the reign of Sophi Munta—"

"Who reigned three centuries ago, and whose law has long since fallen into disuse! For over a century, the courts have held that to slay one's slave at one's own discretion be a basic human right! Let not this cheap mountebank—"

"Hold your tongue, charlatan!" shouted Klung. "Honorable Captain, this convicted criminal can bend every law to his purpose of the moment—"

"Humbug!" yelled Pwana. "I challenge you to a magical duel, ashore, you fat pretender—"

Both wizards screamed threats and insults. Kerin quietly rose, went around the table, and said in Captain Yambang's ear:

"Sir, if I might speak to you apart for a moment. . . ."

The captain nodded and said to the disputants: "I call a recess for a few moments, to let you *gentlemen*'s tempers cool." He gave "gentlemen" a sarcastic emphasis and spoke rapidly in his own tongue to one of the two marines standing behind his chair. Turning back, he said: "I have commanded that if any more such outbursts occur, the marines shall drop you over the side, to sink or swim. Come, Master Kerin."

The captain led Kerin into the bedroom of the suite and closed the door. "Very well, young barbarian, what say you?"

"You've heard the claims, sir. What propose you?"

"To be honest, I must return the woman to those blackguards from the temple. They were in hot pursuit when she took refuge on the ship, and the treaties betwixt His Imperial Majesty and the Sophi provide for return of stolen property under those conditions. It is not as if she were your wife; Kuromonian law is strict against the breaking up of families. Hence when a Kuromonian is convicted of a capital offense, the spouse is beheaded along with the culprit."

"If Princess Nogiri were my wife, would you give me back to Pwana's men along with her?"

Yambang came as close to laughing as such a dignified man could. "Nay, youngster. This person would give her the same protection I extend to you."

Kerin thought until the captain made a motion as if to return to the sitting room. Then he said: "Captain, I've heard of nations whose sea captains are empowered to perform marriages. Does that apply to Kuromon?"

A shadow of a smile flickered across Yambang's grave countenance. "Not in this case, since neither of you is a subject of His Imperial Majesty."

"My cabin mate is the Reverend Tsemben, a priest of Jinterasa. Could he perform the office?"

"I suppose he could utter the needed phrases, although without the procession from the bride's house to the groom's, the written contract, the exchange of gifts between the parents, the soothsayer's prophecies, and the other formalities, this would be a marriage of the lowest category above simple cohabitation."

"Wilt excuse me a moment, Captain?"

"So long as you attempt not to leave the ship ere this matter be decided."

Pwana and Klung were still growling maledictions. Kerin touched Nogiri on the shoulder and motioned her to follow him out. On deck, he sighted Tsemben leaning on the rail and watching the sailors hoist the cargo aboard. Kerin said:

"Reverend Tsemben, will you unite Princess Nogiri and me in marriage, instanter?"

"Why—why—very well, my son, if you insist; albeit this is somewhat irregular. Doth she consent?"

"Aye, truly," said Nogiri.

"Then join hands and repeat after me—yeouw!" The little priest leaped into the air and clapped a hand to his shoulder. "Something stung me!"

Nogiri gave a cry of pain and clutched at her bare flank; then Kerin felt Belinka's sting on his knee. "Belinka!" he cried. "What in the seven hells do you?"

"Preserving your chastity for Adeliza!" tinkled the sprite, buzzing about the impromptu wedding party like a large, semi-transparent insect.

"But this is necessary to save Nogiri's life!"

"I care nought for your brown barbarian!" shrilled Belinka. "I know my duty!"

"We shall see about that!" said Kerin. "Nogiri, stay with the Reverend for a moment."

He dashed off and presently emerged from the captain's suite with Klung waddling after. To the balimpawang he said:

"My familiar gives trouble again. Wouldst please tell your hantu to get her away? Chase her, seduce her, beat her, or whatever be needed to leave us alone for a while."

Klung's round face crinkled into a smile that hid his slanting black eyes. "Aha! I see ye be taking a desperate measure to get your princess out of Pwana's clutches. It is not for me to lecture you on the advantages of single blessedness. Oh, Sendu! Hither, and sprackly!"

Klung muttered to an invisible presence. Kerin heard a diminishing wail: "You inhuman monster! I'll get even. . . ." The sound, like the buzz of a departing insect, died away. Kerin said:

"Very well, Reverend Tsemben, proceed!"

The priest joined Kerin's left hand to Nogiri's right and rattled through a speech in Kuromonian, of which Kerin caught only a few words. Then Tsemben thrust out a hand, palm up.

"How much do I owe him?" Kerin asked Klung in Novarian.

"One Kortolian eagle were generous."

Digging the coin out of his money belt, Kerin asked Klung: "What befell whilst I climbed that rope?"

"Pwana first told the doublegoer to begone. When the spirit would not, Pwana made a sign to his sentry, who swung his kris; but the blade passed through the entity as if it were smoke. Then the being ran, as I had commanded, with the others after it—all but Pwana, the first to realize it as a simulacrum lacking substance. It was all I could do to keep from laughing and betraying my hiding place. Ah, would ye had seen it, my boy!"

"I had enough on my mind at the time," said Kerin.

Pwana departed down the gangplank. Ashore, he shook his bony fist at the *Tukara Mora* and croaked: "I will send a wind demon to sink you all! I will teach you to thwart the will of the mighty Bautong!"

Klung tapped Kerin's shoulder. "Farewell, lad; and I hope ye enjoy a greater marital felicity than I have. Forget not your contract with me!"

As Klung trudged away, Captain Yambang said: "Well, Master Kerin, this person hopes your presence on my ship will cause no further disturbances. I have told my sailors to move your gear from Number Eighteen to Number Two."

Kerin stared; his thoughts had not run so far ahead. Nogiri's expression was unreadable, but she seemed neither surprised nor disconcerted. As Captain Yambang walked off, she said:

"Had we not better see that your things be rightly stowed?"

"Of course, of course," said Kerin, flustered.

They descended to the cabin deck and went to Number Two. After a long silent minute, Nogiri, standing by the bed, said:

"Well, my lord?"

"Hm," said Kerin. "Dost love me, Princess?"

She showed a puzzled frown. "Nay, certes. But what has that to do with your husbandly rights?"

"In my native Kortoli, love is the main excuse for marrying."

"What a backward, barbarous land!" she cried. "A proper marriage is securing of a family tie, joining of resources, and the building of a stable family unit. These things form a much more lasting basis for marriage than simple sexual lust."

"It sounds cold-bloodedly calculating to me."

"So what? If people acted more by reason and less by the whims of passing emotions, half the world's problems were solved. Of course," she added thoughtfully, "if a pair cohabit harmoniously for years, they may come feel for each other something like this 'love' you speak of. In the present case, I have no family or estate. I know nought of yours, and in any case they are far away. So you, my lord, have done me a great favor, making a wife of a mere thing. Think not but that I am grateful."

"I try to help my friends," mumbled Kerin. "But I wouldn't take unfair advantage. . . ."

"I know not what you mean. I am your wife, am I not? So what about it? It were indecent to hold aloof from me. Let me suggest that, if we take not advantage of your familiar's absence, she may complicate intimacies later on."

"Methought your—ah—misfortune had made such things repugnant."

"That memory has faded, and I am always ready to do my plain duty in any case. Let us to it!"

Kerin broke into a grin. "Good girl!"

The newlyweds were resuming their garments when Kerin said: "I ask your pardon, Princess, for not giving you greater pleasure. I am in need of practice."

"Hast had none for long?"

Kerin squirmed, feeling himself flush. "To tell the truth, this was my first."

"Amazing! You must be subject to some strange tabu amongst the round-eyes. I regret that I cannot say the same for myself. So why apologize? A man is not expected to give his woman pleasure, and you were gentler than those pirates. All you need is experience—"

A tiny voice interrupted: "Master Kerin! Oh, Master Kerin!"

"Yea, Belinka?"

"What dost? It looks as if you and your barbarian were about to indulge your beastly lusts despite all!"

"Belinka," said Kerin sternly, "Princess Nogiri and I are man and wife. So we—"

"Oh, you vile creature! Whilst my back is turned, you break poor Adeliza's heart! How can you be so cruel?"

"I had to, to save Nogiri's life."

"A poorish bargain! At least I shall be here to stop indulgence of your animal lusts. Back in civilization, you can dissolve this so-called marriage."

"I won't dissolve it," said Kerin. "As for 'beastly lusts,' you're too late."

"You mean—eeek!" Belinka gave a tiny shriek, dancing about the cabin semitransparent. "You have ruined not only yourself but me as well. Madame Erwina will torture me!"

"I'll put in a good word for you, if we ever win back to Kortoli. Meanwhile you might as well accept—"

"Never! You shall either leave the woman here in the East and say nought about her on your return, or else you must take both her and Adeliza to Janareth or some such place where multiple wives are legal."

"I'll do no such thing. And, unless you promise not to interfere with normal married usages, I'll borrow Klung's hantu to keep you in order!"

"Fiddle-dee-dee! I can twist Sendu round my little finger!"

"Then I'll tell Erwina how you lied to me. If you don't leave us alone, I'll get Klung to turn you into a puddle of slime. Aroint!"

"Aiyee!" came the tiny screech. "Doom, doom! I have failed! What is left? On my own plane, I could immolate myself in a volcano, but that's impossible here."

Kerin regretted his burst of temper. "Now, Belinka, be reasonable!" he said soothingly.

"I'll not, not, not, you arrant satyr! Since I have failed to keep your purity, I will no longer be yoked to the cause of my disgrace. So farewell, you mass of slimy lust! I shall return to Erwina and take my punishment. I go!"

"Belinka, please—" But Kerin soon realized that he was talking to air. He sighed, pulled on his jacket, and left the cabin for his language lesson.

·VIII·
The Ship
Tukara Mora

When Tsemben had finished drilling Kerin in the honorifics of Kuromonian, the priest said: "Master Kerin, the food at the common table leaves somewhat to be desired: ever salt pork and rice. To be sure, the officers enjoy a more delicate diet, and the captain has his personal cook."

"Then how do we passengers manage?"

"We bring our own dainties aboard. Take care that you fetch nought that will soon rot."

"Thankee," said Kerin. He looked towards the quay, on which stood a pair of guards from the Temple of Bautong, tossing dice on the cobblestones and glancing towards the *Tukara Mora*. Kerin was sure they would set upon him the instant he stepped ashore.

Not having Belinka to run errands for him, Kerin went to the rail and crooked a finger at a dockside loafer. The man was persuaded to come aboard and, for pay, to take a message from Kerin to Klung, to get him a basket of nonperishable foods.

The sun was low when Wejo appeared with a basket, with which Kerin started for Nogiri's cabin. Passing him on deck, Purser Zummo said:

"Ah, this person sees that you are taking precautions. May I look in the basket, to make sure there be no contraband within?"

Kerin uncovered the basket, disclosing a myriad of unfamiliar edibles: little cakes, pots of sugary preserves, and so on.

Zummo gave a low whistle. "You must have a gigantic appetite, Master Kerin, for one so lean."

"How so?"

"We shall reach Koteiki in nine or ten days. Meseems you have enough here for a month."

"Oh? This is for Princess Nogiri as well as me."

"So? Perhaps you know not that she will mess with the officers' wives, in consideration of her rank. Her fare, I do assure you, will be adequate."

"Thank you; but then where shall I eat?"

"At the common table with the merchants. I grant there is a contradiction here, since normally a husband outranks his wife, even a royal wife; but the regulations of the Merchant Marine are precise. And speaking of rank, it were unseemly for a Kuromonian gentleman to bear his own burdens. As a barbarian you would not know that; but I would help you to learn decent Kuromonian manners. So permit me to summon a sailor to carry your basket." He spoke to a boatswain's mate, who in turn sent a deckhand off to find a sailor not otherwise occupied.

Kerin, beginning to miss the informality of the little *Dragonet*, asked: "Where should I eat if I were of royal rank?"

"Albeit a foreign devil, you would rank with the junior officers. Otherwise you are but a middle-class foreigner."

"My mother claims I'm a tenth or eleventh cousin of King Fridwal of Kortoli."

Zummo chuckled. "Alas, not close enough. Far enough back, we should doubtless find we are all related, being sprung from the first human pair, whom Jinterasa made from the Five Elements: earth, wood, metal, fire, and water. But harmonious intercourse requires established rules."

At dinner, the merchants ignored Kerin until he tackled his bowl of rice with chopsticks. Trying to eat it a grain at a time, Kerin observed a curiously strained expression on his neighbors at the long table. This puzzled him until he realized that they were trying to keep from laughing.

"Go ahead and laugh," said Kerin genially. "In my land laughter is thought good for the digestion."

The merchants broke down in a spasm of giggles. One said: "Watch me, honorable barbarian!" He picked up the little bowl, held it against his chin, and shoveled in the rice with the chopsticks held close together but not quite touching. After some fumbling, Kerin managed a fair imitation. The merchant who had spoken said:

"This person is happy to see a foreigner learning civilized manners."

The next few days passed peacefully, save for the threatening mien of the temple guards on the quay. Kerin went about his routine. He practiced Kuromonian with Tsemben, did swordplay exercises, exchanged amenities with the officers, watched the stevedores manhandle cargo down the after hatch, and retired to Nogiri's cabin to make love. After an early one of these encounters he said:

"Darling, did I do better this time?"

"Aye, my lord. In fact I, too, enjoyed it—something I never thought I should."

Kerin was finishing his dinner at the merchants' table when a sailor touched him and beckoned. He followed the man up to the weather deck, where Second Mate Togaru said:

"Master Kerin, the wizard Pwana seeks words."

Pwana stood on the quay, while four marines lined up at the rail with fauchards ready. Kerin called across the gap: "Well, sir?"

Pwana said: "I give you one last chance. Either send the wench ashore—ah, here she comes!—send her ashore, or I will send to fetch her a demon from the Fifth Plane. You could not stand against such a being."

"Meanst one of those red things with bat's wings?"

"Ay, indeed."

"The kind that can't appear in daylight, because sunlight sickens them?"

"That is the reason I have waited until sunset. Nay, forget your sword. Their flesh is so tough you could not even scratch it."

Kerin had partly drawn his blade. Now he said to Nogiri, who had come to stand beside him: "Dear, go back to your cabin and lock yourself in, quickly! Argue not!" He turned her about by her shoulders and gave her a little push; then to Pwana: "Very well, Doctor, bring on your spook!"

Kerin felt less brave than he sounded. While he had no wish to lose his life, he could not supinely let a demon carry off his bride without a fight.

"Then have at you, rash boy!" screeched Pwana. "After her, Uqful!"

Overhead came the sound of beating wings; their wind stirred Kerin's hair. Looking up, he saw the Fifth Plane demon against the darkling sky, dimly lit by lanterns hung about the ship. As it descended, Kerin saw a being of roughly human size and shape, supported by huge batlike wings. It was covered with a scarlet skin, which showed no external organs of sex and exhibited taloned extremities like the feet of birds of prey.

The four marines, too, looked up. With a simultaneous screech, they dropped their fauchards and ran for the forward hatch.

As it circled closer, the demon glided towards the forward hatch, down which Nogiri and the marines had gone. Kerin snatched up a fauchard and ran to the hatch. He arrived just ahead of the demon. Gripping the polearm, he thrust the curved blade at the creature's body. The point thumped home but failed to penetrate; it was like thrusting at a leathern cuirass with a blunted weapon.

"Ouch!" snarled the demon. "That hurt! Stand aside fellow, and let me do my duty!"

"I'm doing mine," growled Kerin. When the demon tried to dodge around him, he thrust again, hitting it in the throat.

"Gah!" roared the demon. "I told you not to do that! Know that I am the mighty Uqful, who could tear you limb from limb! I will, too, an ye force me to."

"You'll have to catch me first," said Kerin, lodging another spear thrust in Uqful's belly and bringing a squall of pain. The demon tried to seize the shaft of the fauchard; but since its reactions were slower than those of an alert human being, Kerin was able to jerk his weapon back out of reach.

The demon made several more tries, but Kerin blocked each one. Ashore, Pwana screamed orders and advice. At last the wizard said: "Dematerialize, stupid, and return to this plane in the woman's cabin!"

"Oh?" said the demon. "Now why thought I not of that?"

Uqful stepped back, turned itself around, spun faster and faster until it became a blur, and vanished with a rush of air.

While Kerin pondered what to do next, he heard a muffled scream from down the hatch. Soon Uqful appeared at the base of the ladder with Nogiri, shouting and beating the demon with her fists, in its arms.

"By the heavenly bureaucrats!" said Purser Zummo, appearing beside Kerin with a sword. "You lead an eventful life, Master Kerin! What betides?"

"That is Pwana's pet demon, sent to rape away my bride," said Kerin. "If you'll close the after hatch, we shall have it trapped on the cabin deck!"

"But what needs the ship with an imprisoned demon—"

"Just go and close the hatch!" shouted Kerin, waving his fauchard, "unless you want to lose paying passengers! And fetch that ship's sorcerer I hear about!"

"I trust you know what you do," the purser grumbled; but he went away to carry out Kerin's demand. At the after hatch he shouted at the sailors whose heads peeked over the coaming to watch the drama. Two sailors climbed out on deck, replaced the hatch cover, and battened it down. Then Zummo disappeared into the sterncastle, from the doors and windows of which the officers likewise watched.

As the demon started to climb the ladder, Kerin aimed his fauchard down the hatch. The demon hoisted Nogiri above its head as a shield, with the result that the girl squirmed out of its grip and almost fell. Uqful caught her arm with a sound of ripping cloth.

Ashore, Pwana screamed: "Let no harm befall the maid! I need her intact!"

Still holding the girl, the demon struggled up the ladder again. Kerin sent a thrust into the being's open mouth. He pushed hard as if to force the blade down into the demon's viscera. The demon freed a clawed hand long enough to grasp the shaft and thrust it back up. Then it had to release the shaft to fend off Nogiri's clawing at its eyes. Uqful made spitting and gargling sounds.

"Curse you!" it mumbled at last. "Ye have done me evil scathe! Master Kerin, wilt *please* stand aside and let me carry out my mission? Ye do but struggle against the inevitable."

"We shall see about that," said Kerin. "Let the princess go, and I'll let you up on deck."

The demon wheedled: "But my dear sir, I cannot! It were against my master's command!"

"That's your hard luck. If need be, I'll keep you there all night. When the sun comes up—well, you know what happens."

"An ye let me not up, I will tear your wench limb from limb!"

"But you can't do that, either. Pwana ordered you to deliver her unharmed."

"Ye are a hard, cruel mortal! It is always thus with you Prime Planers, snatching us from our native planes and forcing us to serve without pay. Ye compel us to commit deeds we should never dream of on our own planes." It may have been a trick of the light, but Kerin was sure he saw a couple of tears roll down the being's cheeks.

"Blame me not," said Kerin. "I never commanded you to snatch my mate. Now just release the princess and go your way, and we'll say no more about it."

"But I cannot—" Taking advantage of Kerin's momentary inattention, the demon made a sudden scramble up the ladder. But Kerin aimed his fauchard at the creature's hairless skull and brought the weapon down with all his strength. He felt the point bite into the tough, resilient flesh. Uqful tumbled back down the ladder with ichor, black in the murky light against its scarlet skin, leaking from a small scalp wound.

"The curse of the green slime upon you!" it shouted. "That is the second time ye have wounded me! I will be revenged!"

Kerin forebore to answer. The standoff continued, with the demon alternately cursing, threatening, and wheedling. Officers and men of the ship's crew gathered cautiously around Kerin, staring awestruck and murmuring words of advice or encouragement. Purser Zummo reported that Kushingu, the ship's sorcerer, had gone ashore, none knew whither, and in any case would not be available for help against Uqful until his return.

Kerin yawned; the time was well past midnight, and still Uqful crouched on the ladder with one taloned arm around Nogiri, awaiting a chance to spring up.

"Look me in the eye, mortal," gargled Uqful, swaying its head from side to side. "Ye grow sleepy—sleepy—sleepy. . . . Soon ye shall be unable to keep your eyes open. . . . Sleep—sleep—sleep. . . ."

Kerin found himself beginning to doze off. He awoke with a jerk of his head. "Stop that!"

"Sleep—sleep—sleep—Cease your struggle and let sweet sleep claim you. Sleep—sleep. . . ."

"What betides here?" said Balimpawang Klung's familiar voice. "I see; ye have trapped one of Pwana's servitors."

"I can't hold it forever," said Kerin, "but if I let it out, it will carry Nogiri off to the Temple of Bautong. The ship's sorcerer is absent and cannot help. Can you magic the demon back to its own plane?"

"Nay, Master Kerin. Only its master, the accursed Pwana, can do that."

"I blocked its way when it first tried to go down this ladder. So it dematerialized and reassembled itself in Nogiri's cabin. Why can't it carry her out the same way?"

"Because, whilst it can pass through walls in its astral form, it cannot dematerialize your princess to bear her along."

"I've heard they fear sunlight."

"Fifth Plane demons have what we in the profession call an allergy," replied Klung.

"So if I can stay awake and keep it there till dawn, I can strike a deal, to let it go without Nogiri ere the sun rise. But—"

"I have just the thing for you," said Klung, producing a flask from his robe. "Drink this."

Kerin cautiously put the flask to his mouth and tipped it. A lukewarm, slightly bitter fluid issued from the flask. "What's this, a magical potion?"

"Nay; a drink called qahwa. It is a kind of soup made from the berries of a bush that grows in Macrobia, far to the south; and it banishes sleep for a while. I take this flask to meetings of my guild, which oft wax tedious when members argue over rules of admission, dues, and changes in the by-laws."

"How didst happen to come here?"

"I fetched him," came the tiny buzz of Belinka's voice as the little blue light swooped around Kerin. "Seeing you in peril, I flew to his house; but he was off presiding at his magicians' meeting. As soon as he returned, I apprised him of your plight. Whilst I no longer deem myself in your service, I could not let you be destroyed. And now farewell forever!"

"Thankee. Where's Pwana now?"

"Being older than we," said Klung, "the scoundrel needs his sleep. He had departed when I arrived."

"My brother Jorian tells me a professor at the University of Othomae claims Fifth Plane demons do not exist. He says no being of that size and weight could fly, because muscle of beasts is not strong enough to flap the wings of the needed size with adequate vigor. Yet I saw Master Uqful fly to the ship."

"Your professor should be here to cope with Master Uqful," said Klung. "Beings on the Fifth Plane are made of tougher stuff, as ye discovered, than we, and their thews embody more power for their size than ours."

Kerin yawned. "May I have another swallow? I wax sleepy even with it."

For hours, Kerin remained at his post, with Klung sitting cross-legged on the deck nearby. They kept each other awake by telling tales; Kerin repeated some of the stories with which he had regaled Malgo's pirates. He said:

"Doctor, I never imagined that a combat like this would become tedious. Such contests are not supposed to become boring."

"How should they go?"

"I ought to be fighting for my life with a sword against Pwana's henchmen, whilst you cast a mighty spell to make Uqful vanish with a clap of thunder."

Klung laughed. "My boy, deeds of derring-do oft entail much boresome watching and waiting." He looked up. "An I mistake not, I see the first flush of false dawn, or zodiacal light as the astrologers call it. That means true dawn will not long delay." He called down the hatch opening: "Oh, Master Uqful! The false dawn glows in the east. Hadst not better get you hence whilst ye can?"

The demon growled something unintelligible about treacherous Prime Planers. Then came a sharp sound, a kind of *floomp* from below. Nogiri called up:

"My lord! Kerin! It's gone!"

"Eh? What happened?"

"After Doctor Klung spake to it, it set me down, spun around faster and faster, and vanished. I took some scratches from its claws."

"Darling!" said Kerin. "Wait till I get down—"

"Nay; first I most urgently need to get to the cabin alone."

"Come to think, I have a like need," said Kerin; then to Klung: "Methinks none will now mind if we use the rail."

All next day, Kerin watched the shore and waited apprehensively for another attack. When nothing had happened by mid-afternoon, he sent Belinka, who still hung around despite her last farewell, ashore to ask Klung what was up. An hour later she returned, with an elfin giggle as her blue light danced about. She said:

"Doctor Pwana would have assailed you and your barbarian bride by other means, save that today he presents to the Sophi a wizard from Mulvan who, he saith, can infallibly stiffen the royal member for its multiple duties. Rumor hath it that His Majesty hath offered not only to wed one of Pwana's daughters but even to make her his Number One wife. This were an opportunity wherefor even the vindictive Pwana will forgo his revenge. Besides, if the Mulvanian's spell doth work, he will no longer need your barbarian to sacrifice. And now farewell forever!"

"Just a word, Belinka. This is the third time you've said good-bye forever, but on the other occasions you came back."

"The first time was to save you from Uqful; the second, when I realized I had forgotten the dress you bought me. Couldst leave it out in your cabin, pray?"

"Better than that." Kerin dug the scrap of cloth out of his wallet. "I've been meaning to ask Sendu to give it to you. But what should I think of this farewell?"

"This time I truly mean it, Master Kerin. I have decided to tarry in Salimor to store up strength for the long flight back to Kortoli. Besides, my dear Sendu and I have much in common. So when your ship sails, 'twill sail without me. Try not to fall overboard again!"

The little blue light zipped away. Somewhat reassured, Kerin still shot suspicious glances shoreward when he was trying to concentrate, under Tsemben's tutelage, on the Kuromonian verbal auxiliaries. As the sun declined, the balimpawang appeared, saying:

"How goeth it, my boy?"

Kerin told of the message from Belinka. Klung said: "Now I must be off. Tomorrow brings me a wealthy client, so I may not be able to bid you a final farewell. Take no needless chances, and forget not our contract!"

The *Tukara Mora* left the harbor in midmorning, with a banging of gongs and drums, creaking of cordage, and shouts of command. One by one the four great slatted brown lugwails rose, jerk by jerk, as lines of deckhands hauled on the halyards.

Once clear, the *Tukara Mora* swung to follow the coast of Ambok northwest. All day the ship forged ahead, keeping the coast barely in sight to starboard. When Kerin came up on deck after dinner, he found the ship pursuing the same course, rendered easy by a brilliant moon just past half full.

Early next morning, the ship passed the last headland of Ambok and swung northeast. Kerin watched to learn how the ship was navigated. A group of officers, distinguished by little round black hats, gathered on the fantail. With them came a small, wizened Kuromonian whom Kerin had not seen. A pair of deckhands carried a heavy box by handles.

"Reverend Tsemben!" said Kerin. "Who is the oldster?"

"The ship's sorcerer, the honorable Kushingu. It is his duty to protect the ship against any magical mischief that hostile wizards, like him who sent the demon against you, might attempt."

"He wasn't very helpful on that occasion," grumbled Kerin.

"Alas! He was ashore indulging his one vice, which is gambling."

"Who in his right mind would gamble with a magician? By a trivial spell he could control the fall of the dice, the turn of the wheel, or—"

"Owners of gambling places take measures. Some have magicians as partners, who put counterspells on the house; others hire familiar spirits from pawangs to detect the use of magic by gamesters."

"Does Master Kushingu also navigate the ship?"

"Aye."

"This I must see," murmured Kerin, starting towards the group. Before he reached them, a pair of burly marines blocked his way, pointing their fauchards and exclaiming:

"Keep back! Keep away!"

"I am merely fain to watch—" began Kerin, but they only shouted louder and waved their weapons.

Tsemben plucked at Kerin's sleeve. "Pry not into imperial secrets! Men are slain for less."

Kerin backed away until the marines grounded their fauchards, though they continued to glower. Later, the *Tukara Mora* passed a group of smaller islands. Around the end of one came a swarm of canoes, some almost as long as the *Tukara Mora*, twin-hulled and driven swiftly by scores of swarthy paddlers. On the ship, gongs banged and whistles blew. The marines lined up at the rail. At the sight of the hedge of steel, the canoes swerved away and disappeared.

"Pirates from Nintava," explained Tsemben. "That isle has an evil repute."

For a few days things were quiet. Every day at noon, the same officers and hands appeared with the little sorcerer and the mysterious box, performed their rite, and went away. Kerin exercised, walked the deck, watched whales and flying fish, and enjoyed Nogiri's company. They were coming to know each other well enough for each to anticipate the other's thoughts. When Kerin confided the details of his deal with Klung, she observed:

"A year as a bondservant in Kwatna were not so terrible, with an easygoing master like Klung."

"Maybe not to you; but I have my own mission, and my family and business back in Novaria. I must return. Besides, if we were living in Kwatna, who knows what devilment Pwana might not cook up?"

"True."

"If I could only get a look at this thing they do on the fantail, it might advance our quest. If I could fasten a mirror at an angle to the fourth mast. . . ."

They discussed this possibility, that with such a mirror in place, Kerin, ostensibly busy with his sword exercises, could sneak a look into the midst of the ship's officers in the mirror. But Nogiri pointed out that such a mirror would interfere with raising and lowering the sail and therefore would almost certainly be forbidden by the officers, even if they did not suspect its true objective. The argument waxed heated until Kerin rose angrily, saying:

"Methinks I'll hunt up Tsemben for another language lesson."

He stalked off. After the midday meal, he found Nogiri in her cabin. Twisting his feet and staring down at them like a delinquent schoolboy, he stammered an apology for his bad temper.

"Oh, forget it!" said Nogiri, embracing him. "A Salimorese husband would have beaten me for daring to oppose him, and *never* would he admit to being in the wrong. You are so much more likable than the men of my land that I wonder all our maidens migrate not to the West for such husbands."

"I know not that all Novarians be like me," said Kerin. "I merely stumble and fumble along, striving to do my best."

Kissing escalated to full lovemaking. When it was over, Nogiri said: "My lord, you grow daily better at this sport. It is you and not that stupid old Sophi who should have had the thousand wives!"

Reaching for his clothes, Kerin grinned. "Thankee; but methinks I'd better learn how to please one wife ere essaying to manage a flock of them. And by the way, dearest, much as I should like us to have children, it were better to await our return home. Hast been using your contraceptive spell?"

"Aye; my thoughts run ahead of yours."

"They often do, I've noticed," said Kerin, looping the chain of Rao's package over his head.

"What's that, my lord?" said Nogiri. "A protective amulet?"

"Not exactly." Kerin paused, frowning. "I might as well confide in you, for I need advice." He told of the Mulvani Rao and the message he was supposed to deliver to the Kuromonian court. He also told how Rao had given Kerin the package and then vanished at Akkander.

"May I see it?" she said. Turning it over, she remarked: "It is some sort of paper folded in a silken envelope."

"Pwana opened and resealed it on the island," said Kerin. "According to him, it is a set of directions for making a magical fan of some sort. The thing makes me uneasy, for who knows what might come of it? At the same time, I am reluctant simply to drop it into the sea. I promised Rao to make at least an effort to deliver it. What shall I do with the thing?"

"Since you are going to Kuromon anyway, you might as well give it to some authority. They might even reward you."

A day of storm sent huge green waves sloshing across the *Tukara Mora*'s weather deck, while the ship plodded imperturbably on her course. The crew had lowered the sails in their rope tackles until only the upper halves were still spread. Between waves, the crew scampered about their duties without excitement, although the storm was more severe than that which had tossed the *Dragonet* about at the start of Kerin's journey.

Koteiki harbor was the largest anchorage that Kerin had seen; and the number of ships of all sizes, from little rowboats up, exceeded those at Vindium and Janareth combined. All the sailing vessels bore bamboo-battened sails; most of their hulls were gaily painted in gaudy colors.

When the *Tukara Mora* dropped anchor in the outer harbor, a big galley-barge approached and drew alongside. Several Kuromonians climbed the boarding ladder. One, in an embroidered robe and a round cap with a crimson button, appeared to be the leader. Others wore a kind of uniform tunic bearing a squiggle in Kuromonian writing. Then came another man, a small, plump, older one with a thin gray beard and a fancy green robe, but with a different design.

Captain Yambang met the delegation. He and the leader exchanged low bows, over and over until Kerin felt a sympathetic backache. They exchanged documents and conversed, too fast and colloquially for Kerin to follow. The leader from the galley sent his men scurrying about the ship, Kerin supposed to check the captain's manifest against the cargo.

Days before, Kerin had asked how to deliver a message to the Imperial Court. The officers had told him to find the harbor master, who would set him on his way. When the official from the galley was momentarily unoccupied, Kerin asked:

"Sir, are you the harbor master?"

"Nay; this humble worm is but the second assistant to the noble harbor master. What wouldst?"

Before Kerin could reply, the older Kuromonian approached, saying: "Your pardon, but are you not Master Rao of Mulvan, with a document for our invincible government?"

"Why—ah—" stammered Kerin, at a loss. While he wondered whether to try to explain how he came to have the little package, the older man produced a sheet of paper bearing several lines of Kuromonian writing and a sketch of a man's face.

"Ah, yea," said the man, bowing. "You are indeed this eagerly awaited courier. Hast that you were sent to bring?"

Kerin reached inside his jacket and showed the package of oiled silk. "Here it is."

"Excellent! If you will step aboard . . ." He indicated the galley.

Kerin whispered in Salimorese to Nogiri: "What shall I do? Hadn't I better confess the mistake now, ere it be too late?"

"Nay!" she breathed. "We shall have better treatment if they think you the original messenger."

"But if they find out later, the gods know what they'd do—"

"And if they find out now, they may chop off your head for murdering Rao and stealing his package, hoping for a reward!"

"My conscience bothers me." Kerin turned back. "Sir, to whom have I the honor of speaking?"

"This person is civil servant Toga, *gwan* of the tenth rank and fourth assistant secretary of the Foreign Barbarian Section of the Bureau of Internal Travel Control of the Department of Roads, Canals, and Shipping, at your service."

Kerin did not know what *gwan* meant but inferred that it was some sort of term for "official." His command of Kuromonian was not yet firm enough to follow sentences at normal rate of speech. He was therefore often compelled to ask his interlocutors to repeat what they had said more slowly. Now he bowed, saying:

"May I see that paper, pray?"

The man turned the paper, and Kerin saw a recognizable likeness of himself—in fact, both of himself and of the vanished Rao. The latter was much darker of skin, but this inkbrush sketch ignored that difference.

"Thankee, Master Toga," said Kerin. "Permit us to collect our baggage, and we shall join you."

Soon Kerin and Nogiri climbed down the ladder into the galley. Kerin was in his everyday jacket, trousers, and boots, while over her sarong Nogiri wore the embroidered Kuromonian jacket Kerin had bought her. The vessel pushed off and headed for shore with vigorous strokes of its twenty oars.

When they climbed out on a pier, Toga said: "Have the goodness to step hither." He led them along the pier to the shore, where a group awaited them. There were five armed men, wearing brass helmets and long cuirasses of hardened leather studded with bronzen buttons. They had swords at their sides and leaned on fauchards like those of the marines on the *Tukara Mora*; one wore on his helmet a gilded ornament suggesting that he commanded the rest. There were two litters and several thickset, drably clad Kuromonians to man them.

"Wilt take this chair, Master Rao?" said Toga, gesturing.

"Whither go we?" asked Kerin.

"Why, to Chingun, for you to present that which you bear to the appropriate official."

"Then where is my wife to ride? In the other?"

"The woman? We had not anticipated her presence. She can find lodging in Koteiki to await your return, or she can follow us afoot."

"Nay, sir!" said Kerin, feeling gallant and a bit reckless. "Her transport shall equal mine own."

Toga looked puzzled. "But she is a mere woman!"

"Our Western ideas differ from yours; and she is also, after all, a princess."

"Oh!" said Toga, bowing to Nogiri. "This vile excrescence begs Your Highness' forgiveness. This heap of nameless filth did not know. Pray take the other chair whilst this inferior one rounds up a conveyance for his humble self."

Toga went off. Kerin stared about, taking in the throngs of working-class Kuromonians in faded blue jackets and trousers, with conical straw hats tied beneath their chins. He thought he ought to get a hat of that sort, since the climate at Koteiki was almost as hot and humid as that of the Salimor Archipelago.

Then he examined the chairs as eight men of their escort picked up these conveyances and readied them for use. Each chair, without covering or enclosure, was attached to a pair of shafts extending fore and aft. The shafts were affixed at seat level; a pair of downward extensions, corresponding to the front legs of a normal chair, supported a footboard for the rider. The shafts were braced near their ends by crosspieces, and from each crosspiece a dowel rod descended, so that the porters could set the weight of the chair on the ground.

From the ends of each crosspiece, a rope was belayed to the midpoint of a carrying pole about six feet long. The rope had sufficient slack so that, when the pole was in use, it was about a foot higher than the shafts on either side. Four porters manned each chair, two bearing the ends of the forward pole and two the after, the second of the front pair and the first of the rear pair standing between the shafts. Another man in workman's costume waved to the chairs, saying:

"Sit! Sit!"

At least that is what Kerin thought the man said, although the local dialect differed from the Kuromonian that Tsemben had taught him. He and Nogiri climbed into their chairs and watched the crowds. Kuromonians of the mercantile and official classes could easily be picked out by their embroidered ankle-length robes, bearing patterns of flowers, birds, and other designs, and pillbox hats. They seemed to be mostly stout men, fanning themselves as they walked with slow and dignified gaits.

After another wait, Toga reappeared astride a small gray ass. He barked a command, whereupon soldiers shouldered their pole arms and porters picked up the bags of the passengers' possessions.

"Go!" said Toga. In single file, the chair porters heaved the carrying poles up to their shoulders, raising the passengers' feet a foot above the ground; and all started off for distant Chingun.

· I X ·
The Prohibited Precinct

Kerin had vaguely supposed that being borne on the shoulders of men would give one a feeling of grandeur. The reality turned out different. His four chair porters plodded in single file, keeping in step by a little chant in local dialect. They sang the same stanza in rotation, over and over. After a hundred or more repetitions, the fourth man called out. The porters lowered their poles until the dowel rods touched the ground and took the weight. Then all four shifted their poles from one shoulder to the other. On they went, murmuring the same little song.

Kerin found that chair shafts have a natural period of oscillation. His weight set up a resonance, so that the chair bounced, with a loud, rhythmic creak, with each stride of the porters. At first Kerin did not mind the motion; but after an hour his clothes began to chafe where they rubbed with each bounce, and his stomach felt queasy.

Since the day was advanced when the *Tukara Mora* anchored at Koteiki, Kerin's porters had covered only a couple of leagues when, with darkness looming, Toga called a halt at a little wayside inn. The official bustled about, getting Kerin and Nogiri settled in the hotel's fanciest room and the others placed elsewhere. Kerin took time before dinner to learn the locations and use of the facilities.

Kerin was now adept with chopsticks. Toga said: "This person must say that, for a barbarian, you adapt readily to civilized ways."

Kerin paused in his stoking. "Master Toga, my brother, who has traveled widely, warned me that, wherever I went, I should find the folk believing themselves above all other human beings; that they are the wisest, bravest, truest, and politest people on earth. So I do not let myself be disturbed when folk of other nations call me a barbarian."

"Your brother is shrewd, Master Rao. Of course, when we of the Heavenly Empire think thus, it is no mere boast, because we are in sober fact superior."

Kerin suppressed a smile. "Another matter. Are these chairmen supposed to haul us all the way to Chingun?"

"Aye. It is a mere fortnight's walk."

"Were not horses or carriages speedier?"

Toga spread his hands. "Doubtless; but only holders of the colored cap buttons—the upper nine grades of the civil service, called mandarins—may ride horseback or travel in chariots without special permission. And if I filed a request for this permission, the document must needs make its way through various bureaus and would keep us waiting a month in Koteiki. So in practice, it is quicker to walk."

"What said he?" asked Nogiri. "I missed some words."

When Kerin explained, she said: "Oh, I am happy that you did not get horses! I have never ridden, and they terrify me."

Kerin grinned. "You, the bravest woman I have known? Well, we all have weaknesses, I suppose. I hate spiders." He turned back. "Honorable Toga, I should like to ask a favor, namely: to trade places tomorrow, for me to ride the ass and you the chair. I like not being bounced like an infant's ball."

"Oh?" said Toga. "If you insist. A chair implies a higher status than an ass; it was meant as a delicate compliment. Your trouble, Master Rao, is that you are too lean. A well-fed merchant or official, far outweighing you, would not bounce. But it shall be as you desire. Could we feed you properly for a few months, we could give you the obesity proper to a gentleman."

"Thankee, but I like myself as I am. On a perilous journey, one must be ready for violent action."

Toga gave a little sigh. "This inferior person will never understand the barbarian mentality."

When Kerin was on his way to his and Nogiri's bedroom in the rambling one-story structure, he passed the common room, into which the soldiers and porters had crowded. They were crouched around a little bowl on the floor, into which the head porter poured chick-peas. The head porter began taking out peas, a few at a time, while betting grew frenzied. When almost all the peas had been removed, those who had bet on the number remaining gave shrieks of triumph.

"It is called *fantan*," said Toga. "Wouldst take a hand?"

Kerin hesitated, but Nogiri said in Salimorese: "Husband, you would not fall into the trap that caught that other fellow you spake of, now would you? You are in a strange land."

Kerin said: "My princess is a-wearied, Master Toga. I thank you for your kindness, but we must retire."

Retire they did; but they were long kept awake by intermittent howls of "One! Three! Four! Two!" from the common room.

•　•　•

Next morning, Kerin had trouble with the ass, which rolled its eyes and shied as he approached it. Toga explained: "It is your barbarian smell, Master Rao."

With porters holding the ass's head and tail, Kerin mounted. The stirrups proved too short, even after the straps had been let out to the last bucklehole.

"This person will find a worker in leather—" began Toga; but Kerin said: "Bother not. At the first stop I shall make the needed holes with my dagger."

Toga sighed. "You would do manual work that you can hire others to do for you? Ah, barbarians!" Shaking his head, he climbed into the chair vacated by Kerin.

The little caravan plodded northward along a muddy road lined with endless brown-and-green fields of crops. Often they passed by fields at the corners of which coffins were stacked. Toga explained that the owners' families had not yet gotten around to burying their dear departeds. Some coffins had been in place long enough for the ends to have rotted out; pigs poked their heads in the openings for anything edible.

Kerin's saddle, a simple wooden frame with a square of blanketing fastened over it, proved rather uncomfortable; but it was better than being forever bounced. Kerin noticed that Toga's tubby form held the chair steady as his own lesser weight did not. Nogiri did not seem to mind the bouncing.

On the third day, a downpour caught them on the road. Toga brought out rain capes of yellow oiled silk for himself and his charges. The soldiers and porters had to plod on unprotected, stooped and squinting.

The group wound its way beneath a low, gray sky through a country of low but rugged hills. Farms were few here; the inhabitants mainly raised livestock. In the inn that night, Toga said:

"Honorable Rao, this is bad country for robbers. We must keep a sharp watch."

When he retired, Kerin dug out Pwana's spyglass. The next day he stuck the telescope into a jacket pocket.

They continued through the hill country. At the midday halt, Toga muttered about brigands. Kerin got out his spyglass and scanned the hills.

"I see none," he said.

"Good, honorable barbarian! Then let us eat. I have a bottle of wine that is not altogether disgusting."

Kerin was shoveling in the first chopstickful of rice when a porter sprang up, crying out and pointing. A group of men had erupted out of a gully and were running towards the caravan, waving weapons.

In a scramble, all the porters rose and fled. The five soldiers snatched up their pole arms but then ran after the porters. The ass galloped off in the midst of the crowd.

"Run!" shouted Toga, lighting out after the soldiers.

"Come on, Nogiri!" said Kerin. "We can't fight the whole band alone!"

Hand in hand, Kerin and Nogiri ran after the rest. The porters fled up a long incline. Kerin soon passed the stout Toga, laboring and puffing. He and Nogiri overtook the soldiers, slowed by the weight of their arms and buffcoats.

The rise went on and on, until Kerin also began to pant. He paused to look back. A group of their attackers had seized Toga and were dragging him back to the luncheon site. Others were eating the food that the caravan had abandoned.

Kerin finally reached the crest. The ground dropped sharply on the other side, and in the draw before the next rise the porters and soldiers huddled, talking. The ass placidly grazed.

Kerin strode up to Captain Mogami. "A fine lot of brave soldiers you are!" he snorted.

Mogami clasped his hands, bowed, and spoke. It took a couple of repetitions in his dialect, but at last Kerin understood him to say: "But honorable barbarian, they outnumbered us three to one! Since no help could be expected from the porters, to stand and fight were futile."

"But they were also a ragged, starveling lot, with a miscellany of weapons and no armor. Besides, you let them capture Master Toga."

The officer shook his head. "Indeed, sir, ye have shamed me. Be so good as to take this!"

He thrust his fauchard into Kerin's hands, pulled off his crested brass helmet, knelt, and bowed his head. Kerin supposed the man to be praying. After Mogami had knelt silently for a while, Kerin asked:

"What do you?"

"I wait for you to cut off my head," said the officer. "I do but beg a single, clean stroke."

Kerin recoiled. "Now what on earth do I want with your head, without the rest of you?"

"Honorable barbarian, since ye have shamed me before my men, it is the only way I can recover my lost face."

"Excuse me; I must think." Kerin strolled back up the slope until he could just see over it to the luncheon site. Through Pwana's spyglass he watched the sixteen robbers feasting and passing Toga's bottle of wine around. Toga they had tied up, and one was heating his sword blade in the smoky little fire. He and others laughed and pointed to Toga. Kerin guessed that they were thinking of interesting things to do to the civil servant.

Kerin rejoined the group at the bottom of the draw, where Captain Mogami still knelt, and said: "Art fain to recover your face?"

"Aye. Therefore I begged a quick, sure stroke."

"I have a better idea. If you will follow my orders, you may not only live but also gain glory. Up!"

As Mogami rose, Kerin handed him his fauchard. "One of you hold this beast whilst I mount it. Follow me, all five of you!"

Kerin rode up the slope and halted where he could make out the robbers. "We shall charge downhill. If you are all quiet, we may get close ere they see us. When they espy us, I shall call on you to shout and scream. If any stand his ground, we shall slay him. Do you all understand?"

They topped the rise. Kerin waved his sword, saying: "Charge!"

The ass trotted; the five soldiers ran. Halfway to the luncheon place, a bandit saw them and cried out. In a trice the robbers were scrambling for weapons.

"Shout!" called Kerin. He and the soldiers burst into roars and screams of threat and invective.

The robbers formed a ragged line. As Kerin galloped closer, waving his sword, one robber dropped his spear and ran. Then another turned tail, and then the whole sixteen were in flight, dropping pieces of loot.

Filled with the lust of battle, Kerin galloped after them; but the ass put a hoof into a hole and pitched on its head. Kerin went flying, coming down on a patch of muddy road. By the time he had regained his feet, scraped some of the mud off his face, and assured himself that he had no broken bones, the robbers were out of sight. The ass was placidly munching grass again.

Kerin limped back leading the ass. The porters and Nogiri were straggling down the slope. A soldier had cut Toga's bonds, and the civil servant was rubbing his hands to restore circulation. He bowed, saying:

"This negligible person is eternally grateful, and not merely for saving his worthless life."

"What else?" asked Kerin.

"Why, they were going to try a red-hot sword blade on me."

Mogami spoke: "A terrible thing to do with good steel! It ruins the temper."

Toga continued: "I should not so much have minded dying. But I feared that, by crying out under torture, I should lose face before those scum."

Kerin said: "Pray explain something. . . ." He drew Toga aside and told of Captain Mogami's invitation to Kerin to behead him. "Did he really mean it?"

"Of course he meant it!" said Toga. "That is what any Kuromonian gentleman would do. Although Mogami is a mere soldier, he hopes to rise above that status, which amongst us is one of the lowest grades."

"If a soldier is deemed such a contemptible fellow, no wonder they ran away!"

"True; but what would you? Admire one whose sole skill lies in slaying his fellow beings? That were to stand civilized values on their heads! But tell me, honorable Rao, in view of their numbers, how knew you the robbers would run from your charge?"

Kerin chuckled. "Something I learned of the habits of the Mulvanian wild buffalo. A fellow named—" He had been about to name the original Rao, but checked just in time as he realized that he was supposed to be Rao. "I forget his name, but he'd traveled in the jungles. He told me there was one coward in every herd. Tell me, what would have happened if I had cut off Mogami's head?"

Toga shrugged. "His soldiers would have stripped the body of aught of value. If they were honest, they would give these things to his widow on their return home. The corpse would have been left for the pigs and wolves."

"Would nought have befallen me for the slaying?"

"Nay; why should it? He offered you his life before witnesses, and under the circumstances you were entitled to take it."

Kerin sighed. "I find the customs of the Heavenly Empire as confusing as you would doubtless find ours."

Toga chuckled. "This person blames you not. After all, you have not had the advantage of a civilized upbringing."

Later, when Kerin was alone with Nogiri, she said: "My lord, you are a true hero. Were you not at all frightened?"

"Forsooth, I was; but not of the robbers. I feared that my gallant soldiers would flee at the last instant, leaving me to fight the banditti alone!"

The rest of the journey saw few incidents, save that it took twenty-five days instead of the promised fourteen. When Kerin twitted Toga about this, the official said:

"Ah, Master Kerin, you have not yet learned this feature of polite civilized discourse. The first principle in answering a question is to give the questioner an answer that shall please him, even if one must bend the literal truth a bit."

At every halt during the day, Kerin ordered the soldiers to post at least two of their number as sentries. Since he had proved his prowess, they obeyed his commands with alacrity. Whether or not the sentries discouraged evildoers, there was no more sign of robbers during the journey.

On the night before reaching Chingun, the caravan stopped at a village where dwelt a cousin, Hizen, of civil servant Toga. After Toga had settled the party in the local inn, he took Kerin and Nogiri to his cousin's house for dinner. Nogiri was sent to eat separately with Hizen's women.

Although Kerin was circumspect in his behavior and cautious in his drinking, Toga and Hizen got slightly drunk and sang ribald songs. Anon, Toga lurched to his feet and plucked Kerin's sleeve, saying:

"Come, honorable Rao. It is time to visit the garden."

"Garden?" said Kerin, puzzled. "At night, when the moon is hidden by clouds?"

Toga giggled. "Of course, how stupid of this inferior one! Know that in the Heavenly Empire, it is polite, when one has dined at another's house, to leave nightsoil in his garden afterwards." He wagged a finger. "Waste not, want not!"

As they neared Chingun, Toga persuaded Kerin to change places with him again, "as a matter of face." Toga, now astride the ass, led the way to one of the colossal gates in the buff-colored outer wall. He produced a sheaf of papers from his scrip, which the officer of the guard went over one by one before returning them and waving the caravan through.

In Koteiki and in the towns they had passed through, Kerin had seen the features of Kuromonian architecture: the lavish use of vermillion, black, and gold; the hip rafters curving up at the end like the toe of a Mulvanian slipper; the rows of little gilded figurines of guardian monsters along the hip rafters.

In Chingun he saw the same features but on a larger scale. Like Janareth and Kwatna, the city had some broad, straight avenues and, between these, tangles of narrow, crooked streets. But the scale of Chingun was so vast that Janareth and Kwatna, if moved to Chingun, would have been merely two more wards of the metropolis.

Kerin bounced in his chair along one avenue, and another, and another. The streets swarmed with Kuromonians, mostly in the universal working-class blue jackets and trousers worn by both sexes. The middle class wore ankle-length robes. Men's hair was worn long and tied in topknots. The streets were noisy with the bells, gongs, horns, drums, whistles, and other noise-makers used by itinerant tradesmen such as barbers, knife grinders, and sellers of snacks.

The local feature that most startled Kerin was one he had not seen elsewhere. On the well-paved streets of the capital, many did not merely walk but glided along on roller skates. Each skater wore a pair of high-topped, metal-framed shoes to which were journaled two wheels, forward and aft. Kerin inferred that, since paved streets were rare in smaller towns and villages, the device would not be useful there.

The caravan entered a public square in which a string of two dozen camels awaited loading for the journey northward into the steppes. Some had not yet shed all their winter fur, so that they presented a patchy appearance.

Beyond the camels, a small crowd was gathered. Amid this crowd a group of men stripped to the waist knelt with their hands tied behind them. An executioner was going down the line with a short, broad-bladed, two-handed sword. Two bodies already lay prone on the pavement with their heads detached and crimson blood pouring out. As the caravan passed, the executioner swung, and *chug!* off went another head. The head bounced and rolled while the spouting body fell *plop* on its chest.

"Who are those?" Kerin asked.

Toga shrugged. "Miscreants of some sort. Chingun swarms with cutpurses and other criminals. In my native village there was none of that sort of thing."

They passed the spectators and came to a two-story tower. On the roof, reached by an outside stair, stood a cluster of astronomical instruments, protected by a canopy. Below, the tower had a series of openings, stacked vertically, in which appeared a series of figurines about half life-size, carrying squares of board on which symbols were painted. The tower emitted clattering and splashing noises. As they passed, a gong sounded. One of the figures moved out of sight, while another appeared in the opening. Kerin called:

"What is that?"

"The great astronomical clock, built by the ingenious Hukuryu. It tells not only the time but also the date, the phases of the moon, and the motions of the stars and planets."

This, Kerin thought, I must see at more leisure. The caravan plodded on until the party reached a walled section in the center of the city. At the gate into this interior wall, the whole tedious business of checking papers was again undergone.

At last Kerin and Nogiri were borne into the enclosure, which Toga explained was called the Prohibited Precinct. Within each side of the wall stood a row of large one-story buildings. Within the square formed by these structures, a vast plaza spread, bedight with bronzen dragons, armillary spheres, monumental stone stelae, and other ornaments.

Kuromonians bearing scrolls and sheaves of papers bustled about this plaza, some afoot and some whizzing by on skates. They streamed in and out of the buildings like ants in their nests. At the center of the plaza rose an even larger building, covering several acres. Its gilded roof flashed blindingly in the sun.

"That," said Toga, "is the Proscribed Palace, where dwells the Son of Heaven."

"Are we going thither?" asked Kerin.

Toga gave a mirthless little laugh. "Any wight who sought to enter the Forbidden Interior uninvited would find himself shy of a head before he could blink."

"Then whither go we?"

"You shall see. We must pass you through official channels.

First I must report to my superior, the honorable Third Assistant Secretary Aki of the Foreign Barbarian Section."

Toga led the way to one of the large buildings of the outer square. He dismounted, helped Kerin and Nogiri out of their chairs, and led them inside. The corridors swarmed with Kuromonians in clean but sober dress, afoot and on skates. Sometimes Toga had to push through the throng, crying: "Borrow light! Borrow light!"

When the crowd thinned, Kerin asked: "Honorable Toga, who are all these people?"

"Clerks and officials."

"Why on earth are so many needed?"

"Because the Heavenly Empire rules millions of subjects, and a government cannot control so many and promote their welfare without this apparatus."

"I should think so many would get in one another's way and duplicate one another's work. Or else they would spend more time in intrigue and peculation than at their proper tasks."

"True, Master Rao. One of our problems is that, as the size of an organization grows, it become harder and ever harder for even the ablest and most upright administrator to keep an eye on every official, clerk, and other underling so that he perform his duties with diligence and honesty. We must therefore hire people to watch them, and this increases the total number and aggravates the problem of keeping an eye on all. So we must hire still others to watch the watchmen, and so on."

"Well," said Kerin, "methought our little Kortolian monarchy and its Chamber of Burgesses an ineffectual, ramshackle sort of government, but on the whole I prefer it to this."

"Ah, but if your kingdom had a population like unto ours, you would encounter all our difficulties."

"Then is the Empire simply too large to be well-run?"

"In a sense, perhaps. But when Kuromon was divided into a

host of contending kingdoms, ever warring and ravaging one another's lands, things were even worse."

Toga gave his name to a guard at a door. The guard disappeared, and Toga and his charges stood so long in the corridor that Kerin asked: "What's the matter now?"

Toga chuckled. "It is usual for an official to keep a subordinate waiting to see him. Thus he gains face and proves his status."

Eventually the guard returned and ushered the trio in. They found a stout man seated at a desk, and flanking that desk two smaller desks at which sat clerks with writing brushes. The stout man wore a device new to Kerin: a pair of reading glasses in a frame that fitted over the bridge of his nose and were secured in place by a pair of ribbons tied at the back of his head. He rose, and he and Toga exchanged so many bows that Kerin fancied he could hear their spines creak.

"Ineffable superior," said Toga, "permit this lowly one to present the honorable barbarian, Master Rao of Mulvan. Master Rao, you stand before the honorable Third Assistant Secretary Aki."

Kerin bowed as he had seen the Kuromonians do. Aki stared at Kerin as if he smelled something offensive and gave a slight nod.

"Has he the document from King Lajpat?" asked Aki.

"Show it to him, Master Rao," said Toga. Both Kuromonians ignored Nogiri, who stood at Kerin's side.

Aki clapped his hands, and a young Kuromonian woman appeared with a tray supporting a teapot and two small cups without handles.

"Seat yourself, honorable Toga," said Aki. "Pray partake." He and Toga began a rambling conversation, devoted to gossip about promotions, bureaucratic intrigues, and competitive examinations, leaving Kerin and Nogiri standing and ignored.

Kerin grew angrier and angrier, but as a single foreigner in the midst of thousands of locals he dared not give vent to his feelings.

Toga finished his tea and rose. He and Aki exchanged more bows, and he led his charges out. Glancing at Kerin's angry face, with its thin lips and narrowed eyes, he said soothingly:

"This person must apologize for the honorable Aki's manners. His faction would cut off all contact with barbarians. He hates them all, having lost kinsmen to pirates from the Gwoling Islands and nomadic raiders from the steppes. Now we shall visit his superior."

They entered a larger office. Kerin was presented to Second Assistant Secretary Ushio, who said: "From Mulvan, eh? I should have expected a man of darker hue."

Kerin gulped, fearing that his imposture was on the verge of exposure. "It—it depends on what part of that land one comes from."

"Toga!" snapped Ushio. "Where hast been? You were expected a fortnight past."

"Exalted superior, this vile creature brought the honorable barbarians as quickly as the chairmen could walk."

"Walk? I sent down orders for you to be furnished with a horse for you and a cart and driver for Master Rao."

"Your order never reached me, sublime sir. Methinks Secretary Aki may have detained it. You know his sentiments anent barbarians."

"Huh! Belike he did; but if we accuse him, he will put the blame on his clerks. Oh, well, the main thing is that you are here."

More tea was brought, and Ushio ordered his clerks to furnish Kerin and Nogiri with seats and teacups. Toga plunged into a discussion of the proper channels for bringing Kerin before Imperial Wizard Oshima. Ushio said:

"I could not authorize a direct approach. Belike my superior, the honorable Kaga, could if the Secretary have authorized him to conduct interdepartmental contacts. Let me see. . . ."

Ushio got out a chart, unrolled it, and placed it on his desk with small objects at the corners to keep it from rolling up again. Kerin saw a spiderweb of lines connecting characters in Kuromonian writing.

"Now," said Ushio, "we can go up this way, and across thus, and down thus. . . . Or else we could go to the bureau head, the honorable Sendai."

"If all else fail," said Toga, "this person could apply to the Lord High Mandarin of Roads and Shipping. . . ."

"Methinks we need not go to that extreme," said Ushio. "Being unwell, the exalted Aoba had delegated many duties to assistants. If the honorable Kaga can get you transferred, well and good; if not, you must needs go through Sendai. Convey my respectful regards."

Leaving Ushio's office, Kerin asked: "If I am supposed to report to the Imperial Wizard, why can't we go straight thither? Why all this roundabout skirmishing?"

"This person would not expect you as a barbarian to understand," said Toga. "To keep confusion to a minimum and prevent the different branches of the government from acting at cross-purposes, we need rules of who may do business with whom. It is called 'going through channels.' It is a nuisance, but not half the nuisance we should have if everybody rushed about from department to department without their superiors' knowledge. Of course, old hands like this person know how to take shortcuts without causing trouble.

"The wizard Oshima works in the Magical Bureau of the Department of Health and Welfare. To get from one department to another . . ." Toga launched into the complex rules of the civil service. By the time he finished, they had arrived at the office of First Assistant Secretary Kaga.

"The honorable Sendai is on vacation," said Kaga, "and has deputized me to act in his place. I shall write you a pass to the Health and Welfare Building. There you shall report to Secretary Huso. If he be unable to receive you in person, he will authorize your conveyance down the channels to the proper office in the Magical Bureau. Have a cup of tea; you, too, my dear barbarians. . . ."

A dozen cups of tea later, Second Assistant Secretary Hiei of the Thaumaturgical Laboratory of the Magical Bureau of the Department of Health and Welfare led Kerin, Nogiri, and Toga down a hall, saying: "This person had better take you himself, since our Imperial Wizard is not the most affable man in the Empire."

They entered a large room cluttered with apparatus. Fiddling with the equipment was a small, wrinkled man with a straggly white beard. The man ignored his visitors while he made an adjustment, then said:

"Well, Master Hiei, what folly hast come to demand of me now? A magical rug that shall fly to the moon?"

"My good wizard," said Hiei, "the barbarian is Master Rao, with a message from the King of Kings of Mulvan. If you will momentarily bridle your churlishness, he has something for you."

"Oh, I remember. It is that deal betwixt the Son of Heaven and that so-called King of Kings, eh? Lajpat has surely taken his time with his part of the bargain. Well, where is it?"

Kerin handed over the little oiled-silk package. "You are Wizard Oshima, I take it?"

The little man snorted. "Certes! If Master Hiei had not forgotten his manners, he would have presented you properly. And this I suppose is your fancy woman?"

"My wife," said Kerin, thinking that Oshima's cantankerous manner was enough to subvert any system of etiquette.

"Wife, eh?" snarled Oshima. "Does she respond with invigorating delight when you mount her?"

"Uh—" said Kerin, feeling himself flush. He tried to answer, but so violent was his embarrassment that only inarticulate sounds came forth. He wanted to say: "None of your futtering business, you damned old clown!" but dared not. While he struggled for utterance, Nogiri quietly remarked:

"We manage to our mutual satisfaction, my lord."

"Good!" barked the wizard. "Any fool can see you are the more intelligent of the pair. The trouble with the Heavenly Empire is that women are deemed mere things of no account, thus depriving the society of the effective use of their talents."

"Take him not to heart, Master Rao," said Hiei. "He likes to utter absurdities for the pleasure of shocking his hearers."

"Nought shocks the multitude like an unwelcome truth," growled Oshima. "Now let us see."

Oshima broke the seal on the package and unfolded the paper. He scanned the lines of Mulvanian writing, grunting: "Hm, hm." At last he said:

"This seems to be the formula for making Ajendra's fan— or to be exact, Tsunjing's fan brought hither by Ajendra. Making and ensorcelling the thing will take at least a month, and we cannot send Master Rao on his way until we know if the fan does work. So, Master Hiei, you must needs find quarters for the barbarians, where they can live until we release them."

"Excuse me," said Kerin, "but what is your part of this bargain with Mulvan?"

"Oh, it is merely the secret of the device for finding the true north—"

"Enough!" barked Hiei. "You should not talk about it."

"Since Master Rao will doubtless break the seal and read the contents, as I suspect he have already done with this one, it makes little difference. Well, get on with it! I must concentrate on deciphering these Mulvanian squiggles."

As they left the wizard's oratory, Hiei said: "Now I shall find you quarters. If there be a vacancy in the Diplomatic Village, you shall reside there whilst we await the result of Oshima's experiments."

"Wilt take care of that matter, Honorable Hiei?" said Toga. "This lump of iniquity has not yet been home to his wives and children. I must also pay off the chairmen. You will take care of the baggage porters, I trust?"

"Run along, Master Toga," said Hiei, "ere you burst your breeches with unrequited lust. At least you are not a boy lover like Secretary—but I had better not name names before these foreign devils. Come with me, my dear barbarians."

Following Hiei, Kerin said: "Your wizard seems—ah—different from other Kuromonians."

Hiei chuckled. "You allude to his appalling manners, eh? By the fifty-seven major deities, anyone else would have lost his head for his temerity long ago! Oshima keeps his attached by virtue of being the ablest wizard in the Empire and by the fear he inspires. All believe that if one made a hostile move against him, he would instantly evoke some demon or dragon to destroy one. Fortunately he has no lofty ambitions. So long as we furnish him with a well-equipped oratory for his researches, he is satisfied."

Followed by the baggage porters, Hiei led Kerin and his bride to a walled enclosure in the farthest corner of the Prohibited Precinct. Inside were smaller enclosures—Kuromonians, Kerin thought, must have a passion for building walls around things—each containing a little house with a garden. At the gate outside the Diplomatic Village, guarded by soldiers in brazen helmets and gilded cuirasses, Hiei spoke with a man in the office beside the gate. He told Kerin:

"Master Sinsong says he has just the place for you, save that the present tenants are but now departing. If we sit on this bench, he assures me you shall soon be settled. Meanwhile he will have tea brought. I must compliment you on your progress with the language of civilization. Why, I can understand what you are driving at more than half the time!"

"Thankee," said Kerin. "Tell me, pray, the story of this magical fan!"

"I suppose it will do no harm," said Hiei. "The tale begins centuries ago. The wizard Tsunjing made it for the then King of the Gwoling Islands. With it one can fan any creature out of existence and bring it back by tapping the wrists and head according to a code. When Prince Wangerr, grandson of that king, encountered a dragon on Banshou Island, he fanned it away.

"Generations later, the fan came into possession of the Mulvani ascetic Ajendra, together with the code book listing the taps to summon back beings of every category."

Nogiri spoke, as she had seldom had a chance to do that day. "What befalls the vanished beings?"

"None is certain," said Hiei. "One school holds that they be translated to another dimension, coexistent with this one. Another believes they be dispersed into their constituent atoms, to be reassembled by the signal for recall. To continue: Holding to a principle of harmlessness, Ajendra had no use for the fan; but he wanted money to endow a temple to his favorite gods in his native village, where he could pass his remaining days in meditation of the Thatness of the All.

"Since the Mulvanian king was straitened by the costs of a

recent war and so could not afford to help with the project, Ajendra brought the fan to Chingun in the reign of Tsotuga the Fourth. He persuaded the Son of Heaven to pay ten thousand golden dragons for the fan and the code book, with a military escort back to his native land.

"Tsotuga was not an evil man, but testy and irascible. When one of his ministers argued too strongly against some project the ruler had set his heart on, Tsotuga sometimes fanned the unfortunate mandarin out of existence. Meanwhile he had packed the code book away in a special place, to be sure of finding it in emergencies—but now he could not remember where he had put it.

"After the disappearance of the mandarins of the departments, the rule fell into confusion. Underlings devoted themselves to intrigue, peculation, and private business interests instead of to their proper work. Hard times came upon the land, aggravated by the paper-money inflation that Tsotuga had launched against the wish of Finance Minister Yaebu. Misliking Yaebu's advice, Tsotuga had fanned him away.

"At last Tsotuga took counsel with his consort, Empress Nasako, and hired an able supervisor of provincial roads and bridges, Zamben of Jompei, as Prime Minister. Tsotuga did not know that Zamben and Nasako were secret lovers who plotted to get rid of the Emperor.

"Zamben inveigled Tsotuga into a game of *sachi*. Whilst they fumbled on the floor for a piece that Zamben had dropped, the Prime Minister managed to trade fans with the Emperor, and a wave of the magical fan did the rest.

"Zamben married Nasako and became the Dowager Empress's consort. He improved administration but also set himself to reconstruct the missing code book for recovering beings banished by the fan. He tried out combinations of raps, with

a secretary to record the kind of being recalled for each procedure. Amongst others he restored Finance Minister Yaebu.

"Eventually he inadvertently gave the combination that recalled the dragon that Prince Wangerr had vanished long before.
The dragon snapped up Zamben, fan and all, ere Zamben could
defend himself and fled from the Proscribed Palace.

"Prince Wakumba, though a stripling of fourteen, became
Emperor. After the ceremony he pulled off the plumed and
winged crown, complaining of its weight. Whilst poking about
this complex headpiece, he caused a metal flap to spring open,
revealing the missing code book. Tsotuga had hidden the book
in the secret compartment. Since, however, the fan was gone,
and nobody in the Empire knew how to make another, the book
was filed away in the archives.

"Our present Ruler of the World, the divine Dzuchen, wished
to possess a magical fan to go with the code book. So he tracked
down the spiritual descendants of the ascetic Ajendra, hoping
that amongst them the formula for making such a fan might
still exist, having been passed down from guru to chela. With
the help of Doctor Oshima's divinations, the magician Ghulam
was found to possess these instructions. So our Son of Heaven
agreed with King Lajpat to trade this secret for something else,
possessed by the Heavenly Empire. Therefore—"

Hiei broke off as a party approached the gate from within. It
comprised a group of stocky, brown-skinned, flat-faced men in
sheepskin coats, left open because of the heat, bulbous fur hats,
and big felt boots. A gaggle of baggage porters followed them.

"The nomad envoys," murmured Hiei.

Kerin became aware that these men could be smelled almost
as far as they could be seen. He could not tell how much of
their mud-brown hue was natural and how much a coating of
dirt. They marched out, ignoring Kerin and his party, and
barked commands. Grooms appeared with a train of horses.

When the baggage had been secured to some of these, the no-mads mounted, gave a wild yell, and galloped off, heedless of any pedestrians in their path.

As Kerin and Nogiri were being settled in the cottage as-signed to them, Kerin asked: "When may I depart, pray?"

"When the fan has been completed and tested," said Hiei.

"In other words, this is a polite form of imprisonment?"

"Say not so, honorable Master Rao! Since you are destined, if the fan prove successful, to carry the returning message back to Mulvan, we must assure ourselves that you will be available when the time arrives."

"May we leave the Diplomatic Village at will, then?"

"Certes, so long as you remain within the Prohibited Pre-cinct."

"Suppose we wish to see more of your great city?"

"If you will send a message, this person will arrange your escort. It will be for your personal safety, since it is easy to lose oneself in Chingun or fall prey to criminals, whereof we have, alas, a plethora. And now, honorable barbarians, I must return to my duties. As said the wise Dauhai, nought encourages dil-igence in a subordinate like the sight of his superior practicing that virtue!"

As Hiei walked off, radiating self-importance, Kerin turned to Nogiri and said softly in Salimorese: "Didst hear what old Oshima said, ere Hiei shushed him, about their secret navi-gating device?"

"Nay. I caught only the word 'north,' for they spake too fast for me."

"Well, you know my bargain with Klung. If they hand me directions for the device and send me off—as they suppose, to Mulvan—there's half our problem solved." Kerin's face took on a worried look. "But I know not. If I promise to convey the secret to King Lajpat and then give it to Klung, I shall be a faithless . . ."

"Were I you," said Nogiri, "I should wait upon the event. If we be lost at sea or slain by pirates betwixt here and Kwatna, you'll never have to wrestle with your thorny conscience. And in Salimor, Master Klung may not even be amongst the living."

"Sensible, as always," said Kerin.

· X ·
The Forbidden Interior

Kerin sat on the pavement outside the gate to the Diplomatic Village with his feet, in overshoes with roller skates, stretched out before him. He scowled up at Nogiri, who stood shaking with laughter.

"Damn it, woman," he growled, "if you be so clever, let's see you manage these devilish contraptions!" He angrily yanked the straps on the overshoes as he took them off.

"Your pardon, my lord," she said as she mastered her mirth. "But after your boasting of how easy it seemed, you looked so droll."

She sat on the bench and put on her own skates, while Kerin climbed painfully to his feet. "I shall have a sore arse tomorrow," he grumbled. "Kuromonian wives are more respectful."

Nogiri sailed away on her skates. She wobbled a little at first but soon caught the knack and came flying back in a long curve. Then away she went in a figure-eight.

"By Imbal's iron pizzle!" said Kerin. "Hast been practicing on the sly?"

"Nay, my lord," she said, ending with a pirouette. "I did but watch the locals. If you would really prefer a Kuromonian wife, I daresay you could find some civil servant willing to trade."

"Good gods!" said Kerin. "Don't even think such thoughts. I may have more than half our thews betwixt us, but you have more than half the wit. I'm sorry I lost my temper; I must indeed have looked a blithering ass."

"And I regret laughing. Wouldst try again, more cautiously?"

An hour's practice made Kerin fairly proficient, and the two skated off to tour the Prohibited Precinct.

Kerin knocked on the door of Doctor Oshima's oratory. He heard a snarl from within: "What is it this time?"

"Rao the Mulvani," said Kerin. "We wondered how you did with the fan?"

"Oh, come in, come in! But waste not my time in useless chatter!"

Kerin pushed open the door. He and Nogiri had their roller skates tied together over their shoulders. Within, Oshima was holding one end of a tube of glass while a spindly, frightened-looking apprentice held the other end.

Oshima snapped: "Begone, Dong!" The apprentice scuttled out. Then to Kerin: "I take it you are learning to skate?"

"Aye, sir," said Kerin.

"Whence gat you the skates?"

"We begged the honorable Hiei. As I said, how are you—"

"You say you be from Mulvan?"

"Aye, sir. But how—"

"And your woman, from appearance and accent, is a Salimorese."

"Aye, she is. But—"

"That is odd. I have known other Mulvanians, but all were of much darker hue than you, like unto tea boiled all night long."

Kerin made a desperate lunge for a plausible excuse: "I have been out of the sun much lately."

"Hm, hm. I daresay you know your own origins, even though one could take you for one of those pallid, round-eyed barbarians from the Far West, who seldom reach the Empire. The honorable Aki dropped in a few days since, voicing suspicions of your authenticity; but he ever suspects the worst of barbarians. Well, what is your question? Hurry, now; I am a busy man!"

"About the fan, sir. How goes it?"

"It goes, but slowly. I need slabs of jade of a certain quality, for which I must needs send to Jade Mountain Province. What business is it of yours, anyway?"

Kerin let his irritation show. "Very much my business, because you people won't let me go my way until the thing be tested."

"Hm. Well, is there aught else?"

"Nay, sir. But—"

"Then good-day to you. Oh, Dong! Come back and get to work, you lazy losel!"

"Damned old churl!" muttered Kerin as they closed the oratory door behind them. "I wonder he still has his head attached, despite the fear he inspires."

"Be careful with him, my lord," said Nogiri. "Whatever his faults, he's a shrewd old curmudgeon."

"Right, as usual," grumped Kerin.

Kerin and Nogiri skated up to Hukuryu's tower outside the Prohibited Precinct. With them skated two soldiers in gleaming brass, to make sure that they were not lost or waylaid; and also, Kerin suspected, to see that they did not leave Chingun. The door in the tower opened to Kerin's knock, and a middle-aged Kuromonian bowed over clasped hands.

"To whom owes this inferior person this visit?" said the man.

Kerin explained that he was a traveler from afar who, hearing the marvels of Hukuryu's clock, had come to examine it, "if such inspection be permitted this humble barbarian," Kerin finished in Kuromonian style.

"The honorable barbarian honors this incompetent care-taker," said the man, bowing. "Enter by all means."

The interior was even noisier than the outside, so that Kerin had to raise his voice to converse. Shafts creaked, the escape-ment clattered, water splashed, and from time to time came an outburst of bells, drums, and gongs. Caretaker Zuikaku, a grandson of Hukuryu, was eager to explain the workings of his grandfather's clock:

"This person is delighted to find a barbarian willing to learn the rudiments of civilization."

The tower was about thirty-five feet high, counting the pent-house. Water, flowing through pipes and vessels, filled the thirty-six scoops of a water wheel, one after another. An es-capement controlled the rotation of the wheel, allowing it to turn one scoop interval at a time. The wheel revolved once in nine hours, while water fell from the scoops into a basin below the wheel.

The wheel turned a wooden shaft with iron bearings. This shaft, by means of a crown gear, turned a tall vertical shaft, which worked the other machinery. This included the armil-lary sphere in the penthouse and five large horizontal wheels bearing jacks. Some of these jacks, in the form of mannequins, bore signs to indicate the hours, the tenths of an hour, sunrise, sunset, and the watches of the night. Other jacks marked these events by ringing bells and beating gongs and drums.

Kerin gave the most attention to the escapement. This was a system of tripping lugs, which held the water wheel against rotation until one scoop had been filled and then allowed it to move just far enough to bring the next scoop into the filling position.

"Whence comes the water?" asked Kerin.

"From the storage tank above. If the honorable barbarian will follow me up this ladder . . ."

"Skates off first," said Kerin. When he had climbed to the second story, he asked: "What dost when the tank runs dry?"

"Every day a convict is brought in to refill it," said Zuikaku. "He turns this crank, which pumps up water from the well."

"Sir," said Kerin, "you have given me more information than my poor little barbarian mind can absorb all at once. I trust I may visit you again?"

"This insignificant mechanic will be delighted, honored sir."

Skating back to the Prohibited Precinct, Kerin said in Salimorese: "That was too easy."

Nogiri replied: "I should think you'd be pleased, to achieve your main goal without trouble."

"That's just the point, dear. In my experience, when things seem too good to be true, it usually means that they are. Belinka was a nuisance in ways, but I wish she were here to warn us."

In the cottage, Kerin spent the evening drawing diagrams on paper furnished by Hiei, showing the escapement mechanism. Apparently the Kuromonians had never heard of the quill pen. They used slender brushes, which gave Kerin much trouble until, by dogged experimentation, he learned to paint a fine line with one.

. . .

Days passed; the heat of summer waxed. Since the air of the city was less humid than those of Kwatna and Koteiki, Kerin minded it less. With his escort he revisited Hukuryu's clock tower to compare his drawing of the escapement with the actual thing. Wearing a Kuromonian clerk's jacket and cap, he roamed the corridors of the great departmental buildings unchallenged.

Once in the building of the Department of Roads, Canals, and Shipping he passed the stout Third Assistant Secretary Aki in the hall. A glower flickered across Aki's bespectacled face and then faded into bland impassivity. Neither spoke.

One evening, when Kerin was trying with little success to master Kuromonian ideographic writing, a messenger boy arrived on skates, saying: "The honorable Kaga presents his compliments to the honorable barbarian Rao and requests the said Rao to meet him at the entrance to the Proscribed Palace at the third hour tomorrow. He is commanded to the Forbidden Interior."

After the boy had left, Nogiri asked: "Was nought said about me?"

"Nay, darling. I suppose—"

"Forget it! In this land women are of even less account than in mine own. You shall go whilst I wash your hose."

Kerin found a cluster before the entrance to the Proscribed Palace. Kaga and Ushio were there, and Toga arrived just after Kerin. There were other officials as well.

Toga touched Kerin's arm and beckoned. Aside he murmured: "Honorable Kerin, I trust you know the proper procedures in the Forbidden Interior?"

"Hiei has rehearsed me."

"Good! A word of warning. Rumor has it that the Son of Heaven is in an irritable frame of mind, for having had to leave his Summer Palace—a far more splendid residence than this old semiruin, with spacious grounds, bejewelled pavilions, duck ponds, and other amenities—to subject himself to the stifling heat of the Proscribed Palace. He would never have come had not his eunuchs convinced him that the importance of the deal over Ajendra's fan made his presence necessary. When he is in this mood, the least error in ceremony can cost the offender parts he were loath to part with, such as his head."

"I'll do my best," said Kerin with a sinking heart.

The doors groaned open, and a fat man called out in a squeaky voice: "Enter, honorables; the Ruler of the World awaits you."

The soldiers at the entrance bowed as the bureaucrats passed between them. The fat man led the party to an audience hall, where a score of courtiers already stood at attention. At the far end sat Emperor Dzuchen, swathed in voluminous robes of brilliant hues—scarlet, emerald, and gold—on a throne on a dais. The dais was five feet high, as if to make up for the fact that Dzuchen was a small man. He wore the towering, winged crown of state, bedight with peacock plumes and glittering with precious stones. Soldiers stood beside the dais, while eunuchs padded around it.

The fat usher lined up the party in a single rank. He led them forward three paces; at a signal, all dropped to their knees and thrice touched their foreheads to the floor. Watching the others out of the corners of his eyes, Kerin followed their actions.

All rose, advanced another three paces, and repeated the obeisance. They rose, advanced, and genuflected once more. All were careful not to look the Emperor squarely in the face, because of the pretense that one who did so would be blinded by his awful glory.

"Rise!" said the Emperor. "Wizard Oshima, stand forth!"

Oshima and his apprentice Dong stepped out from the shadows at the sides. Oshima held a large, costly-looking fan, which he started to hand up folded to the Emperor. Between the height of the dais, however, and the smallness of Oshima's stature, Dzuchen could not reach the fan unless he got off his throne and stooped. To avoid such a breach of imperial etiquette, Kerin called out:

"Divine Autocrat, suffer this heap of slime to render aid!"

Putting his hands atop the dais, he vaulted up, got a knee over the edge, and scrambled into a kneeling posture. He reached down, took the fan from the wizard, and handed it to Dzuchen.

The courtiers traded startled looks. Kerin held his breath, uncertain whether to expect praise or instant condemnation. The Emperor said:

"And the code book, good subjects!"

Oshima produced the book from one of his baggy sleeves and handed it to Kerin, who gave it to the Emperor and lowered himself to the floor. His heart raced with apprehension. When he had climbed the dais, the act had seemed merely the normal, considerate thing to do; but among these etiquette-mad folk it might yet prove suicidal.

Dzuchen opened the fan, exposing the painted dragon designs. He almost fanned himself but stopped in time. He muttered: "Curse this heat!" Kerin saw drops of sweat escape from under the huge crown and roll down the Emperor's face. Aloud Dzuchen said:

"Our foremost task is to test this thing. Who will volunteer to be fanned away and returned to existence?"

The courtiers exchanged regards again. There was a general shuffling of felt slippers as each tried to hide himself behind his neighbors.

"What, no volunteers?" said Dzuchen, scanning the court.

Oshima spoke: "O Superior One, my worthless apprentice, Goodman Dong, will be delighted to accept the honor!"

The wizard pushed his apprentice forward. The lad rolled his eyes and uttered a faint croak. Kerin judged that the youth was too terrified to protest; he was on the verge of fainting.

"Ah, just the thing!" said Dzuchen. Whipping open the fan, he leaned his body forward and swept the fan past Dong's intimidated face. The youth disappeared with a sound of displaced air.

"Now to fetch him back here. . . ." murmured the Emperor, turning the pages.

"Look under 'apprentice,' Your Imperial Majesty," said Oshima.

Dzuchen found the reference. He folded the fan and tapped his left wrist four times and his forehead once. Instantly Dong reappeared. This time he did faint, slumping into a heap on the floor.

"Guards!" barked the Emperor. "Revive this stripling, give him one golden half-dragon, and send him home for the day. Well done, Doctor Oshima! Now it remains but to meet our part of the bargain with King Lajpat." He fixed his gaze on Kerin. "Art not the youth who brought the specifications for the fan from Mulvan?"

Kerin bowed deeply. "Indeed, Your Imperial Majesty, I am that negligible one."

"You have achieved merit. You shall be rewarded with—"

"O Sovran of the World!" cried a voice. "Your Imperial Majesty has been cozened, deceived, and put upon!"

"Eh? What's this?" said Dzuchen. "Whoever spake, let him stand forth!"

Third Assistant Secretary Aki strode forward, followed by another Kuromonian. The two dropped to their knees and touched their foreheads to the floor. When they did this a second time, Dzuchen snapped:

"Enough formality; get to the point!"

"Superhuman Sire," said Aki, "this puddle of filth has with him Master Litsun of Jobé, a respected merchant. He has just returned from his latest trading visit to Mulvan. On a previous journey, he met Wizard Ghulam and his chela Rao. Now he assures me that he who stands before you, professing himself that Rao, be nought of the sort."

"Thine Ineffable Majesty!" cried Toga. "This mote of dust has proof that the self-styled Rao be indeed he! Behold, O Master of the Universe!"

From one of his baggy sleeves, Toga produced the paper bearing the sketch by which he had identified Kerin at Koteiki. Heads, including the Emperor's, craned to view the picture. Aki cried:

"O Sovran of the Universe, heed not this notorious barbarian-lover Toga! Anyone can draw a picture. How know we that he have not limned it within the hour, for this very purpose?"

"Liar!" cried Toga. "You blind ass, this is the very paper you gave me to identify the barbarian—"

"You white rabbit, ever truckling to dirty foreigners—"

"You thing!" Both were screaming and waving fists.

"You less-than-a-thing!" yelled Aki.

"Shut up, both of you!" barked the Emperor. "Down on your bellies, to beg our divine forgiveness!"

Both officials broke off and flopped down in the *kotou*, murmuring: "O Universal Ruler, forgive this heap of excrement. . . . O Surrogate of the Gods, pardon this slimy slug. . . ."

After a few minutes, Dzuchen said: "Enough! Get up and continue the business at hand. Hold that drawing closer. Ah, it doth indeed match the features of our present Master Rao; doth it not, Aki?"

"Now that I scrutinize it," said Aki, "I confess that it doth. How say you, Master Litsun?"

"True," said Litsun; "but if this loathsome worm may offer

his opinion, it also resembles the visage of the genuine Rao, the Mulvanian one. If he who stands before us be the true Rao, he must have been soaked in a tub of bleaching fluid. The other Rao, when I saw him last year, was as dark as if stained with walnut juice."

The Emperor fixed his slit-eyed gaze on Kerin, with a nasty little smile. "Well, Master Rao—whichever of the twain you be—how answer you this, ere we sentence you to the hundred-cut dismemberment?"

Kerin opened his mouth, but for a few heartbeats no sound came forth; such was the terror that gripped him. At last he pulled himself together. "Your Divine Majesty, it is true that I was darker of hue when I left my native land. Wights from my part of Mulvan are naturally lighter, but exposure to the sun in the more tropical sections darkens them. Since I have been traveling above three months and have been under cover much of that time, my skin has paled." Turning to Litsun, he spoke a rapid sentence in Mulvani that he had been mentally rehearsing: "How like you our northern weather for a change?"

When the man hesitated in answering, Kerin added: "Now doubt you that I be an authentic Mulvanian?"

Litsun spread his hands. "He seems to speak fluent Mulvani, albeit with an accent."

"That is the normal speech of my province," said Kerin.

"There appears to be more here than meets the eye," grumbled the Emperor. "Let us not rush to judgment but have the matter thoroughly and impartially investigated. Let us see; for inquisitors, whom shall we appoint—"

At that instant the sweating Dzuchen, having absent-mindedly opened the fan, fanned himself. Instantly the Emperor disappeared with a rush of air. The fan clattered to the dais.

Outcries arose. Two guards who had stood beside the dais whipped out swords and rushed around the structure, peering around each corner as if expecting an assassin to spring upon them.

"Master Rao!" cried the piercing croak of Wizard Oshima. "Secure the fan and code book, quickly!"

His wits keyed up, Kerin instantly saw the sense of the wizard's command. Whoever possessed the fan could dictate terms. He vaulted back atop the dais, snatched up the fan, and took the code book from where it lay on an arm of the throne.

"Give them here!" cried Oshima, reaching up.

"Why?" said Kerin. "Think you to make yourself Emperor?"

"Nay, fool! Me, spend my days performing rituals, hearing petitions, and questioning spies? Rubbish! Nor could a foreign barbarian like you aspire to the throne. If we bring back Dzuchen, he *may* be grateful."

"I'll do it," said Kerin, opening the book. Then he realized that the book was written in Kuromonian characters, of which he knew a mere handful.

"Here!" he said, extending the book. "We must work together on this. You shall tell me the code whilst I do the raps."

"Sense at last, I see," growled Oshima, turning pages. "Here we are: 'Emperor,' three left, three right, four to head. No, no, idiot! By 'left' it means holding the fan in the right hand and rapping the left wrist, not holding it in the left!"

Kerin went through the procedure. There was another *foomp* of air. A bulky man of late middle age, wearing a plain green robe over black silken trousers, materialized on the throne. On his head sat a round hat of a long-obsolete style, on top of which sparkled a diamond the size of a small hen's egg.

Kerin started back, saying: "Who are *you*?"

The man goggled, mumbling: "Who dares—what—where are we?" He stared about. "This looketh like unto our throne of audience, in our Proscribed Palace. . . . But all is different—

the costumes, the décor—and we see none we know. Ye, young barbarian!" His speech had an archaic flavor.

"Aye, sir?" said Kerin.

"Who are *ye*?"

"Rao the Mulvani, on a mission for the Emperor and the King of Mulvan."

"What Emperor?"

"His Imperial Majesty Dzuchen."

"But we are—at least we were—the Emperor, Tsotuga the Fourth. How explainest that? We were having a quiet game of *sachi* with our Prime Minister, and then *pfft!* Here we are."

"Superhuman Sire," said Oshima, looking up from the floor. "Suffer this pile of ordure to explain."

"Who art thou?"

"Imperial Wizard Oshima, Omnipotent One. Doth Your Ineffable Majesty recall a magical fan, brought hither by a Mulvani ascetic?"

"Aye. We begin to understand. The accursed Zamben must have exchanged fans and fanned us away. Now we have been recalled. *When* is this?"

Oshima said: "The sixth month of the Year of the Camel, in the Cycle of the Tortoise."

"That is as least two centuries," mused Tsotuga. "All our contemporaries maun be dead, including that sharp-tongued consort of ours. Who, said the young Mulvani, was now Emperor?"

"Dzuchen the First, Majesty. You see, in a careless moment he fanned himself away."

"Aha! Is that the same fan in the young man's hand?"

"A replica, Sire, made by this incompetent bungler. The original vanished when your former Prime Minister, having made himself Emperor, inadvertently evoked a dragon. The creature devoured him, fan and all, ere he could defend himself. After

His Majesty Dzuchen vanished, we sought to recall him according to the code but got Your Sublime Self instead. Doubtless when one taps 'Emperor,' one gets them in the order wherein they were filed away. Another set of raps might fetch him back."

"Be not hasty, Doctor Oshima," said Tsotuga. "Methinks one Emperor at a time be all the Empire can afford. What wilt take for the fan and the code book? Ask not for the Imperial throne; we are sure neither of you be eligible. But ye shall not find us ungrateful to those who have restored us. Ye first, Doctor Oshima?"

"All I ask, Sire, is to continue my magical researches in the Department of Health and Welfare, and not to have to squabble with the Imperial Treasury over appropriations for the supplies and equipment I need."

"Ye shall have your wish. And ye, Master—Rao, was it?"

"I need to complete my mission for King Lajpat of Mulvan, Majesty. An ample travel allowance, to leave me something over when I get home, and an escort back to Koteiki by horse or carriage would suit me well."

"Ye shall have it, also. The fan and book, pray!"

Tsotuga held out his hands. Kerin handed over the fan and passed the code book from Oshima to Tsotuga, with a trace of hesitation. While he considered nothing so impractical as aspiring to the throne of Kuromon, he mistrusted rulers, knowing too many tales of the perfidies their power tempted them to commit. But, isolated in the midst of this vast and populous land, he could not think of a viable alternative.

Oshima turned to the whispering, jostling throng, who seemed too paralyzed by the rush of events to interfere. "Hail His Imperial Majesty, Tsotuga the Fourth, whom the fifty-seven major deities have given us in place of the late Emperor Dzuchen!" he shouted.

Turning back, he performed the *kotou* to the throne. Little by little, all the others in the Hall of Audience followed suit. Kerin slipped down from the dais and did likewise.

Tsotuga clapped his hands. "All rise! Is the Imperial Historian present?"

A man with a long gray beard stepped forward. "Your abysmally humble servant, Majesty."

"Good!" said Tsotuga. "Ye shall remain with us, to bring us up to date on the events since our—ah—vacation. The rest of you, return to your duties!"

Kerin and Nogiri stood at the rail of the *Warabi Mora* as the ship entered Kwatna harbor. Kerin slid an arm around Nogiri's slim brown waist and gave her a slight hug. She said thoughtfully:

"My lord, all my life I have been warned against that excited state called 'falling in love.' The right thing, they told me, was to achieve a stable state of mutual respect with one's spouse. But I fear I have developed that kind of passionate attachment towards you that I was warned against. You don't even seem ugly to me anymore, despite your staring eyes and great beak of a nose. Think you I've done wrong?"

Kerin laughed. "By Astis' ivory teats, no! I've been trying to tell you I feel the same towards you. So I'm delighted—"

"Master Kerin!" said a faint, tinkling little voice.

"Eh? Who's that? You sound like Belinka!"

"And why not, since forsooth I am Belinka?" said the sprite. Barely visible in the sunshine, the little blue light danced above the deck on a level with Kerin's face. "It joys me to see you returning safely. For a month I have haunted incoming ships seeking you."

"Methought," said Kerin, "you were returning to Kortoli?"

"I was. But I tarried in Kwatna to build up strength for the journey; and then I became close friends with Sendu, Doctor Klung's hantu. He is a sweet fellow, if betimes a trifle stupid. We have been—we are—"

"Carrying on a love affair, like a Prime Plane pair?"

"Well—ah—in a way; albeit we do it differently from you. But pray, when you return home, tell no one! Madame Erwina would punish me."

Kerin grinned. "If you will keep quiet about my blunders, such as twice falling into the sea, and my flight from Janji, and letting Malgo disarm me, I won't betray your little intrigue. But think not I'll give up my princess here, either!"

"Oh, I am reconciled to that. When I think of other mortal women, I realize you could have done far worse. But I must needs warn you! Doctor Pwana is still hostile, the spirits tell me, because that temple guard whom you sworded died."

"I'm sorry for the guard, albeit 'twas self-defense. But about Pwana?"

"If he learn that you have returned, as he probably hath already from his spirits, he will do you mischief."

"Why? With his Mulvani magus, he had no more need for Nogiri."

Nogiri: "Pwana is a man of fixed ideas. Since you defeated him by carrying me off and slaying his guard, he will lust for revenge as long as he lives, for aught you can do."

Kerin grunted thoughtfully. "Belinka, we cannot long remain aboard, unless we wish to buy passage back to Koteiki. So methinks to pay Doctor Klung a speedy visit." As the *Warabi Mora* inched her way up to her quay with shouts of sailors and rattle of rigging, his glance raked the waterfront. "I see no temple guards or priests lurking. But if they appear—how is the paving to Klung's house? There was something about the Sophi's plan to pave the main streets with flagstones."

"Excellent," said Belinka. "The new Sophi hath carried out the plan of the old, to pave the streets and show the haughty Kuromonians he be as civilized as they. So flagstones have been laid down over the dirt and the old cobbles—"

"How comes there to be another new Sophi, after so brief a reign by the previous one?"

"Vurkai died; his nephew, the son of the previous Sophi, succeeded as Dimbakan the Fourth. What dost?"

Kerin dug their roller skates out of his bag and handed Nogiri hers. "We may wish to move swiftly to Klung's. Belinka, pray get word to the balimpawang to expect us."

When the gangplank was hoisted ashore, Kerin and Nogiri rolled down it. Kerin bore their duffel bag slung over his shoulder by a strap. As they reached the waterfront street, Belinka squeaked:

"Master Kerin! They come!"

Some temple guards emerged from a side street and started towards them, shouting: "Halt! Stop! Ye are prisoners!"

"Away!" said Kerin. He and Nogiri skated swiftly off, ignoring stares and exclamations. Waving krises, the guards broke into a run.

"Beware of tripping!" said Kerin. "Oh, oh, look ahead!"

Out of another side street erupted a squad of the Sophi's palace guard. These, also, clattered towards Kerin and Nogiri, shouting: "Halt! Stop! Surrender! Ye are under arrest!"

Kerin drew his sword, saying: "I know not what the Sophi's men want with us, but I doubt they mean us good. Follow close!"

He skated towards the nearest soldier, waving his sword and uttering a bloodcurdling screech. "Way for the fierce barbarian!" he yelled.

Seeing this apparition rushing upon him, the soldier made a tentative swing of his kris. Kerin parried and, as he whizzed past, gave the man a mighty push that tumbled him to the flagstones. He could easily have killed the fellow, but that would have only further complicated matters. Another soldier, unnerved, turned away; Kerin whacked his buttocks with the flat as he flew past.

"Still with me?" he gasped, not daring to look around for fear of tripping.

"Aye," said Nogiri, "and now they all run after us. Turn left at the next street."

A couple of arrows screeched past, but the zigzag course of a skater working up speed threw off the archers' aim.

Sounds of chase pursued the fugitives after they were out of sight of their pursuers. They skated up to the entrance to Klung's domain. As they entered, several of the magician's clients, waiting in the courtyard, cried out.

Abruptly Kerin stumbled on the irregularities of the rolled earth, pulling Nogiri down with him. Hastily, they arose, unfastening their overshoes.

"Why, Master Kerin!" exclaimed Wejo. "The learned doctor is with a client but will be out forthwith. We got the message from your hantu—"

"Tell him, unless he protect us instanter from all the villains of Salimor, he'll lose that which I bring him."

Klung appeared; in a few words Kerin explained their plight. Klung ordered away the woman who had been consulting him and the other waiting clients. As the clients jostled their way out the gate, the pursuers' clatter waxed.

A crowd of temple guards and royal guardsmen appeared at the gate. An officer pushed his way in shouting: "Doctor Klung, we demand—"

"Keep out!" shouted Klung. "Back, unless ye would be turned to toads!"

The officer nervously backed away. Klung shouted, gesticulated, and threw a handful of powder into the air. A wall of flame sprang up across the front of the grounds. With more words and gestures, Klung extended the flames clear around the house.

Through the flames, Kerin glimpsed a temple guard departing at a run. "Come in," said Klung. "'Tis not a real fire, albeit hot enough, but an illusion created by a class of hantus that you call salamanders, in my service. Didst bring the secret?"

"Aye," said Kerin, hauling out the package of papers.

The magician glanced over the rows of ideographs. "It will take time to translate this; but it saith something about stroking an iron pin with a lodestone. It is the right paper, certes. Would we had real rag paper like this here."

"My conscience bothers me," said Kerin.

"My husband has a tender conscience, as others have sore joints or itching scalps," said Nogiri.

"Cherish him, my dear," said Klung. "Few enough have any conscience at all. What plagues you, Kerin?"

"They gave it me thinking me the true Rao of Mulvan, to convey to King Lajpat. So methinks it properly belongs to him."

"Hm!" said Klung. "Could I but get the new Sophi and that king bidding against each other. . . . But that's for the future."

"How came the succession?" asked Kerin.

Klung chuckled. "Recall you that Mulvanian whom Pwana presented to Sophi Vurkai? The Mulvani's potency spell proved all too effective. Vurkai commanded his thousand-odd wives to line up in the corridor outside his bedchamber, whilst he futtered them one by one. In his folly he tried to go through the entire harem at one sitting, if that be the right word. He gave each as long as it takes to soft-boil an egg ere calling for the next.

"When he mounted Number Seventy-Five, howsomever, his aging heart gave out. The woman shrieked; the flunkeys rushed in and hauled the Sophi off, but too late. I daresay he died happy. His nephew ascended the throne and, as is the custom, ordered all his brothers and half-brothers slain."

"That's a beastly custom!" said Kerin.

"But had the third Dimbakan pursued it, Vurkai had not been alive to seize the throne out of the proper line of succession."

"Why does the new Sophi take Pwana's part now?"

"Dimbakan thinks that Pwana compassed his uncle's death on purpose to make him ruler, and he is grateful. It were not to Pwana's advantage to admit that the Mulvani's Spell of Inordinate Lust was a mere blunder with a man of Vurkai's years."

"How went the election for balimpawang?"

"Tied, nine to nine, curse it! We shall hold another—"

"Master Klung!" cried Wejo, putting his head in the door. "The Pawang Pwana has arrived, and the ring of fire dwindles."

"Curse of the purple pus!" cried Klung. "Come! It is my besetting weakness that when engrossed in talk I lose track of time."

Outside, Pwana stood amid the besiegers, incanting. Over the tops of the dwindling flames, the officer shouted: "In the name of His Majesty the Sophi, admit us!"

Klung made passes and uttered words, and the flames sprang up again.

"Surround the grounds!" came the voice of the officer, now hidden behind the wall of pseudoflame. Pwana's voice rose to a screech.

"Great Vurnu!" cried Klung. "Look at that!"

Over the fire loomed the upper parts of a herd of elephants. Astride the neck of each elephant sat a robed, hooded, bat-winged figure.

"Who are the winged mahouts?" asked Kerin.

"Fifth Plane demons. Pwana hath found a way to protect

them from sunlight. Why thought not I of that? Come inside;
the fire will hold them for a half-hour, but I cannot keep it
going for ay despite Pwana's opposition. When the fire fails,
the elephants—methinks from the Sophi's herd—will smash
my house to bits unless I get you away. Ye would not wish to
remain in any case, since Captain Huvraka hath filed a claim
against you for the theft of his ship's boat, and the kinsmen of
that guard you slew have sworn vengeance."

"That was self-defense!"

"No matter; they'll slay you anyway. Come!"

In Klung's oratory, the wizard opened the door to the cagelike
apparatus, saying: "Wejo, fetch the sack with our visitors' ef-
fects. Kerin, pray enter with your lady!"

"What dost?" asked Nogiri.

"I send you back to Kerin's native land, with the help of some
Fourth Plane entities I control. Then I shall invite those without to enter and search for you."

"That sounds risky," she said.

"Of course it is risky! But what choice have we?"

Kerin said: "You told me you had not yet adjusted the ma-
chine so it moved inanimate objects. Has that been corrected?"

"Aye; or so I believe. First I must cancel your protective spell,
what is left of it. . . ." After a series of magical operations,
Klung resumed: "Now, Kerin, hold Nogiri's hand in one of
yours and grasp your bag with the other."

Klung slipped out of the cage, made adjustments, and moved
a lever. The cage hummed; violet light played around the bars
and wires. The scene faded, and Kerin felt as if a mighty wind
were bearing him aloft.

"Darling!" he shouted. "Art with me?"

"Aye, love!" she called, as if from a distance, although Kerin
still grasped her hand.

The windblown sensation went on and on. Kerin could see

nothing but a blur, as if he were flying through clouds, some lighter and some darker.

In Kortoli City, in the Temple of Shumal, the Fediruni god of righteousness, and his consort Kawais, goddess of purity, the prophet Ikbar was working his sermon up to a climax: "Woe unto those who expose their integuments to the sight of other mortals! None but gods may see the persons of persons; to do otherwise is an abomination. The holy Shumal hath told me that, when he and's consort purpose to beget godlets, they doff not their robes but employ certain cunning openings to make such congress possible!"

Standing before the altar, the Reverend Ikbar waved his arms, so that the baggy sleeves of his long black robe flapped like the wings of a Fifth Plane demon. Long gloves covered the arms that his gestures exposed, and a veil hid all his face but the eyes.

Before him stood several hundred worshipers. Ikbar considered pews a decadent luxury. The congregation all wore hooded robes and were gloved and veiled like their prophet. Ikbar continued:

"Oft have I told you how, years agone, the divine pair appeared unto me on this material plane as I prayed in the temple. Oft have I, without success, besought them once more to manifest themselves before my virtuous worshipers in this very fane. Today I shall essay once more to prevail upon these incomparable deities to bestow upon us this boon."

Turning his back on the audience, he raised his arms and cried: "O divine Shumal, O ineffable Kawais, deign to show your holy faces here before your worshipers. Come! Come! Come!"

There was a flash of blue light, a sharp sound as of a small thunderclap, and a rush of displaced air, which blew the prophet's hood back from his head.

Standing between him and the altar appeared two persons. One was a young man of middling size, lean but well-built, with a curly brown beard. The other was a black-haired young woman with a skin of golden brown and slightly flat-faced, slant-eyed features. Both were completely naked, without so much as an ornament.

A gasp arose. Ikbar staggered back, crossing his arms as if to ward off a blow. "Great Shumal and Kawais!" he gasped. "What do ye?"

Kerin muttered: "Follow my lead, darling. I know who this fellow be." He raised his arms and, lowering his voice to an artificial bass, thundered:

"Thou art guilty of a monstrous error, perverse mortal! Thou hast distorted and misconstrued our teachings. These deem the body holy, to be covered only as the exigencies of climate and occupation require. Down on your faces, to beg our divine forgiveness!"

With a wail of terror and repentance, priest and congregation flopped down on the mosaics. Kerin took Nogiri's hand and led her swiftly through the masses of black-robed worshipers, stepping over and around the prostrate figures.

Outside, a fine rain fell from a leaden sky. Looking around, Kerin sighted a rank of horses, mules, and asses tethered to a row of hitching posts. Some were saddled; others stood in the shafts of gigs and carriages.

"This way!" said Kerin. "Run!"

Minutes later, a patrolman of the Kortolian constabulary goggled to see a horse galloping down the main avenue of Kortoli City. The peace officer put his whistle to his lips, because no pace above a trot was allowed in the streets. But then he stood with mouth open as he saw that the horse drew a gig, and that the gig was driven by a naked man, standing up and flicking the horse with a whip, while on the seat behind him sat an equally unclad woman.

While Kerin dried himself with a towel, Nogiri struggled into an unfamiliar dress, hastily borrowed from Kerin's sister-in-law Margalit. Kerin explained to his kin:

"Klung's spell brought us hither. But that final adjustment, to transport also our clothes and gear, is still not right. So all our possessions, including my money belt, and that jeweled sword, and some nicknacks I bought in Kuromon for gifts, remain in Kwatna." Wistfully he added: "I had saved a liberal sum from the money the Emperor gave me for the return journey, too; but it would be silly to try to go back to Salimor for it."

"We're so glad to see you," said Margalit, "that we should never have thought about homecoming presents. And you seem to have changed."

Kerin's eyebrows rose. "How?"

"You were such a shy fellow, so easily embarrassed. And here you come galloping up in the gig of the wine merchant Morcar, borrowed without his permission, and banging on our door without a stitch on, as if it were the most normal thing. Didst get the facts of the escapement?"

"Aye; but my drawings are in my bag at Klung's house. I suppose that sprite Adeliza hired to watch over me will be along when she wearies of her fairy lover."

"Adeliza will be wild," said Gytha, Kerin's other sister-in-law. "She might bring an action against Mistress Nogiri for filching her betrothed."

"We weren't—" began Kerin, but Jorian interrupted: "Hadn't

you heard? She's wedded young Cenred, the village trouble-maker. Eomer's the wild one."

Kerin grinned: "So hiring that sprite to haunt me was effort wasted?"

The practical Margalit said: "Hadn't we better get you some garments? The pair of you got soaked. And what if someone come in?"

Kerin knotted the towel around his loins. "One thing I need more than clothes right now is pen and paper, to redraw the diagrams of the great clock from memory. I can do it, but on conditions."

"Eh?" said Jorian. "My dear little brother, becoming a sharp haggler? What conditions?"

"That I be left alone without interruption whilst doing it; and that the family pay my tuition at Othomae University. I don't think I shall ever see my own money, left in Salimor, again. Ah, thankee, Margalit."

Taking the pen, ink bottle, and paper that his sister-in-law handed him, he headed for his bedroom.

About the Author

L. SPRAGUE DE CAMP, who has over 95 books to his credit, writes in several fields: historical, SF, fantasy, biography, and popularizations of science. But his favorite genre of literature is fantasy.

De Camp is a master of that rare animal *humorous fantasy*. As a young writer collaborating with the late Fletcher Pratt, he set forth the world-hopping adventures of Harold Shea. These are available today in one book: *The Compleat Enchanter*. Together, Pratt and de Camp also wrote the delightfully zany *Tales from Gavagan's Bar*, a book which has remained in print for forty years.

In 1976, at the 34th World Science Fiction Convention, he received *The Gandalf—Grand Master Award for Lifetime Achievement in the Field of Fantasy*. The Science Fiction Writers of America presented him with their *Grand Master Nebula Award of 1978*. Alone, and with his wife and sometime collaborator Catherine, de Camp has been a welcome guest of honor at fan conventions throughout the United States.

De Camp belongs to many scholarly, professional, literary, and social organizations, speaks several languages, and has traveled widely to get material for his books in North, Central, and South America, Europe, Asia, Africa, and the Pacific. He has been chased by a hippopotamus in Uganda and by sea lions in the Galápagos Islands, seen tiger and rhinoceros from elephant back in India, and been bitten by a lizard in the jungles of northern Guatemala.

The de Camps live in Plano, Texas. They have two sons: Lyman Sprague, and Gerard Beekman, both of whom are distinguished engineers. De Camp works sixty to seventy hours a week, reading one to three hundred source books for a typical non-fiction book of his own. When not traveling or writing, he devotes himself to reading, gardening, and classical recordings.